# GRAVE SINS

## Jenna Maclaine

St. Martin's Paperbacks

This is a work of fiction. All of the characters, organizations, and events portrayed in this novel are either products of the author's imagination or are used fictitiously.

GRAVE SINS

Copyright © 2009 by Jenna Maclaine.
Excerpt from *Mortal Sins* copyright © 2009 by Jenna Maclaine.

For information address St. Martin's Press, 175 Fifth Avenue, New York, NY 10010.

ISBN: 0-312-94617-1
EAN: 978-0-312-94617-3

Printed in the United States of America

St. Martin's Paperbacks edition / February 2009

St. Martin's Paperbacks are published by St. Martin's Press, 175 Fifth Avenue, New York, NY 10010.

10  9  8  7  6  5  4  3  2  1

*For You.*

# ACKNOWLEDGMENTS

I would like to thank my wonderful editor Rose Hilliard for being so very patient with me and with this story. Also, to everyone at St. Martin's Press who works so hard to make all of this come together, you have my undying gratitude! Thank you to P.N. Elrod—if I'm ever lucky enough to meet you in person, I owe you a drink . . . or ten! As always, I have to thank my parents for being my biggest fans, and all my wonderful friends for their support. You guys are the best! But most of all I want to say how thankful I am for all of my readers, some of whom have waited a very long time for this book. I hope you all enjoy it!

# CHAPTER 1

*Love. Such a small word, really. Four little letters. And yet it is the axis upon which our lives revolve. We live for it, die for it . . . kill for it. It is the impetus that propels us to do extraordinary, or terrible, things. It has created and destroyed lives, kingdoms, empires. It is the light and the darkness within us all. It is the best of us, and the worst of us.*

*Love is, in short, the most powerful magic in the world. And I know a little something about magic . . .*

Ravenworth Hall, near London
October 1828

I looked down at the child, her face flushed in sleep, and smiled. Reaching out, I ran the backs of my fingers over the old gray cat sleeping next to her. The cat meowed softly and scowled at me before tucking her nose back into the fluff of her tail and closing her eyes.

"Grumpy old lady," I whispered. "Don't worry, Prissy, I won't disturb your girl."

Bending down, I kissed Janet's forehead. I was tucking the covers more snugly under her chin when I heard a soft laugh from the doorway.

"Any other mother would die of fright to see a vampire leaning over her sleeping child," Fiona said, settling her shoulder against the doorframe.

"I would sooner stake myself in the heart than harm a child, especially *your* child, Fi, and well you know it," I scoffed.

I crossed the room and looked down at eight-year-old Ian, shaking my head. "By the gods, he even sleeps like a boy."

Ian's covers were in a wad at the foot of his bed. His arms were flung over his head, and one leg was trailing off the edge of the mattress. I gently moved his leg back onto the bed as Fiona straightened the blankets. When her son was tucked tightly back into bed, Fiona walked over and slid her arm around my waist. I returned the gesture and leaned against her.

"You've done well for yourself, Fi," I said. "You have a lovely family and a good life."

"Yes, well, I can thank my cousin Dulcie for dying and leaving me this estate and a substantial income."

"You're welcome," I said with a laugh, "but I didn't have anything to do with these babies."

Fiona shrugged. "No, but thanks to your legacy I was no longer the housekeeper's daughter and I was considered a proper enough wife for Lord Bascombe's youngest boy."

I snorted. "John Bascombe could have married any girl he chose, be she a duke's daughter or a scullery maid. It's not as if he needed to worry about his father disowning him."

Fiona smiled wickedly. "Yes, who would have thought that scrawny John Bascombe would return home from years in India, all grown up and handsome as the devil," she said, holding up her hand so that the candlelight flickered and danced off the huge sapphire in her wedding ring, "and rich as Croesus to boot."

"Ah, so now we know the truth! You married him for his money, did you?"

"Ha. John has qualities much more . . . compelling . . . than his money."

"Oh, stop," I said. "I'm getting very naughty mental images of the rising young star of the House of Commons."

Fiona elbowed me in the ribs. "Be naughty with your own husband."

"Oh, I am," I said with a wink. "Frequently."

We giggled and walked arm in arm to the door. It was as if we were children again, as if I'd never left. As if I'd never . . . I stopped and looked back at the children. Fiona smiled and squeezed my hand.

"Do you ever regret it?" she asked.

Did I? Even in the quiet moments when I couldn't lie to myself?

"No," I said, honestly. "I did what I had to do or Kali and Sebastian would have killed us all. You have a good life, Fiona. You have the life I was supposed to have. But this isn't my world anymore and I'm happy with the path I chose. I have an incredible man who loves me. I have adventure and purpose. And every year I get to come home for two weeks and see my family."

I didn't add that every year it killed something inside me to see them grow up and age when I would never grow old, would never die. I didn't add that it worried me that someday we would get caught sneaking off to Ravenworth for two weeks of solitude— that one year John or someone else who knew that I was "dead" would find me here. I didn't add that sometimes I missed being plain Dulcinea Macgregor Craven, only child of Viscount Ravenworth, instead of being Cin Craven, the Red Witch of The Righteous, judge, jury, and executioner for the Dark Council of Vampires.

"You've never wished you had children?" Fiona asked.

I snapped my head around, pulling myself out of my reverie, and smiled. "Not really," I replied, cocking my head to one side. "Especially when your youngest screams his head off day and night."

"I don't hear him," Fiona said, frowning.

"You don't have a vampire's sense of hearing," I replied. "I can hear him all over this house."

"I'm sorry, Dulcie. I'd better go see what the problem is. I swear he is the neediest child I have. He's such a boy, just like his brother. Janet slept through the night from the beginning, but not my boys. He wears me out, that one," she said, but she smiled as she said it. "Apparently no one told Mackenzie Bascombe that thirty-five was entirely too old for his mother to be having more babies."

"He was something of a surprise," I agreed.

"We have another surprise," Fiona's mother said as she came down the hall. "And I'm not sure it's one you're going to like, dear."

Fiona's mother, Jane Mackenzie, had been my nanny and, later, Ravenworth's housekeeper. She had been there for everything in my life. She had been at my mother's bedside when I was born and she'd been at my bedside that night, thirteen years ago, when I had risen as a vampire. I'd left Ravenworth Hall and a sizable annuity to Fiona in my will, and now Mrs. Mackenzie was no longer a housekeeper. She still ruled Ravenworth as she always had, but money bought her the respect due to a dowager.

Mrs. Mackenzie was still a beautiful woman at fifty-two. Her chestnut hair was graying at the temples, and her face was softly lined around her eyes and mouth. Those lips that had kissed me good night every evening of my twenty-two human years were now pursed in consternation.

"What's wrong?" I asked.

"There's a man at the door."

"A man?"

"A vampire. Well, I'm practically positive he's a vampire. He's asking for Devlin."

My whole body stiffened. "You didn't invite him in, did you?"

Mrs. Mac snorted. "Of course not."

I relaxed somewhat. Devlin and Justine were out hunting with Michael, but they should be back soon.

"Fiona, go check on the baby. Mrs. Mac, stay here with the children. I'll handle this."

I strode down the hallway, my temper rising with every step. By the gods, I got two weeks of peace and quiet a year. I wondered what sort of suicidal idiot would be foolish enough to show up at my door, uninvited, with my family in residence. He would be lucky to leave Ravenworth with his head still attached to his body.

The idiot was definitely a vampire; I could sense that within moments of opening the door. He was old, too, even older than Devlin, perhaps. He had dark hair and his skin looked tanned, which meant that he was originally from somewhere far more exotic than England. He was of average height and build. In fact, there was nothing about him that wasn't average. He wasn't beautiful like Michael or overwhelmingly masculine like Devlin. He wasn't anything out of the ordinary . . . until he turned his pale eyes to mine and smiled.

"Miss Craven," he practically purred as he raised my hand to his mouth. "A pleasure to make your acquaintance."

He brushed his lips across my knuckles and I

breathed a soft, involuntary "oh." No, he was not classically handsome, but there was something so raw and earthy about him that you didn't really notice. Watching his lips linger on my fingers made me think of those lips moving across other, more intimate places. *So this is what it feels like to be bespelled,* I thought. No. No, that wasn't right. One of the good things about being a vampire is that another vampire, no matter how old he might be, cannot use mind tricks against you.

I jerked my hand from his, frowning, and narrowed my eyes. "Who the bloody hell are you?"

"I am Drake, Sentinel of the Dark Council." His voice was rich with an exotic accent, eastern European perhaps. It gave me mental pictures of shadowy castles and dark, misty mountains. "I've come to speak with Devlin, indeed with all four of you. I have a personal request from the High King himself."

"You'll have to wait. The others are out at the moment." My voice sounded hollow even to my own ears.

"Then I shall wait. May I . . . come in?"

The inflection of his voice when he said *come in* sounded almost like a proposition, and I had no doubt that he'd meant me to take it that way. For a moment it was tempting, but the faraway sound of Fiona's baby crying brought me sharply back to my senses.

"Actually, no," I said with an icy smile, and then I shut the door in his face. I leaned back against the wood and rubbed the chill bumps from my arms. Lord and lady, what was that all about?

"Who was it, dear?" Mrs. Mac asked from the landing of the stairway.

"Trouble," I said, simply. When she frowned in confusion, I elaborated. "He says he's from the Council. Let Devlin and Michael take care of it when they return."

"You're just going to leave him out there?"

"I am. You and Fiona go on to bed. You're the only ones who can invite him in, and I don't want him in this house under any circumstance. He may very well be a good man but he . . . disturbs me."

I passed her on the stairs and leaned over to give her a kiss on the cheek.

"Oh, and Mrs. Mac? When are you going to marry that man?"

She flushed and stammered, "What? What are you—"

"Don't bother to deny it. I've smelled him on you for the last eight summers. Lord Bascombe's been a widower for ten years now. Don't you think it's time you made an honest man of him?"

I smiled wickedly and floated up the stairs, leaving Mrs. Mackenzie on the landing with her mouth open and her face a charming shade of pink.

# CHAPTER 2

I stood at the window of the empty guest room across the hall from my bedroom and watched as Michael, Devlin, and Justine came from the woods and approached the house. Devlin, the leader of our group, had his arm around his consort and was whispering something in her ear, her blonde hair caressing his face. Michael was laughing with them until his gaze snapped toward the house and his hand came to rest lightly on the sword strapped to his hip.

*Good man,* I thought.

Drake walked from the shadows and was greeted by Devlin and Justine as if he were an old friend. Drake and Michael simply exchanged respectful nods. Well, that was interesting. Perhaps I wasn't the only one disturbed by our unexpected guest.

As they talked, Drake motioned toward the house and Devlin frowned. Michael's head came up and his eyes scanned the windows of the second floor. Even though I was standing in a darkened room on a moonless night, I knew he could see me. He arched a brow at me, and I crossed my arms over my chest and shook my head slowly from side to side. Michael gave an imperceptible nod and turned back to Drake, putting one arm around his shoulders in a brotherly gesture. I watched as he steered Drake toward the kitchen garden, Devlin and Justine following in their wake. There was a comfortable little gazebo out there that would do nicely for whatever business they had to conduct.

I breathed a sigh of relief as I returned to my room. Michael was my consort, my lover, my partner. He would respect my wishes in this, but eventually I would have to explain myself. That, I did not look forward to. I flopped down on my bed and stared at the ceiling.

What was it that disturbed me so much about Drake? That I found him attractive? While a rare thing, it was hardly a crime. I could barely remember the faces of the two men I had been physically attracted to before I'd met Michael, one a lord and the other a footman in my father's house. Each of them had once made my heart race, but now they were both no more than a blurry watercolor in my memory. Michael fired my blood now, and only Michael. Feeling an attraction to Drake, even if I had no interest in doing anything about it, somehow seemed like a betrayal. Justine would tell me that I was being ridiculous, that there was no harm in looking as long as your lips didn't follow your eyes. Since she was a 150-year-old vampire and former courtesan, I tended to take her word in such matters. I had nothing to feel ashamed of, truly, but there it was all the same.

What should have concerned me more was what kind of power Drake wielded. I knew he couldn't bespell me. Certainly Drake was old but even Kali, who had been well over two thousand, hadn't had that power. It just wasn't possible, which meant that whatever magnetism Drake possessed had little or nothing to do with being a vampire. It made me wonder what Drake had been as a human.

Everyone has some sort of innate talent, and there is something in the magic that makes a vampire that amplifies what we were when we were human. I'd been a witch and my magic was stronger now, though different in some ways, than it had been when I was alive. Michael had been a swordsman, and his proficiency with a blade was legendary among our kind. Devlin had been a soldier, a knight and a champion, and few in the undead world could claim to equal his skill and leadership, on or off the field of battle. Justine had been an opera singer and courtesan to kings. I'd often wondered if her incredible voice had been made more perfect by the transformation when Devlin had turned her, but it had always seemed too rude a question to ask. It was her past as a courtesan, however, that put me in mind of Drake. I'd seen the way men, and women for that matter, looked at Justine when she walked into a room. She was sex incarnate. Drake had that same appeal, in a masculine form, vibrating off him in waves.

Yes, it definitely made me wonder how our Sentinel had made his living when he'd been human.

When Michael walked in I was sitting in the middle of my bed, wearing only my green satin nightgown, my knees tucked under my chin and my arms wrapped around my legs. I was staring at the painting on the wall. I hated it, though I'd never tell Michael that. He had painted it for me the first year after he'd made me a vampire. It was a nearly life-sized portrait of me and so expertly crafted that it seemed as though I could have walked right off the canvas. I was wearing the scandalously cut red courtesan's dress I'd had on when we first met—which was why it was hanging in here and not in one of the public rooms. My hair was pulled up in an artful array of curls the color of fine rubies. When I was a child my mother had said that my hair was beautiful, but that it was an unnatural color, and she had taught me to use glamour to make it appear a normal copper. I rarely used the glamour anymore, unless I was out among humans and needed to blend into the crowd. Michael loved my hair and had painted it in all of its blood-red glory. The technique was flawless. He had once told me that given ninety years to practice, one could become accomplished at almost anything. I had yet to master the piano so I assume that, unlike me, he'd had some talent to begin with.

It wasn't his skill with a brush that I'd taken exception to; it was the cold, arrogant look he'd given me.

The set of my chin, the arch of my brows, the look in my eyes, all screamed *Bitch*. Michael and I had had a huge fight about it. He had never quite come to terms with the fact that he was a poor crofter's son and I was a viscount's daughter. From the beginning he had not felt himself worthy of me. When our relationship was new the subject had come up frequently, but in the intervening years it had become less of an issue between us. I'd been horrified when I'd first seen the painting and asked him if this haughty creature was truly how he saw me. He had been genuinely shocked at my dismay, and to this day we've agreed to disagree about that painting. He once told me that it was my strength he had painted and that one day, when I was ready, I would see it, too. I'm still waiting for that to happen.

I tore my eyes from the canvas, laid my cheek on my knees, and looked at Michael lounging against the closed door. By the gods, he was beautiful. Even after all these years he still took my breath away. His dark blond hair was cut shorter than it had been when we'd met, and the shorter length gave it a bit of curl. The neatly trimmed sideburns accentuated the knife-edge sharpness of his cheekbones. His blue eyes were dark with worry as he pushed away from the door, his hard, lean body moving with supernatural grace. He sat down behind me, gently pulling me between his legs and against his chest as he reclined against the pillows.

"Tell me," he said simply, his lips briefly caressing my ear.

I leaned my head back against him and relaxed in the protective circle of his arms. The warm summer air clung to him, along with the spicy fragrance of his lime-scented soap and the barest coppery hint of the blood he'd drunk tonight. He smelled like home, he felt like a god, and I nearly laughed out loud that I'd even given Drake a second thought.

"I don't like that man," I said.

"Drake? He's very old and very powerful. He's the messenger of the High King and not a man who's accustomed to being insulted. He is trustworthy, Cin."

"Well, I thought Sebastian was harmless, too, once upon a time," I pointed out. Sebastian had been a childhood friend of mine and nothing more than an unwanted suitor until he'd become a vampire and tried to kill me.

"I understand why you didn't invite him in, we all do. You had Fiona and Mrs. Mackenzie and the wee ones to protect. Drake understands this."

As if I gave a damn one way or another whether or not I'd offended the man. "That wasn't the only reason I wouldn't let him in," I said coldly.

I could feel Michael stiffen behind me. "Did he attempt to seduce you already?"

"Well, I wouldn't go as far as to say that, but he certainly made me uncomfortable."

"Rotten bastard," Michael muttered.

I laughed. "I got the impression the two of you aren't exactly great friends. You might as well tell me all of it because something tells me Drake will anyway."

Michael was quiet for a moment. He and I talked to each other about everything, and his reticence made me certain this story involved a woman. I had long ago ceased asking him about the women who had come before me. On some level I was grateful to them for making him such an amazing lover, but secretly I was just as content to pretend he'd been a monk before he met me. Hearing anything about his previous lovers always sent me into a jealous pout, which frustrated Michael and accomplished nothing but making me think less of myself for it. Therefore, past loves were a subject we both avoided.

Finally, Michael said simply, "I took a woman from him once."

"Really?"

"Don't sound so impressed. He didn't truly care for her or I probably wouldn't have succeeded."

*Did you care for her?* I was tempted to ask, but I kept silent and let him finish the story.

"I shouldn't have done it but I was young and foolish. This was after the war," he said, as if there'd only ever been one and I should know which one he was talking about. I assumed that he meant the Jacobite Rebellion of the last century, when Devlin had found Michael mortally wounded from an ambush by English soldiers and had turned him into a vampire to save him. I nodded silently, encouraging him to continue. "I don't think Drake was truly angry, but his pride was wounded. He'll try to even the score with me by having you, if he can."

I laughed. "Well, since I haven't seen pigs flying around the estate recently I don't think you should worry. Besides, now that your business has been concluded we may not see him again for years, if not decades."

"Well, as to that . . . ," Michael said, running his fingers slowly up and down my arm in a nervous gesture.

I turned in his arms until I could look him in the eye. "Michael?"

He sighed. "We have a job."

I narrowed my eyes. "When?"

"We leave tomorrow at dusk."

"Michael, you didn't agree to that!"

"Cin, it's an order from the High King himself. It cannot be ignored simply because we're on holiday."

"Two weeks, Michael!" I yelled, poking my finger at him. "Two weeks! All year we travel the whole of Europe, hunting down rogue vampires, bringing death and destruction in our wake, and all I ask is two weeks of peace and quiet with my family. You promised! We've only been here for five days," I said, with a firm jab to his chest.

He reached out, grabbed my wrist, and in one smooth movement I found myself flipped onto my back with Michael's body pinning me to the bed, his hands shackling my wrists above my head.

"Quit poking at me, woman," he growled. "I'll talk to Fiona in the morning and schedule a time when we can come back for a full fortnight. I did promise you and I'll make good on it, but we have to do this." He buried his face in my hair and kissed my neck. "Ah, darling, you know I wouldn't take you away if it wasn't necessary."

Yes, I did know that. I sighed. "Damn Drake anyway. I should have followed my instincts and cut his head off the minute I opened the door."

Michael laughed against my neck and pushed himself up, his hands pressing my wrists into the pillows. "So, lass, other than rescheduling your holiday, what can I do to make this up to you?"

I smiled at the devilish way his eyebrow arched as he said it. Sliding my legs around his waist, I pressed myself against him. Well, he was certainly ready to make amends!

"Hmmm . . . We could start with this." I closed my eyes and called up my magic. An instant later we were both naked, his hard body flush against me, and our clothes in a pile on the floor beside the bed. Michael chuckled and began to explore my newly exposed skin with his mouth.

"I'm so glad you finally mastered that," he said between kisses. "I was getting tired of ending up on the floor while our clothes stayed in bed."

"It is a handy bit of magic," I agreed, my breath catching in my throat as his mouth closed over the peak of my breast.

"How would you like me to make it up to you?" he murmured as one extended canine grazed my nipple back and forth, back and forth. "Quickly or slowly?"

"Michael," I whispered.

He knew me well enough to know my moods, my every whim and desire. He released my wrists, grasped my hips and drove into me in one deep stroke. I arched my back and braced my palms against the headboard as a low moan escaped from somewhere deep in my soul.

The sheets were tangled in a heap at the foot of the bed, there was dried blood on both of our necks, and I was so bonelessly content that I could have purred. I rested my head on Michael's chest and traced my fingers across the square muscles of his stomach.

"I love these little ridges," I muttered, absently. "Michael, you never told me what the job is. Where are we going?"

His mouth tightened and he laid back and closed his eyes. Finally he said simply, "Marrakesh."

It was enough. That one word tied my stomach in knots. I dug my nails into his biceps. "You're not serious."

He opened one eye and looked down at me. "I wish I weren't."

I laid my head back down on his chest, thinking. "Dear Goddess. Marrakesh."

# CHAPTER 3

There are plenty of things that I love about being a vampire, but the process of getting from one place to another is definitely not one of them. Oh, certainly Devlin's new coach provided the finest comforts that money could buy. The seats were soft and deep, in my favorite shade of dark red, and the paneling was a soothing off-white with just a hint of pink undertone. There was contraband whiskey, fine champagne, and a small selection of fresh fruits to make the journey more bearable. For all that the coach was spacious and comfortable, however, we were still traveling hour upon hour and night after night in a windowless box. No matter how fastidious Devlin was about maintenance and repair, there was always a chance that something would break and leave us stranded by the side of the road as the sun came up; therefore the windows were heavily painted over in black to prevent us from burning to a crisp if such a thing should ever happen. There were nights, though, such as this one, when I would have gladly traded the chance of ending up in a ball of flaming agony for a window with a view. I should have ridden up top with Devlin when he offered at the last stop.

We didn't employ a human driver, and Devlin often preferred to take the reins rather than ride in the coach. I couldn't blame him. The conveyance was spacious, but Devlin was nearly six and a half feet tall and built like a brick wall. He didn't like being confined, and Michael had reluctantly agreed to ride up top with him on the last leg of the trip. Justine was sitting next to me, knitting. It always made me chuckle a bit inside to see the former courtesan and vampire slayer doing something so domestic. Her pale silver-blonde hair was pulled back, hanging in large curls down her back and over one shoulder. She cursed under her breath as she pulled out several stitches and started again. I chuckled inwardly. I wasn't sure that anything actually resulted from all of Justine's knitting—she was simply one of those people who couldn't stand to have idle hands, and it kept her occupied during long trips. I ran my fingers over the gothic novel that sat unopened on my lap and finally, almost reluctantly, turned my gaze to the man sitting across from me.

In an effort to overcome my initial dislike of him, Drake seemed to be making a concerted effort to win me over. During the trip he'd turned the full force of his rather darkly appealing charm in my direction, and I found it disconcerting the way he seemed to get better looking the longer I spent in his company.

His dark hair was short and curly, his face pleasantly square. If his nose was a bit too large and his lips a bit too thin to be truly handsome, you didn't notice it once you looked into his eyes. He watched me now, like a predator watches its prey, and I had no idea what was going on behind those haunting, deep-set moss-green eyes. There were dark things behind the mocking arrogance of his eyes, hurtful, angry things. Things I didn't ever want to know about.

Justine had whispered when we'd been alone, "You can't help but wonder what it would be like to have him, can you?" No, I suppose you couldn't. He would not be a gentle lover, though you could see, somewhere deep down, that he might have been in the past, in another life. No, the Drake that sat across from me now would consume you and drag you down into whatever hell he lived in. I don't think any woman of passion could help but wonder, from a safe distance, what it would be like to stand in the center of that storm.

"How long will this take?" I asked him.

He cocked his head to one side. "Are you so eager to return to your humans?"

*Goddess, yes,* I wanted to scream.

Ravenworth was my anchor, my last tie to the human world. It was home and those who lived there were my family—not the family I had been born into, but the family I had created. My blood relatives had turned their backs on me after I'd become a vampire. Aunt Maggie, my mother's sister, thought I was evil. Even my cousin Thomas, whose life I had once saved, preferred to keep me at a safe distance. But those at Ravenworth treated me as though I was the same girl I had always been.

I wanted to watch Fiona's children play with Prissy's new litter of great-grandkittens. I wanted to see how things turned out with Mrs. Mac and Lord Bascombe. Young Tim, who'd been just a stable lad when I'd become a vampire, was now a grown man, married to Chloe Harper and expecting their first child next month. He was John Bascombe's stablemaster, and I longed to sit in a stall with him all night, waiting for my old mare Missy's granddaughter to give birth to her first foal. Was I eager to return to my humans? Yes, because back there was life and birth and young things at play, and where I was going there would only be heartache and fighting and death. I gave him a look that said as much and turned my face away.

"It is no easy thing, to depose a monarch," Drake commented.

"You should know," Justine muttered.

"Yes, I do," he said, coldly. "I was King of the Eastern Lands for many centuries but madness took me, just as it seems to have taken the Queen of the Western Lands. The Furies came for me then, just as The Righteous comes for her now."

The Furies were three sisters who were our counterpart in eastern Europe. I'd never met them, but it was said that they could not be swayed by a pretty face. Michael had told me that Drake had lost the woman he loved, a human woman, to the plague before he could turn her. Drake had gone mad and become a danger not only to himself, but also to those who depended on his leadership. The High King had ordered his removal and had sent the Furies to escort Drake to Castle Tara, deep in the Connemara Mountains of Ireland. He had spent many long years there, and when his grief had lessened he had become the High King's Sentinel, his messenger among the lesser vampire courts of the world.

"Are we to take her to the High King, then? That's what the Furies did with you," I observed.

"I had not killed humans," he replied. "You know the penalty for that is death. It is what you do."

"Do you believe she's guilty?"

He shrugged. "I never believe anything without proof, which is why we're here. This will not be an easy task. If she is guilty, her king will not let her go without a fight."

I sighed. If she had been killing humans, then as the High King's enforcers we were duty-bound to execute her. If she was simply insane, then the High King would take wardship of her, and we would escort her to Castle Tara. I'd heard more than one vampire call it Castle Terror, though in defense of the High King these were not vampires who were in his good graces. Drake seemed to have come out of it all right, but I certainly would not like to be the one to tell the King of the Western Lands that we were removing his queen from the capital. The thought of having to execute her, though, was terrifying. Among our kind you did not get to be king by an accident of birth or fortune. No, among vampires you had to fight to claim a kingdom, and there was a reason that kings were rarely challenged for their thrones. These were not creatures you wished to cross.

"What is she like?" I asked.

Justine laid her knitting in her lap and looked at me, the sadness in her eyes speaking volumes. I had forgotten that this was a woman Justine counted as a friend. "She is beautiful. She is just and fair in her dealings with her subjects. She is loyal to her king and loves him beyond measure. And she's the most frightening woman I've ever met." Justine gave a Gallic shrug. "She is everything a queen should be."

I looked back at Drake, thinking that if it were up to me I'd tell the High King he could bloody well get his ass on a boat and come do this himself. Taking in the mutinous look on my face, Drake swiftly changed the subject.

"You have not yet come to Tara to make your obeisance, Miss Craven."

"I have several years yet. I'm required to make an appearance in the first twenty years after my death. I've only been a vampire for thirteen."

Drake waved a hand dismissively. "It is no matter. The High King has given me leave to tell you that you need not trouble yourself with the trip. I will report my impressions to him and he may judge your character for himself upon the next Council meeting."

"He doesn't want to see me?" I asked, a chill creeping up my spine at the implications of that. All vampires were required to pledge their allegiance to the High King and sign their name written in the Book of Souls. Not to do so meant that you lived outside the rule of the Dark Council; that you had no honor and no promise of protection under our laws. It also meant that you were not bound to abide by those laws, and that one day The Righteous, or someone like us, would most likely hunt you down and kill you. To be excused from such an important ceremony made my stomach clench. I'd never heard of the High King doing such a thing before. Why make an exception for me?

As if he knew what I was thinking, Drake cocked his head to one side and said, "You are rather an anomaly among the undead. We haven't had a witch-turned-vampire before, you know. To be quite honest with you, the High King is wary of your power."

The shock I felt must have registered on my face, because Drake chuckled and settled more deeply into the velvet cushions.

"Oh, yes, you're quite famous among vampires the length and breadth of Europe."

Justine snorted. She, at least, still thought of me as a little sister who needed to be protected and taught how to survive in our world. Even though I'd fought by her side for over a decade, she still seemed to think of me as the twenty-two-year-old sheltered aristocrat's daughter she'd first met. How innocent I must have seemed to her back then. By the time she was twenty-two, Justine had long been a famous opera singer and the mistress of two kings. There were times when I thought she would always see me as that young girl, no matter how many years passed.

"It's true," Drake said. "They say your name in whispers. For five hundred years Kali killed or evaded everyone the High King sent against her, and then here you come, a mere slip of a girl not a week turned, and vanquish her."

"I had a lot of help," I assured him.

And I had. I'd had Fiona, Mrs. Mackenzie, The Righteous, Archie, and dear old Mr. Pendergrass, may his soul rest in peace. I couldn't have done it without them, but when the end came it had been just me and Kali. I had walked away and she had not.

"Nevertheless it was quite impressive, and you can understand how a wise man would keep you at a distance, at least until he'd fully taken your measure."

"And yet here you are," I observed.

He leaned across the carriage in a motion so quick that I barely saw it, and grasped my hand. He turned his moss-green eyes to me and smiled. As his lips closed over my knuckles, one sharp canine nicked my flesh and his tongue darted out to taste the blood that welled up. "Ah, but I have a death wish. Everyone knows that."

My breath came out in a rush as I snatched my hand away. For the majority of the trip Drake's conversation with me had been filled with well-placed double entendres, which had annoyed my consort to no end.

"Apparently," I said. "Michael will kill you, you know, if you don't stop flirting with me so brazenly."

"He can try," Drake said with a wicked smile, running his tongue over the tooth that had nicked me.

*"Nous sommes ici. Finalement!"* Justine announced a little too loudly.

I tore my gaze from Drake's laughing face, realizing that while we'd been talking I hadn't noticed that the cadence of the road had changed. The clacking of the wheels on cobblestones meant that we were entering the city. Justine put her knitting in the side compartment all the while muttering in an unintelligible torrent of French as she scowled disapprovingly at Drake. Her voice was too low and fast for me to catch anything more than a word here or there, but I got the distinct impression that he was being scolded.

"Here," she said, as she pulled out a bottle of whiskey and delicately wrinkled her nose in distaste. Justine did not care for whiskey. "You may as well pass it around. We are all going to need it tonight, *n'est-ce pas?*"

I took it and drank a long swallow straight from the bottle before handing it to Drake, who followed suit. What did it say when the judges had to fortify themselves with liquid courage before questioning a suspect? Nothing good, I'm sure.

# CHAPTER 4

I could hear Michael and Devlin jump down onto the sidewalk as I swung the coach door open from the inside. Michael had not come to help me out. Of course, I didn't *need* help, but he was always such a gentleman. The fact that he was standing next to the coach with his back to me, his coat tucked back on one side and his hand lightly resting on the basket-hilted claymore at his hip, gave me pause. I glanced past him and Devlin to the very nice three-story townhouse in front of us—and the two very unusual vampires who stood flanking its door.

They were tall and broad and looked like something out of *1,001 Arabian Nights*. What made them even more spectacular was that they were twins. The gaslights from the street seemed to shine off their bald heads and cast their dark eyes in shadows under their thick black brows. The man to my left had a gold hoop earring in his right ear, and his brother had a matching one in his left. The white linen pants and tunics they wore set off their dark skin to perfection. A crimson sash was tied around each of their waists, the fringed ends hanging nearly to their knees and the tops of their shiny black boots. They looked like a pair of exotic bookends. I suppressed the urge to jump down out of the coach, run up those stairs, and take a better look at them, mostly because the men were all posturing now and it would have ruined their moment. Drake made no move to exit the coach, so I shifted on the seat and settled back into the shadows. Who knew how long this would take?

I had watched this dance, for that is what it reminded me of, on countless occasions over the years. There were times when making nice was easier than others, but the formalities had to be observed, regardless. It was only polite when entering a new territory to make ourselves known to the ruling vampires, though as The Righteous we were not answerable to anyone but the High King himself. Each town, or county in many cases, had a lord or lady who held dominion over the vampires who resided in their territory. These minor lords were ruled by a regent in the closest large city or capital. The regents were governed by their respective king and/or queen, and those monarchs were subject only to the High King of Tara.

The Dark Council was a governing body made up of the regents, the kings and queens, and the High King himself. They met every three hundred years to renegotiate laws and policies, but an emergency session could be called at any time by the High King or by the monarch of the Eastern or Western Lands.

In accordance with the edicts of the Dark Council that sat in the year 1360, Europe was split into two kingdoms. The King of the Western Lands ruled over Britain, the Scandinavian countries, western Europe, and most of what was once the Holy Roman Empire. The Queen of the Eastern Lands ruled all the lands from Poland, Turkey, and the Russias eastward to India. It might seem like a disproportionate split in terms of size, but the world's vampire population was heavily centered in northern, western, and central Europe. In terms of the number of their subjects, the two kingdoms were fairly evenly divided.

Outside Europe the vampire population was sparse, and its fealty to the Dark Council varied. China was not a member of the Council. It was known that there were vampires living there, but there was no way to tell how many. The vampire emperor kept his people strictly confined to his own lands. I'd never known anyone who had seen one of his vampires, or who had traveled into the emperor's territory and returned to tell of it. Our High King was of the opinion that as long as the Asian emperor kept to himself, we would do the same. The Americas were becoming more populated, and it was rumored that the High King would annex the continent under his rule and establish a similar division of powers there when the Council sat again in the next century. Africa belonged to the Western Lands but for obvious sun-related reasons very few vampires lived south of the Mediterranean, or the Caspian Sea. Hell, the only Arab vampires I'd ever seen were now walking down the stairs of the gray stone townhouse in front of us.

"Devlin," the man on the left said, inclining his head.

"Khalid," Devlin replied in an equally respectful, but cautious tone. Both men's faces were carefully blank, though Khalid's brother stood behind him with his massive arms crossed over his chest and a fierce scowl on his face. That was never a good sign.

"We have business with MacLeod," Devlin stated.

"The court has dispersed or retired to Castle Darkness, and my king and queen are indisposed." Khalid's tone was dismissive, as if he expected that we would simply say thank you, drive off, and that would be the end of it. I was fairly certain that he knew why we were here, and I was willing to bet that he wasn't stupid enough to think he could get rid of us.

I noticed Michael's thumb caressing the hilt of his sword as Devlin's low, gravelly voice replied, "The night is waning, old friend, and we are going to need to see him before the dawn. Your door has always been open to me before." He glanced up at the sightless windows of the townhouse. "Or do you have something in there to hide?"

Khalid's face remained impassive as he and Devlin stood mere feet from each other, their eyes locked, waiting to see who would back down first. Khalid's brother was not so patient, and the low growl that came from his throat showed just how much offense he took at Devlin's remark. The man stepped forward, and I saw Michael's hand move to wrap around the grip of his sword. Things were going to get messy for the twins if that blade cleared its scabbard.

Justine pulled one of her daggers from her boot and put a hand on my shoulder, pushing me back into the seat as she moved forward. Drake grasped her wrist, shaking his head, then stepped from the coach in that frighteningly graceful way vampires have, as if pulled by strings no one can see.

"Khalid," Drake said in a tone as carefree as if he'd asked the man if he wanted milk or sugar with his tea.

One word. That's all it took from Drake and the whole tableau shifted. Khalid and his brother bowed low to Drake, and Michael took his hand off his sword.

"Your Highness," Khalid said, his head still bowed.

"Highness no longer, my friend," Drake replied, clasping Khalid's shoulder, "but I would have three rooms for the duration of our visit, and the coach and horses seen to."

"As you wish, my lord." Khalid turned to his brother. "Hashim, make it so."

Drake strode up the stairs to the front door of the townhouse as if he owned the place. He called back over his shoulder, "Oh, and Khalid, show the ladies to their rooms to freshen up and tell the king that we wish an audience in one hour."

Khalid bowed again, and I realized that at some

point in the past Drake had probably been his king. "It will be done," he replied. The words were pleasant enough, but the expression on his face was not. He looked as if he wanted to either kill someone or throw up. I couldn't do anything about the latter, but I could do something about the former.

One thing that Devlin had taught me over the years was to put your enemy off balance every chance you get. I did not want Khalid to decide that violence might circumvent whatever he thought was about to happen to his queen. I let Michael hand me down out of the coach, gave him a warm smile, and then walked to stand in front of Khalid. I was very glad now that I'd worn the dark amber satin carriage dress instead of my usual custom-made breeches. I sank into a low curtsy. When I straightened, I took Khalid's arm and smiled up at him. He looked down at me as if he had no clue what to do.

"Shall we?" I asked, gesturing to the door.

He nodded and escorted me up the steps while Devlin, Michael, and Justine followed behind us. The poor man was clearly miserable and confused, but at least he didn't look like he wanted to rip anyone's head off anymore.

I tried very hard not to laugh. I often envied Justine her height and her incredible long legs, but sometimes, just sometimes, it was helpful to be small and delicate. "Small and delicate" always put a large man off balance, especially if you could manage to throw in "helpless" as well. When Khalid opened the door, I turned my whiskey-colored eyes to him and smiled shyly as I passed through. He didn't exactly smile back, but his face did soften a bit.

Being little and sweet wouldn't be helpful once we were face-to-face with the king—in there I would have to be strong and scary—but for now it had gotten us into the house without anyone starting a fight. Already that was better than a lot of assignments we'd had over the years. There was something in the air, though, that told me that getting into this house was going to be a whole lot easier than getting out.

# CHAPTER 5

Hashim delivered our trunks to our room on the third floor, depositing them unceremoniously with a thump and a scowl before exiting the room in a similar manner. Shaking my head, I opened my trunk and surveyed the contents. Tonight's wardrobe would have to be chosen with care. If this were a normal audience with a territorial ruler then I would have worn one of my splendid gowns, but tonight we had to show that we were strong, that we were The Righteous. Nothing ordinary would do.

I pulled out my black leather breeches, made to fit snugly against my curves, and the thigh-high black boots that went with them. I'd come to prefer the thigh-high boots because I'd found it convenient to have my daggers strapped to each thigh instead of having to waste time reaching down to pull them from inside a knee-high boot. Besides, I thought the taller boots made my legs look longer, which isn't an easy accomplishment when you're five foot five. I pulled out a crimson shirt with tight-fitting sleeves

that ended in points at my wrists, and a black custom-
made frock coat heavily encrusted with crimson silk
embroidery. Laying these across the end of the four-
poster bed, I turned to watch Michael dress.

He noted my choice and pulled out garments to
match. I climbed up the little set of steps next to the
bed and lay down on my side, my head propped up
on one hand, the other hand resting on the curve of
my hip, and watched him tuck the black shirt into
his black breeches and button them.

"Seems such a shame to cover all that beautiful
skin," I mused.

He smiled wickedly, his blue eyes sparkling. "Give
me but a few hours and you can take it all off again."

"Promises, promises."

He buttoned the shirt, leaving it open at the neck.
Michael only wore a cravat if I absolutely made him.
The black-and-crimson-embroidered vest came next,
and he lay his black coat out beside mine.

"Your turn," he said, grabbing my ankle and pulling
me to the edge of the bed.

I stood and offered my back to him. "You'll have
to undo me."

His hands circled my waist and his lips trailed
along my neck, stopping to suck gently over the
faint pulse. "Anytime you want, my lady, anytime you
want."

I laughed softly, wickedly. "I meant the buttons,
dear."

"Oh." His long, battle-scarred fingers slowly undid

the line of buttons that marched down my back until the carriage dress slipped from my body to pool on the floor. My corset and shift quickly followed until I stood naked with my back to him, his hands moving over my skin. "God, lass, you're the most beautiful thing I've ever seen."

"Even after all these years?"

"Even after eternity," he vowed.

His hands drifted over my hips and across my stomach, moving purposefully up to cover my breasts. He rolled my nipples between his fingers, gently at first and then harder. I moaned and arched my body against him, reaching back to plunge the fingers of both hands into his dark blond hair. I tipped my head back and pulled him down to me until his lips met mine. He kissed me gently, tenderly, and every time I tried to deepen the kiss he drew back, nipping at my lips or stroking his tongue lightly against them.

"You're such a tease," I murmured, frustrated.

"Am I? We'll see about that."

His booted foot reached out and kicked the bed steps closer. Picking me up by the waist, he set me down on the bottom step. I turned to question him but he snaked one arm around my waist, pulling me closer until I felt his hard erection pressed against my backside in throbbing need. He planted his other hand firmly in the middle of my back and pushed my upper body forward. I grabbed the smooth wooden post of the bed with both hands and leaned against it.

His hand ran down over the swell of my hip and

then up the inside of my thigh. There was no teasing in his manner now. I spread my legs and his fingers claimed me, stroking me until I moaned his name, and then they slid inside. I pushed backward against him, moving in a frantic rhythm, feeling the long, hard length of him against my butt as his fingers stroked in and out of me. His free hand came up to cup my breast, and just when I thought I'd go mad at the feel of him inside me and against me, he leaned over and placed his mouth on the tender flesh just where my shoulder meets my neck . . . and bit me. His teeth sank into my flesh as two fingers slid hard inside me. My body started to shake and I cried out his name.

"That's it, lass," he whispered against my neck. "Ah, God, you're so tight."

His lips returned to the place where he'd bitten me and he sucked gently. I threw my head back in ecstasy as the tremors shook me. My knees buckled and I clutched the bedpost for support. Michael's arm wrapped tightly around my waist, and he buried his face in my neck.

"Oh, Goddess, Michael, the things you do to me," I breathed in a shaky whisper.

The knock at the door would have made me jump if I'd had one ounce of tension left in my body.

"I do not suppose I need ask what you two are doing in there," Justine called out. "But you have fifteen minutes to finish it up."

I giggled and Michael moaned against my neck.

"Do you think we could both get naked, finish

this up properly, and get dressed again in fifteen minutes?" I asked.

He chuckled. "I'd rather you just owe me one, lass."

I turned in his arms, pressing myself flagrantly against him. "That is a debt I'll happily pay."

There is a fine line between looking aggressive and looking like assassins. I thought we'd all done rather well, though our color palette did run mostly to black. Altogether we probably had enough weapons on us to have stormed the Bastille, but the only blade visible was Michael's claymore. He'd left off the frock coat and instead had the long sword in its sheath at his back. He said it was to remind the king that they were countrymen. This wasn't the basket-hilted broadsword he'd worn earlier, but the great two-handed Highland *claidheamh mòr*. Michael rarely used this sword because it was four and a half feet long and nearly impossible to conceal. It was, however, an impressive weapon and, according to Fiona, not nearly as heavy as it looked. I wouldn't know. Having vampire strength, I found it easy enough to wield with one hand.

I dragged my eyes from Michael as Drake finally made his way down the stairs. The Sentinel made his way to me and ran an appreciative glance over my attire.

"My dear," he said smoothly, "you look deliciously dangerous."

"Why, thank you," I replied.

It was clear that he would have liked to have continued the conversation, but I had noticed the scowl on Michael's face as he overheard the compliment so I politely extricated myself from Drake's company. It was the king's prerogative to make us wait for an audience, but I doubted that we would be standing on the spacious second-floor landing much longer now that Drake was here. I didn't imagine that he would be content to lounge on one of the velvet-upholstered chairs and await the king's pleasure. Personally, I would have been more than happy to retire to my room and miss the whole thing. There was an oppressive feeling in the air that had nothing to do with the decorating scheme, which tended to run mostly to red velvet and heavy gilt. Just as I opened my mouth to ask if anyone else felt it, too, Khalid, dressed in heavily embroidered sage-green silk from his turbaned head to his black-booted feet, threw open the great double doors and ushered us inside.

The room we entered made me catch my breath at the sheer unexpectedness of it. While the rest of the house, from the first-floor receiving rooms to the third-floor bedrooms, looked as if its furnishings had been stolen from Versailles, this room was built like a medieval Presence Chamber. It was the sort of room a centuries-old king would be comfortable in. The tapestry-lined walls were made of the same gray stone as the floor and fitted at regular intervals with sconces holding flaming torches. A row of medieval backless chairs lined the left and right walls, but other than that, the room was devoid of furnishings. Except for the throne and the man who sat upon it.

MacLeod, King of the Western Lands, was not exactly what I'd expected, either. I've met many vampires, and killed more than a few, but MacLeod was the first I'd seen who had been old enough when he'd been turned to have liberal splashes of silver in his dark hair. That being said, I had no problem imagining him on some ancient, body-strewn battlefield, covered in blood, claymore in hand. His face, with its strong, square jaw and deeply cleft chin, drew my attention. It was a face that had settled during his mortal years, so that you knew without a doubt that he was much more handsome in his late forties than he had been in his early twenties. There were lines on that face that remembered squinting into the sun, and he was infinitely more interesting for having them.

No, he didn't look at all like I had expected him to. What he did look like was every inch a king, from his short salt-and-pepper hair to his broad shoulders draped in full Highland regalia. This was a man who was used to giving orders and having them followed without question. He had an air of authority about him, a sense of unquestioning confidence that he could face anyone he encountered and come out the victor. If he had been in a room with a hundred other men, I'd still have known him for a king.

Of course, the throne certainly helped to convey that image. Vampires, I'd come to realize, were particularly fond of thrones, whether they held any claim to one or not. MacLeod wore this one with as much confident grace as he did his kilt and sporran, as if it were an extension of himself and his power. Its centuries-old wood was dark with age and heavily carved, and I wondered briefly what long-dead king or emperor had sat on it before him.

My gaze moved to the king's left, to where Hashim stood dressed in a darker green version of his twin's attire, and finally settled on the petite woman standing at MacLeod's right. She was obviously a vampire, and I wondered if she was the queen. If so, she was exquisite. She wore a gown that had been the height of fashion in the last century, with its wide skirt and yards of tucks and lace. She should have looked outdated, but she didn't. She looked like she had been born to wear it, and I couldn't imagine her in today's less complicated fashions. Her glossy black hair was piled in artful curls atop her head, and every feature on her heart-shaped face was nothing short of perfection. Black brows arched delicately over eyes that looked to be almost violet. She was like a tiny porcelain doll. She did not look like someone Justine would call *the most frightening woman I've ever met.*

Khalid stopped us halfway across the room and said in his deep, accented voice, "Your Highness, King of the Western Lands, may I present Drake, Sentinel of the High King of Tara, and his companions, The Righteous."

"The Righteous?" the woman gasped, her hand going to her throat

Her eyes widened as they traveled over the four of us, and then she did something I never thought I'd see in this new world that I lived in.

The vampire *fainted*.

# CHAPTER 6

The men rushed forward but Justine and I hung back, staring.

"What the—?" I opened my mouth, closed it, opened it again. "Vampires don't *faint!*" I exclaimed in a whisper.

Justine chuckled and grinned at me. "She has your helpless routine down pat, *mon amie.*"

I glared at her, offended. I had never resorted to something as trite as fainting.

"Well, it certainly seems to be working," I said, cocking one eyebrow. "She has *your* man fawning all over her . . . *mon amie.*"

Justine's eyes narrowed as she watched Devlin pull the woman into his arms. Michael was frantically fanning her with his hand. Khalid paced and fretted behind them, and Drake had moved up to watch the whole scene with a bemused expression. Hashim, I'd noticed, hadn't moved an inch. In fact, his gaze stayed riveted on me. MacLeod was watching the woman with concern on his face but hadn't risen from his seated position. Not the queen, then. So who was she? She was about to find herself staked if Michael and Devlin didn't quit drooling over her, and at this point I wasn't sure who would be the one to do the deed, me or Justine.

"Is she all right?" Khalid inquired.

"She'll be fine," Drake assured him. "Who is she?"

"The young lady is new to Edinburgh," Khalid explained, then his voice fell to a whisper. "I believe she had a falling-out with her lover. She arrived by ship with not a shilling to her name. One of the Wardens took pity on her and brought her here. Naturally, the king was kind enough to offer her a room."

The woman's violet eyes fluttered open, and she gasped as she saw Michael and Devlin leaning over her.

"You have nothing to fear from us," Devlin said, his voice so deep and gravelly that I wasn't sure it wouldn't scare her into another swoon. "What's your name?"

She looked at him with wide, round eyes. "Belinda," she whispered, placing one dainty hand on his chest. "But you may call me Bel."

I rolled my eyes and shifted my weight. Justine's fingers were inching ever closer to the sapphire-tipped dagger she had hidden in her boot. I cleared my throat, and Michael turned his head to look at me. I gave him a meaningful look and pursed my lips. His gaze moved over my face, then on to Justine's. He took one look at her and reached down, pulling the woman to her feet as he gently shoved Devlin away from her. Justine relaxed a bit, and I let out a breath. I certainly wouldn't want to be in Devlin's shoes if he were ever foolish enough to stray.

Drake stepped up and took control of the situation. "My dear Belinda, we aren't here to harm you. We are here to investigate the bodies that have shown up in the city in recent months."

MacLeod leaned back and narrowed his eyes. "Let us not play games, Drake. You are here to investigate my queen. You are here because some spy in my court has whispered to the High King that she is guilty. That is why you've brought *them* with you," he said with a sweeping gesture.

Drake inclined his head. "If she is guilty, then she must pay the price."

MacLeod's fingers gripped the arm of the throne, his knuckles turning white. "What will you do, Drake? Have one of them take her head? Lock her away somewhere in the bowels of Castle Tara?"

Drake laced his hands behind his back and paced. "So quick to judge, my old friend. Do you think she is guilty?"

MacLeod's head jerked back. "Of course not. But she is . . . not well. Leave here, and I will take her into the hills to *Caisteal Dubhar,* and not bring her back to the city."

*Caisteal Dubhar,* or Castle Darkness, was the king's country residence north of Inverness. It was remote and well protected, a veritable fortress.

Drake shook his head. "I will not bargain with you, MacLeod. The truth must be uncovered, one way or another."

MacLeod leaned forward. "She is my wife, my world. I will not let you take her."

"With all due respect, Highness, you are outnumbered."

MacLeod leaned back and chuckled. "You are no warrior, Drake, and the red-haired girl is a mere fledgling. Three against three are odds I'll take any day."

Khalid and Hashim flanked their king, and I had no illusion that they were as unarmed as they appeared to be. We certainly weren't. This could get messy quickly. I moved up to stand between Michael and Devlin, and Justine moved in to guard my back.

"With all due respect, Highness," I echoed, holding my hand out, palm up. I conjured a ball of pure magic above my palm, glowing with iridescent golden light. With a thought and a touch of glamour, the ball seemed to burst into flame. It wasn't a true flame, only the illusion of it, but I was counting on the fact that no one would put it to the test. Technically I *could* conjure fire in the palm of my hand, but I would never try it, vampires being so very combustible. "The fledgling begs to disagree. It is a fight you cannot win." I snapped my fingers and the ball of flame disappeared. "So why don't we try discussing this like rational adults instead?"

Five pairs of eyes regarded me with fascination or

horror, or both. Bel's hand went to her throat again and I snapped, "Woman, if you swoon again you'll wake up on fire." She gulped and took a step back, but thankfully stayed on her feet.

MacLeod smiled. "Such power in such a small package. You'd best beware that you don't become so powerful, you are more of a liability than an asset to the High King."

I glanced at Drake, but his expression gave nothing away. It was, in fact, so devoid of any reaction to MacLeod's statement that a cold knot of dread clenched in my stomach. Ah, bugger, that was all I needed. I couldn't do anything about it now, though, so I would worry about it later. At the moment I had bigger problems, like Hashim gliding toward me with the stealth of a serpent.

"She is dangerous, Your Majesty. She will use her magic to effect whatever outcome they desire, whether it be the truth or not." I rocked back on my heels at the force of his fear and hatred. "Let me kill her now."

"Don't be a fool," I snapped. "I have not wronged you in any way, Hashim."

"Your very existence is an affront to Allah. You are an abomination," he spat.

"Oh. Says the *vampire*."

Sometimes I really don't know when to keep my mouth shut, and this was one of those times. Hashim's hand drew back to strike me, and before I could even blink two things happened at once: I heard the slap of flesh against flesh and the sharp hiss of steel clearing a scabbard. I hadn't flinched. I'd known without a doubt that he would never be able to touch me, not with Michael standing at my right and Devlin at my left.

A muscled ticced in Hashim's cheek as he took in the result of his folly. Devlin's hand gripped his wrist not six inches from my face, and the tip of Michael's claymore was pressed into his jugular.

I glanced at Michael and found his face cold as stone. His high cheekbones seemed sharp as a knife's edge when his jaw was clenched in fury. "You lay a hand on my woman," he said in a low, deadly voice, "and you're going to die bloody."

Khalid reached out and jerked his brother back, whispering fiercely to him in Arabic.

I looked at MacLeod. "It's not my magic that you need to worry about, it's whatever magic has been worked here before me. The air fairly reeks of it."

Everyone looked around as if they expected to see magic floating above their heads. I laughed and shook my head. "For people whose entire existence is due to some sort of magic, it always amazes me that vampires aren't more sensitive to it. Someone has been working magic in this house."

"What sort of magic?" Drake asked.

It was a question I wished I could answer. Sensing another witch's magic was one of the first things my aunt Maggie had taught me when I'd come into my power. Just like humans or vampires, there are good witches and bad witches, and it was important, Maggie had said, to be able to sense what sort of magic was being worked around you. What was in this house, though, didn't feel like anything I'd ever encountered before.

"I don't know," I said. "But it's definitely here."

"'Tis impossible," MacLeod said. "I've not even seen a witch in more centuries than I care to count."

"It's not only possible," I replied, "it's happened. If the queen hasn't been working magic, then perhaps someone has been working it against her. You say she's been unwell?"

MacLeod was silent for a moment. There was hope in his eyes, hope that I'd put there, but he still didn't trust me. It was a pity, really, since I was his one best hope to save his queen.

Finally he spoke. "She has. Do you think that her illness is due to some sort of spell?"

I shrugged. "I need to see her. I can't promise anything, but it's possible that I'd know if she has been influenced by someone else's magic."

MacLeod nodded and rose. "You may come up to our chamber, but only you."

I started forward, but Michael grabbed my wrist. "She doesn't go anywhere in this house alone."

MacLeod arched one dark brow at him. "You dare suggest that your woman would come to harm while under my personal protection?"

"She's already been offered violence," Michael

said, motioning toward Hashim. "I'll tell you again, Highness, she goes nowhere alone."

MacLeod glared at Hashim, and then nodded. "So be it. But the rest of you must remain here."

Drake opened his mouth to protest, but I caught his eye and shook my head. He gave me a long look, then inclined his head to me and remained silent. MacLeod was skittish and I for one was willing to humor him. I wanted this whole business over with as quickly as possible.

The whole house was so overly done with red velvet and gilt that MacLeod's bedroom stunned me just as much as his Presence Chamber had. It was a massive, windowless room but, for all that, it wasn't over-whelming. It was comfortable; the sort of room that could keep you occupied through long summer days.

The walls were hung with rich, vibrant tapestries, and the wood floors shined with polish. A heavy oak desk sat at an angle in the left-hand corner of the room, its surface covered in papers and piles of books. The bookshelves that consumed the two walls behind it were similarly crammed with texts and pieces of paper jutting out here and there. A huge globe perched on a brass stand to the left of the desk. Across the room, a fire glowed in the hearth, illuminating the two Roman couches that flanked the fireplace and the low table between them. A large, well-used chair sat directly across from the hearth, making the little sitting area quite cozy. To the right of the door a second fireplace mirrored the first, casting flickering shadows across a huge, low bed swathed in sheer netting. It looked like something you might find in a sultan's harem. My gaze traveled upward to the Italian Renaissance ceiling, painted with scenes of gods and goddesses. I shook my head and smiled. It was exactly the sort of eclectic room that a well-traveled two-thousand-year-old vampire would have, filled with mementos and antiquities. The only thing missing was the queen.

MacLeod's shoulders were visibly tense. "She was here but an hour ago," he said, almost in a whisper.

I could feel the same cloying scent of magic in this chamber, stronger here than it had been in the rest of the house. Whoever was responsible for it had been here recently.

"If she was taken, how did they get in?" I asked.

He looked at me without comprehension, and I nodded to the heavy key in his hand that he'd used to unlock the door. He looked down at it as if he were seeing it for the first time.

"The lock is meant to keep her safe, not to keep her a prisoner." He nodded to the door, and I noticed that in addition to the lock there was a heavy iron bar that could be placed across the door from the inside. This was their retreat, their daytime resting place, and as such would be barred from the inside so that they could get out, but no one could gain entrance from the outside.

"We must find her before daybreak," Michael said.

"Come, Highness, we'll alert the others and split up and search the house."

MacLeod nodded, and the three of us moved rapidly down the hall. When we reached the head of the stairs I stopped. "You two go ahead." I motioned in the opposite direction, toward our room. "I'll get some supplies and see if a location spell will help us find her."

Michael narrowed his eyes at me. He knew very well that it had been years since most of my magic required any sort of spell or ritual to accomplish, and he knew that I carried little with me in the way of magical paraphernalia.

"I'll help you," he offered, daring me to object.

"Thank you," MacLeod said, and at my nod he turned and continued down the stairs.

"What are you up to?" Michael asked when the king was out of earshot.

I shrugged. "Whoever had been using magic in this house has been in that room. I want some time in there to see if I can pick up on anything."

He shook his head. "I'm not leaving you alone in this house."

"Michael, sweetheart, I am not without my own defenses. Besides, we don't know that anything nefarious has actually happened to her. She could be the one working this magic for all we know, and has fled out of fear we'll find her guilty." He gave me a dubious look and I sighed. "I know, it doesn't feel right to me, either, but someone in this house is not on the up-and-up, and I need you to go down there and keep an eye out. Look for anything suspicious. I think we can safely rule out MacLeod as a suspect, but the other three . . . make sure none of them go searching without one of us with them. Now go," I said, reaching up and kissing him quickly. "I'll be fine."

"You have fifteen minutes," he said, "and then I'll be back."

"That's all I need," I called out over my shoulder as I hurried back to MacLeod's chamber.

Once inside I stood at the foot of the bed, cleared my mind of everything, and reached out with my senses. It wasn't my magic, however, that drew my attention to the tapestry on the wall to my right; it was the very faint draft of air that blew along my cheek. I walked over and ran my hand along the cavorting unicorns and faeries, appreciating the master weaver's skill even as I felt for that draft once more. Toward the edge of the tapestry my hand pushed into empty space. I grasped the fabric and pulled it aside. There was a door that had been left open, sliding neatly into a pocket in the wall. Beyond the door were stairs leading up in one direction and down in the other. It would be more logical to take the stairs down—this near to dawn any sane vampire would surely head down—but something drew me inexorably up the short flight of stairs to my left, which ended at a heavy steel hatch in the ceiling. I slid the bolt lock free and pushed the hatch open, climbing out onto the roof.

The sound of weeping drew my attention to a small, tin-roofed gazebo. I glanced around before I approached, searching the shadows for any sign of danger. Other than the woman at the gazebo, I could sense no other presence around me. The heavy latticework kept me from seeing inside the structure, so I walked slowly across the rooftop and around to the front.

The sounds of the city stirring filtered up to me: voices shouting, either in greeting or annoyance; horses' hooves clicking on the cobblestones; the jingle of bridles and the low rumble of heavy carts. Above it all Edinburgh Castle sat high on its rugged stone perch, like a mother dragon nestled down, keeping watch over her children. Only the muffled sobs of the woman in the gazebo disturbed the otherwise ordinary cadence of the waking city. I walked around the corner of the gazebo and stopped short, my hand flying to my mouth.

She was on her knees, her wrists chained behind her back to one of the gazebo's stout support beams. Her long blonde hair hung in tight ringlets, covering her face and her naked body. Her shoulders shook with each racking sob, but she didn't raise her head when I took a step forward. She didn't seem to realize I was there. I reached out a hand to her.

"Marrakesh?" I asked, softly.

# CHAPTER 7

She threw back her head and let out a hoarse scream.
I jerked my hand away. If she was the queen, then
I shouldn't touch her. She had power, this one, the
power to see into your soul at the merest touch of her
hand. And if she wished it, she could destroy you
with what she found there. It wasn't a vampire power,
or witchcraft. It was . . . something else . . . and it was
the reason she was feared and respected by vampires the world over, the reason MacLeod hadn't
been challenged for his throne in centuries. She was
his enforcer, and it was said that the last vampire to
challenge him had run screaming into the sun when
Marrakesh had touched him. She'd felt all the pain
he'd caused over the many centuries of his existence
and had turned that pain back to him, flooding him
with a tide of emotion that had snapped his sanity
and driven him from *Caisteal Dubhar* and into the afternoon sun. I had only been a vampire for thirteen
years, but even I had done things that I didn't want to
relive. And so I stood there, wondering what to do

next, and watching the Queen of the Western Lands cry as if her heart were being wrenched from her chest.

"You would betray me like this?" she wailed.

I took a step back and shook my head. "My queen, I did not do this to you, I swear it."

But how had she ended up here, like this? How could someone have done this without touching her? Perhaps whoever was working the magic that I sensed had used a spell to make him or her immune to the queen's power.

*What I wouldn't give for that spell right now,* I thought.

"I loved you," she whispered, and I frowned and cocked my head to one side. "I became everything you wanted me to be, and more. I tried so hard to please you."

She wasn't looking at me. In fact, she didn't even seem to realize I was there. I moved around so that I was directly in her line of vision, but the look in her eyes was so glassy and faraway that I knew that whatever she was seeing, it wasn't an Edinburgh rooftop, and it certainly wasn't me.

"I loved you," she said again, looking lost and hurt and confused. "You're my husband, Conall. I've given you everything—money and land . . . every inch of my body and soul. How can you do this?"

Well, that certainly wasn't MacLeod. Gods, could she be reliving her *human* life? She had to be well over a thousand years old. What could possibly still hurt this much, after all that time? I shook my head. This was something I shouldn't know anything about, didn't *want* to know anything about. I should leave. I should go and get help. But she looked so heartbroken and vulnerable that I couldn't bring myself to move. I stood there, still as a statue, while the whole gut-wrenching tale tumbled from her lips.

"And you . . ." She turned her head slightly to the right, as if someone else were standing there. "I've loved you like a sister. You were my first friend when I came here as a bride." She laughed harshly, and it was not a pretty sound. "You were even *kind enough* to give me advice about how to please my husband in bed. What a fool I was. I thought you were so wise, but it was easy enough when you knew what he wanted firsthand, wasn't it? Tell me, Nessa, how long have you been sleeping with my husband?"

I waited while she listened to voices only she could hear. Finally she closed her eyes, bowed her head, and slumped down as far as the chains would allow her. I didn't need to hear the other side of the conversation to know the answer to that question.

"So it was all a lie, from the very beginning. By Danu, why would you make me believe you loved me, Conall? I married you because my uncle asked it of me, and he is the *Uí Níall*. I never expected love and would have been content without it."

I barely heard her when she whispered, "You bastard." She raised her head, and her eyes were red, her face wet with tears. "So now you plan to stake me out on this beach with this paltry treasure in the hope that they will take me and leave your village alone. And what will you tell my uncle? That I was killed in a raid? And then you will be free to marry the woman you love. How convenient. Mark me well, Conall, you won't get away with this, either of you."

She started pulling violently against the chains that bound her wrists as she screamed out her husband's name. Finally, she sank back down on her heels, crying and shaking as if she would break.

"Marrakesh?" I said, not really expecting a response. Vampires generally changed their names after they're turned, and if she believed she was in the past, still human, she wouldn't recognize *Marrakesh* as her name. Whatever her human name had been I didn't know it, so I simply petted her hair and said, "Darling, I'm going to get help. I'll be back soon, I promise, and then this will all be over."

She jerked her head up, her eyes wide and wild with fear. "Shh!" she said. "Quiet. They're coming. They're here."

I shook my head. "Who's here? Who are you afraid of?"

Her breath came in shallow gasps. "Vikings."

I rocked back on my heels. He had told her he loved her, slept with her best friend, and then staked her out on a beach as a sacrifice to the Vikings? Bloody hell, what kind of evil bastard *does that*?

"What the hell is going on here?" a male voice snapped from behind me.

I spun around, drawing the short sword that was sheathed down my spine as I did. It was MacLeod. It occurred to me briefly that whoever had done this to the queen either possessed strong magic or was someone she trusted, someone who would not balk at the touch of her power. The man she slept with every day, perhaps? Had one husband staked her out to be killed by Vikings, only to have another stake her out to be killed by the morning sun?

I lowered the sword. He was unarmed, and the look of pain on his face as he stared past me at his wife was so stark that it squeezed my heart. I wanted to believe that he couldn't have done this thing. However, I'm not a stupid girl, so I kept the sword in my hand.

"I found her like this," I said. "I don't know what's wrong with her. She speaks of Vikings."

"She's told me, of course, how she came to be in Marrakesh when I found her, but I've never seen . . ."

The chains rattled behind me, and I glanced over my shoulder to see her struggle to rise to her feet. With a regal toss of her head she slung her hair over her shoulder and stared at MacLeod as if she truly saw him.

"Handsome enough," she whispered to herself.

My gaze swung between the two of them, each staring at the other in rapt attention. I stepped aside, unsure of what was going on.

"Viking," she called. "I have a bargain to make with you."

She stood tall and proud, confident in her beauty, unashamed of her nakedness. She was several inches taller than me and not fat, necessarily, just . . . solid. Lush. It was a figure that had once been fashionable and undoubtedly would be again. She'd been young when she had been turned, in her early twenties I would guess, and was at least twenty years (and several centuries) younger than MacLeod. Her blonde hair hung in tight curls to her waist, and her eyes were like green velvet as they moved over MacLeod's face and frame. He walked to her and stood before her. Even though she was chained and naked, I had no doubt who had the advantage here. She was like a cobra hypnotizing its prey.

"You're hardly in a position to make bargains, lady," MacLeod responded, as if he were an actor in this little drama.

"Am I not? I am lady of yon castle," she said and nodded over her shoulder, pressing her back into the post and arching her body as she did so. Very well done. He was putty in her hands. "And I can assure you that there is more treasure there than the pittance that lies on this beach."

"I need no woman's help to take a keep, or the treasure within," he replied. Obviously MacLeod knew what had happened to her all those centuries ago and was playing the Viking warrior for her. To what end I had no idea, perhaps simply out of his own curiosity. Regardless, I stood transfixed and watched the scene play out.

She laughed. "The treasure is well hidden. You could tear down that keep stone by stone. You could search until Lughnasa and never find it. I will give you what you seek in exchange for two things."

He laughed softly. "You have courage, lady, and spirit. I like those things in a woman. What boon is it you ask of me in exchange for this treasure?"

She raised her chin. "I am the niece of the *Uí Níall* king."

"You wish to be ransomed back to your uncle?"

"I am disgraced," she replied with a bitter laugh. "I can never go back there and hold my head high. But I am a lady, Viking, and have no wish to become a slave. I would be *your* lady. Treat me as a princess should be treated and I'll make you happier than you've ever been, in bed and out of it."

He ran his fingers over her cheek and gripped her chin. "I could have you here and now, lady, and pay no price for it."

She smiled. "You're an old man, Viking. Do you really want a woman in your bed that you have to fight every night? Give me what I want, and I'll give you what you want, freely."

"What makes you think I wish to have you in my bed every night? I could have you once and sell you as a slave to the Moors."

She cocked her head as if to beckon him closer. When he moved in, she leaned forward as far as the chains would allow, her lips nearly touching his. Her gaze moved to his lips, and she licked her own. "You won't let me go without having me. And once you've had me, you won't let me go." She raised her eyes to his. "Give me what I want, and I'll be the best you've ever had."

He swallowed. "Done," he said, when he'd found his voice.

She leaned back against the post and dropped her gaze shyly. It was a coquette's gesture.

"And the second thing you would ask of me?" he prompted.

She was silent for a moment and then raised her eyes to his. Gone was the bold siren or the shy coquette. The hatred that burned like green fire in her eyes made me take a step back.

"Kill them all," she hissed.

# CHAPTER 8

"MacLeod," I said, tearing my gaze from Marrakesh's face and looking over my shoulder. "We have no more time for this. Dawn is here."

MacLeod shook himself and looked at the sky. "Damn it," he swore.

He pulled at the chains, but they were tight and held in place by a sturdy lock the size of my fist. I held out my sword.

"Will this help?" I asked.

He looked at the sword, and then back at her wrists, shaking his head. "Even if I could break the lock with it, I can't get to it."

I sheathed the sword and moved to the other side of her. "The post. Break the post off and we can pull her free. We'll worry about getting the chains off once we're inside."

He nodded, grabbing the wooden post that was as big around as my leg and snapping it like a twig. The edge of the roof fell in as Marrakesh pitched forward into MacLeod's arms. And that's when I noticed her back. Even with the eastern sky turning pink with the dawn, I couldn't help but stop and stare.

Her entire back from her shoulder blades to the base of her spine was covered in one large tattoo. A huge black raven took up most of the center of her back, its wings spread up and out over her shoulder blades, its shiny black feathers sparkling with a hint of gold. Behind the raven a full moon shimmered like liquid silver. The raven's beak held a sprig of hazel, and each talon clutched a spray of fir and elder. The green ink was so brilliant that the plants looked alive. Beneath the bird, waves swirled in several shades of blue and green, tapering down into a V at the base of her spine. Pink and gold salmon swam on those waves, their scales glistening. Surrounding the whole tattoo and filling in any empty spaces were Celtic shield knots, spirals, and circles, making the whole thing like something straight out of the Book of Kells. The colors were so vibrant and shiny that I reached out to touch it, to see if the ink was still wet. It wasn't.

"MacLeod?" I asked.

"She's had it since she was made a vampire," he said quickly as he picked Marrakesh up and cradled her against his chest. He looked over his shoulder at the dawn breaking on the horizon. "Hurry."

We rushed across the rooftop, and I stepped aside to allow him to carry his queen down the stairs ahead of me. I slipped in behind him and closed the hatch, throwing the bolt to lock it from the inside. MacLeod shifted on the stairs, giving me room to move past him and hold the tapestry back. Once we were inside, I closed the door and noticed two more bolt locks carved into the wood panel. Unless her abductor had possessed enough magic to open the locks from the outside, whoever had taken Marrakesh up onto that roof had come in from her bedchamber and not the passage beyond.

*Interesting,* I thought as I slid the locks in place and let the tapestry fall back to hide the door.

MacLeod had laid her on the bed and stripped off his shirt to cover her nakedness. I spared an appreciative glance at his heavily muscled chest, and then went to inspect the queen's bound wrists. I passed my hand over the chains, feeling for any lingering touch of magic. When I found none, I closed my eyes and pushed my power into the lock, whispering, "Open."

The lock snapped open and the chains slid from her wrists.

MacLeod's head snapped up. "Why didn't you do that on the roof?"

I shrugged. "Someone is working magic on her. I just assumed that the lock would be warded. I certainly would have warded it, if I had done this to her."

"And if it had been, then what?"

"I haven't found a ward I couldn't break in ten years, but it would have taken time we didn't have."

He nodded and slipped Marrakesh's arms into the

sleeves of his shirt, murmuring Gaelic love words to her as he did so. It was such an intimate thing that I felt suddenly like a voyeur.

I cleared my throat. "I'll just go and tell the others that she's been found. Try to get her to rest, and I'll be back to see what I can do for her."

My hand was on the bedroom door when he called my name. I turned and looked at him, the proud King of the Western Lands, shirtless and cradling his young queen in his arms. The look on his face was filled with pain and helplessness.

"Thank you," he said, "for believing in her."

I shook my head. "I don't know what I believe, Highness, but I do know that she didn't do that to herself."

He stared at me a moment, as if the force of his will alone could make me believe in her innocence, then nodded and turned his attention back to his lady. I slipped out the door, and ran straight into Michael.

"We found her," I said, gently pushing him back as he craned his neck to get a look inside the royal bedchamber. "But we have a problem."

I explained the circumstances surrounding the queen's return, leaving the juicier parts for later, when we were alone.

He leaned back against the wall and closed his eyes. "Well, hell. This couldn't have been easy, could it? Regardless of the circumstances, we have to tell the others that she's been found, and call off the search."

"Agreed," I said. "And I want to gauge the reaction from Khalid and Hashim when they're told."

I would have liked to have seen something on the faces of MacLeod's lieutenants. Some mark of guilt or irritation at the news that the queen was safe would have been nice. Unfortunately, the twins showed no sign of anything but utter relief. Even Bel fluttered and dabbed at a tear with her handkerchief when she learned that Marrakesh was now safely tucked away in her chamber. It was clear to me that Devlin was looking for the same reaction I was, because he fairly groaned in frustration.

"I want everyone in MacLeod's chamber," he said. "Now. I want this whole story told from the beginning. I do not like not knowing what the bloody hell is going on."

As we all headed for the stairs, Bel chattered away. "Oh, an inquisition! I've never been to one before. Do you think this dress is proper? Perhaps I should go change first."

"Your dress is lovely, dear," I said as she swept past Justine and me to follow the men up the stairs.

Justine's fingers curled into claws as she reached for Bel's shiny, bouncing curls. I slapped at her hands, stifling a giggle as I did so.

"Do you really think so?" Bel asked as she turned on the stairs, the hopeful look on her face giving way to several astonished blinks as she watched me swatting at Justine.

I elbowed Justine in the ribs. It was her turn to make nice, after all. She grunted and then inclined her head, her teeth looking just a bit feral as she smiled at the dark beauty above us. "Very nice, *chérie*."

"Hmm. No, I never did like the taste of it, but perhaps a good Bordeaux would go well with an inquisition. What do you think, Michael?" Bel asked as she smiled and turned, leaving Justine and me standing openmouthed at the foot of the stairs.

Justine and I sat on one of the Roman couches in MacLeod's bedchamber, watching as the king paced before the fireplace, his gaze occasionally drifting to his wife. The queen was asleep in her gauze-draped bed across the room, oblivious to us all. Bel and Drake occupied the other couch while Khalid and Hashim stood like good sentries on either side of the fireplace. Michael was standing behind me, rubbing slow circles on the back of my neck with his thumb. I drummed my fingers impatiently on the arm of the couch as I listened to Drake gently explain the difference between an inquest and an inquisition to Bel. Finally, I shot a pointed look at Devlin, who leaned back in his chair, steepled his fingers, and said, "Highness, perhaps you would care to start at the beginning?"

MacLeod stopped pacing and looked at Devlin as if he had just remembered that the rest of us were in the room. I had the feeling that pacing in front of that fireplace was a longtime habit of his. He sighed and leaned one broad shoulder against the corner of the mantel.

"Several months ago I learned from an informant in town that there were very fresh bodies being dissected at the Edinburgh Medical College. As we all know, there is, unfortunately, a very lucrative trade for the Resurrectionists these days. The bodies that were being used by Dr. Knox at the Medical College, however, were too fresh to have been robbed from their graves, so I asked Clarissa to make sure these bodies were not vampire victims."

"Who is Clarissa?" Devlin asked.

"One of the queen's ladies and a longtime member of my court. Clarissa frequently hunted near the Medical College, so I asked her to inquire about the bodies when she had one of the medical students in thrall. She reported that the bodies were pristine, no bites or open veins, and no blood loss. Apparently the cause of death on most of them was suffocation. I decided it was a matter for the human authorities and thought that was the end of it."

I leaned forward and caught Drake's attention. "So if these people were not killed by vampires, then why are we here?"

Drake looked at the king. "Do you want to tell it, or shall I?"

MacLeod scowled at him and inclined his head. "You have your spies in my court, so I'm sure you know as much as I do," he said harshly.

Drake didn't seem to be bothered by the tone and continued with the story. "We're here because it has come to the High King's attention that recently, while Clarissa was out hunting, she saw one of the bodies being delivered to the Medical College . . . by the queen herself."

"It's ridiculous, I tell you!" MacLeod shouted. "She wouldn't have done that. She couldn't have! I was with her that night. *All night.*"

Drake looked at him with sympathy etched on his face. "You understand, my friend, why I can't take your word for that. Any vampire who would cross the deserts of northern Africa to steal a woman would have no qualms about lying to save her. The High King cannot turn a blind eye to this, MacLeod, you know that. You are a king yourself and you know that, as such, you must dispense justice equally or you are not worthy of the title. You are a good man, my friend, and a great king. You must let us see this through to the end."

MacLeod stared at him for a long moment before turning his back on us and bracing his arms against the mantel. "Get out," he said in a low, harsh voice. "All of you get out. I've had enough for one night."

We all looked at Drake, unsure of what to do. He closed his eyes and took a deep breath. Then he rose and wordlessly held out one elegant hand to assist Bel up. We took our cue from him and all filed past MacLeod. He never looked up. He was the king, after all, and we had been dismissed.

As I closed the door silently behind us, Devlin turned to Khalid. "Did MacLeod send Clarissa to Castle Darkness with the rest of the court?" he asked.

Khalid looked away, and then met Devlin's eyes. "No, she stayed behind because the king knew you would wish to question her."

Devlin nodded. "I'll do that now, before we all retire for the day."

Khalid squared his shoulders. "That will not be possible."

I groaned inwardly. Devlin had issued an order, and he was not a man accustomed to having his authority questioned.

Devlin arched one black brow at the man, and his face settled into that cold arrogance I had come to know so well. "I said I would question her now, Khalid. I realize that you are the first lieutenant of the King of the Western Lands, but do not forget who I am. I do not await your pleasure, you await mine."

Khalid bristled, looking as if he would challenge that statement; then the tension left his body and he shrugged one shoulder. "As you wish, my lord."

And so it was that the eight of us ended up marching down the grand staircase and through the common rooms to the large kitchen at the rear of the house. Set into the far wall was a thick oak door. Khalid jerked the door open as if it weighed nothing and stalked down the dark stairs to the wine cellar.

"I thought she was a member of the court," I called out. "Why is she being kept down here?"

Khalid paused on the stairs and turned to look at me. "Clarissa was caught in a bit of a quandary. If she told you what she saw, then she felt she would be betraying her queen. If she tried to cover up what she believed to be the truth, then she feared the Red Witch of The Righteous would know her for a liar. She tried to run last night, and when she was caught MacLeod ordered her to be locked in the cell down here until your arrival."

So the vampires of the world thought that I could somehow use magic to tell a lie from the truth? Interesting. In theory, I supposed I could come up with some sort of lie-detecting spell, but spellcraft wasn't really my forte. To be quite honest, I couldn't tell the truth from a lie any better than the next person. It might be useful for others to think that I could, though, so I just nodded and kept my mouth shut.

The cellar was large, with bottles of wine and other household goods stacked along one wall. Mostly, though, it was empty except for the massive holding cell that stood in one corner. This was where we were supposed to find the reluctant Clarissa, but there was no one in the cell. I walked up and laid my hand against the cold iron of the bars. The only thing inside was a cot, a washbasin . . . and a pile of dust on the floor. I looked at the others and each of us turned to Khalid in horror.

"As I told you, questioning Clarissa will not be possible," he said in an icy tone.

"What the hell happened here?" Devlin asked quietly.

Khalid shook his head, and suddenly looked very tired. "I do not know. We were informed that you would be here before the dawn. Hashim was here with her, to guard her and keep her company. Around four o'clock this afternoon he came running up the stairs to tell me she was dead. He saw nothing. One minute she was there and the next—" He gestured to the pile of ash and bone fragments, all that is left when you kill an old vampire.

We all looked to Hashim and he jerked his chin up, that arrogant expression settling across his face as if he dared any of us to question him. Oddly enough none of us said anything until finally Drake moved forward and said gently, "Did you perhaps fall asleep, old friend?"

Hashim turned angry eyes to him and said in a clipped voice, "I did not. I heard a sound upstairs and I turned to look, but there was nothing there. When I turned back . . . she was gone. We have not gone in to collect her remains. We left everything exactly as it was for you to inspect."

"You said you heard something upstairs. Could someone have—" Hashim narrowed his eyes at me and I bit my tongue before the words *slipped past you* could come out of my mouth.

"No one came in and no one went out," he said flatly. "And Khalid has the only key to the cell."

"Oh, God," came a small voice from the rear of

our group. I had blissfully forgotten about Bel until then. "She killed herself," she said, casting those violet eyes to me, "because of you."

I took an involuntary step back, and my elbow banged into the bars of the cell. Turning away from her accusing glare, I surveyed the contents of the cell again.

"There's no weapon," I said. "She couldn't have cut off her own head, and there's no stake on the ground. If she killed herself, then how did she do it?"

Everyone moved a few feet forward and looked into the cell as if some answer would suddenly become apparent. But there was no answer, and looking at what remained of Clarissa I was beginning to suspect that questions were all we were going to find in this house.

# CHAPTER 9

I didn't sleep well that day. I kept dreaming about being locked in a cell, helpless, while someone ran a stake through my heart. It was one of my top five ways not to die. I don't think Michael slept at all, and we were both more relieved than irritated when Devlin knocked at our door in the early afternoon. I sat up in bed, pulling the sheets up around me, while Michael called for him to come in.

Devlin closed the door behind him and flung himself into the nearest chair, running one hand through his black hair in a nervous gesture I'd come to know so well over the last thirteen years.

"Where's Justine?" I asked. "You didn't leave her alone, did you?"

I didn't think any of us were safe in this house, and I couldn't imagine Devlin leaving the love of his undead life asleep and alone.

"No, I sent her to fetch Drake. The five of us need to search this house from top to bottom. It's a large house that's riddled with secret passageways, and despite MacLeod's assurances I want to make damn sure that there's no one in it that we don't know about."

I completely agreed. MacLeod had said that the house was empty except for the five of them, and the five of us, but his wife was a suspected murderer, and after finding Marrakesh on that roof this morning I wasn't so sure I shouldn't be lumping him into that same category. It would be foolish to take his word on anything at this point.

"Tell me something, Cin," Devlin asked. "You know dark magic. What are we dealing with here?"

I arched a brow at him. "I do not *know* dark magic, Devlin. You know I don't practice that."

He held his hand up. "I apologize. I simply meant that you know what it feels like, what it smells like. After Venice, I mean."

I narrowed my eyes. "Do not judge me for that, Devlin. I did what I had to do, or Gage would have killed us."

"Darling," Michael said calmly, "no one is judging you. He was only asking."

Devlin regarded me with very patient, watchful eyes. I blew my breath out and forced the tension from my shoulders. Michael was right. I was overly sensitive on the subject. I had a right to be, though. If an evil wizard abducted you, your lover, and your best friends, and necessity forced you to use dark magic to kill said wizard and nearly a dozen other people in order to escape, you'd be a little touchy about it, too. As far as they knew, I had been cleansed of that evil, was as pure as I had been before we set foot in Venice. I hadn't told any of them, including Michael, but I could still feel it inside me, waiting for an excuse to come out and play. The reasons I had kept this from them were many and varied, and having Devlin insinuate that I knew the dark arts hit a little too close to my guilty secret for me to be comfortable.

"I'm sorry," I said. "It's just a sore subject. I don't really know much about dark magic, but I do know it when I feel and smell it. The magic that's been performed in this house is similar, but it's not exactly like what I felt in Venice. Gage's magic smelled of sulfur and old blood . . . and power. This smells highly of sulfur, not so much of blood, and has the cloyingly bitter odor of . . ." I closed my eyes and inhaled ". . . wormwood maybe?" I shrugged. "I can't tell you what kind of magic it is, but I can tell you that it's powerful and probably very dangerous."

Devlin nodded. "Would you know if you walked into the room where the spells had been cast?"

I thought about it for a moment. "Possibly. The smell would permeate the room where the spell had been cast. But if you think that someone smart enough and powerful enough to work that kind of magic is going to have an altar set up in their bedroom, you're deluding yourself. Unless he's an arrogant fool, he won't make it that easy for us to figure out. I could probably find the room, but I doubt it'll tell us much of anything about who did the casting."

"It is a start, though," he said. "And more than we've gotten so far."

"I understand where you're going with this reasoning, Devlin," Michael interrupted, "but has no one but me figured out the flaw in this theory?"

Devlin leaned forward. "What do you mean?"

"I mean," Michael said, "that we're so used to Cin's magic that we've forgotten that she's the only vampire anyone has ever heard of who is also a witch."

"What's your point?" I asked.

Michael turned to me. "Have you smelled a human in this house?"

I frowned. "Well, no, but the scent of dark magic, or whatever kind of magic this is, might cover it."

Devlin groaned and leaned back in the chair. "But the rest of us can't smell or sense magic the way you do."

Of course. I might not smell a human in the house, but they should certainly be able to. I flopped down against the pillows.

"Damn it," I said to the ceiling. "So, what? We're dealing with another demon in human form? That would mask the scent of a human."

Devlin shook his head. "I would know the scent of a demon. I spent years in Kali's company, after all. Here's a thought: Could a witch or a wizard cast a spell to obliterate his scent?"

I sat up again and tucked the sheets back around

me. "Honestly, I don't know. I've never had the need to try it, but I suppose it wouldn't be too difficult."

There was a brief knock at the door, and before I could call out, Justine stalked in, followed by Drake and Bel. I was surprised to see Bel and wondered what the hell Justine had been thinking to bring her along. I glanced sharply at her but she simply rolled her eyes and put as much distance between herself and Bel as was possible.

Drake propped one shoulder against the mantel and crossed his arms. His gaze lingered on my bare shoulders and the sheet wrapped tightly around me. Seeing that look, I resisted the urge to demand that everyone leave the room so I could dress. Older vampires were immodest to a shocking degree; none of them would have given much thought to being seen in such a state of dishabille. The fact that I was uncomfortable only served to remind me just how young I was.

"My dear, would you care for your dressing gown?" Drake asked, plucking the garment up from the top of my trunk where I'd discarded it earlier. It was a sumptuous thing of crimson silk and delicate Oriental embroidery, imported from China. He held it open, as if I might get up from the bed and allow him to help me into it.

All eyes turned to me, waiting for my response, and I tried to hide the blush that crept into my cheeks. I ducked my head and murmured, "I'm fine where I am, thank you."

Drake shrugged and tossed the robe aside. I glanced at Michael and found his eyes narrowed on Drake, a muscle ticcing in his jaw.

"So," Devlin said, drawing our attention back to the conversation. "It's either a human witch or a demon."

Drake laughed. "A witch or a demon? I think it's more likely that Marrakesh really did murder those people and MacLeod killed Clarissa and then tried to kill Marrakesh in order to cover it up."

"I won't rule it out," I conceded, "but I saw his face when he found the queen and I honestly don't think he had anything to do with it."

Drake shrugged. "You can become quite a good actor in two thousand years, Cin."

I thought about it and then shook my head. "No, I still don't think he did it."

"If we are going to name MacLeod as a suspect, then we must name Khalid and Hashim as well," Justine interjected. "I have known them many years and they would do anything for their king. I do not believe it—I do not want to believe it—but Khalid was the only one with the key to that cell. He could have easily murdered Clarissa to keep her from telling what she had seen, and his brother would have covered for him with that ridiculous story."

"It is the simplest answer," I said, but it still didn't sit well with me. For one, it didn't explain why magic was being worked in this house.

"It still gets us nowhere," Michael said. "Any one

of the three of them could have chained her to that gazebo."

"I think Marrakesh did it to herself," Bel said as she delicately seated herself in the room's other chair and smoothed the ice-blue silk of her dress across her lap.

We all looked at her. Finally I said, "You think that the Queen of the Western Lands took off all her clothes, went out onto the roof just before dawn, and chained herself to the gazebo?"

"Why not?" she said. "It makes perfect sense to me. If you're going to burn up in a pillar of fire, you wouldn't want to ruin a perfectly good dress, now would you?"

I started to ask why any vampire who wanted to greet the dawn would need to chain herself to a building, or how she would even manage to do it alone, but I thought better of it. Instead I said, "Your logic is . . . truly unique."

Bel smiled brightly. "Why, thank you."

I shook my head and turned back to Drake. "Of course, these theories are all nice and tidy, but I've found that, while that works well when dealing with humans, vampires' actions are rarely explained in the simplest of terms."

Drake smiled at me. "So when you hear hoof-beats—"

I smiled back at him. "I think unicorns, not horses. Besides, none of these theories explains the use of magic in the house."

"Ah," Drake said, "but you're assuming that the one has anything at all to do with the other."

I cocked my head to one side. "You're right. Someone in the court could have a human witch who has been practicing some form of the dark arts in this house for quite some time. It would explain the lingering smell and the absence of any human scent. So we're back at the beginning again with a whole lot of questions and absolutely no answers."

Devlin pushed his massive frame out of the chair. "Oh, we'll by God have some answers before the next dawn. First, we're going to search this place from top to bottom, and then at sunset we're going out. I can't trust a thing anyone in this house tells me, but there are people in this city who have no interest in this one way or another, and we're going to talk to them." He looked at Michael. "Have you ever wished you'd gone to university?"

Michael narrowed his blue eyes at his old friend. "No," he said cautiously. "Why?"

Devlin grinned. "Because you're going to get your chance tonight."

# CHAPTER 10

To my chagrin I ended up paired with Bel for the house search. I pulled Justine aside before we started out and asked her why she'd brought Bel into this at all.

"She was coming up the stairs when Drake and I were headed to your room and she somehow managed to invite herself along," she replied.

"And you couldn't have just said no?"

Justine's eyes narrowed. "Trust me, I tried."

"Well, why do I get her?"

"Drake declined to be paired with her, and she is not going with Devlin."

"Or Michael," I agreed.

"And if she comes with me there will be another murder within an hour. So it is up to you, my friend, to take her."

"Thank you ever so much," I said, my voice dripping with sarcasm.

I looked around the drawing room until my eyes

found Drake lounging in a chair by the fireplace. He rose as I approached.

"I don't suppose I could convince you to take Bel for the search?" I asked.

"I would gladly take you," he replied seductively, and I knew he was not talking about the search.

"Ah, but you cannot have me," I assured him.

"Then I shall just have to be content to worship you from afar."

I shook my head. "You are an outrageous flirt."

Drake smiled. "My dear, you have no idea just how outrageous I can be."

Before I could reply, Drake's gaze moved from my face to somewhere over my left shoulder. I turned to find Michael standing behind me. I smiled up at him.

"I was just trying to convince Drake to partner with Bel," I said.

My smile faltered when Michael neither looked at me nor made a reply. His eyes never left Drake's. "It's time," he finally said.

Drake inclined his head. "I will meet you upstairs."

There was malice in Michael's eyes as he watched Drake leave the room. When the other man was out of earshot Michael turned to me. "Must you encourage him?" he demanded.

"I have done nothing of the sort!"

Michael snorted and looked at me in disbelief.

I narrowed my eyes. "I have absolutely no interest in that man and I have never, by word or deed, led him to believe otherwise. He flirts with all the ladies, Michael. If he pays particular attention to me it's just to get a rise out of you. And you, by your own admission, brought that on yourself."

"Oh, so this is *my* fault," Michael snapped and turned to walk away.

I stared after him for a moment, dumbfounded. I'd never heard him speak to me in such a tone, never seen that cold look leveled in my direction. I rushed after him, grabbing his sleeve and pulling him to a stop.

"Michael!" I exclaimed. "What is wrong with you?"

He gritted his teeth and said nothing.

"Oh, for the love of Danu . . . you're jealous!"

I was the one with the jealous streak, not Michael. Certainly many men had flirted with me over the years and I had seen Michael's jealousy piqued on occasion, but never anything like this. I didn't know what made Drake different in his eyes, but the thought I might stray to another man was simply so ridiculous that I laughed.

With a growl Michael pushed past me and strode from the room.

"Michael, wait!" I called out.

I started after him again but Bel suddenly sailed through the door, blocking my exit.

"Are you ready to begin?" she asked brightly.

I sighed and glanced past her, frowning. After we

were finished with the search, I would find Michael and sort this out. For now, perhaps it was wise to leave him be and let his temper cool.

Bel and I were assigned to the second floor, which mostly consisted of the Presence Chamber and smaller receiving rooms and offices. The bedrooms were on the third floor where Drake and Michael were searching, and Devlin and Justine had taken the ground floor and the basement. Bel followed along behind me, her constant chattering intruding on my thoughts of what I would say to Michael later. I tried ignoring her, but she didn't seem to understand that I was doing so. Apparently she was one of those people who couldn't abide silence, because she didn't give me a moment of it. We were nearly finished with our search, finding absolutely nothing out of the ordinary, when something in her incessant babbling caught my attention.

"What did you say?" I turned and asked her.

She looked a bit startled for a moment, as if she wasn't expecting me to be listening, and indeed I hadn't been for over an hour.

"The queen," she said. "She's been crazy for weeks. She was mad as a box of squirrels even before I arrived in Edinburgh. The second night I was here I found her wandering around the halls, talking to the pastries."

I just looked at her, waiting for an explanation, but

she simply stared back at me with that pleasantly vacuous look on her face. "What," I said very slowly, "pastries?"

"You know," she said, waving one hand toward the wall, "the pastries."

I looked at the wall she was pointing to and said through clenched teeth, "You mean the *tapestries*?"

"Yes, that's it," she replied brightly as she continued down the hall. "Talking to the walls." She shook her head and glanced around to make sure I was following, which I was. "I don't know why MacLeod doesn't just let Drake take her off to Castle Tara and be done with it before she kills someone else."

"So you think she's the murderer?" I asked.

She shrugged. "Who else would it be? She was caught delivering the bodies, from what I hear. That's why MacLeod sent the court away, you know. They were already gone by the time I got here, but I heard it from Old Bear down in the Vaults that the reason MacLeod sent the court away is because Marrakesh does his dirty work for him and they'd lose all respect for her if they saw her like she is. Then *he'd* have to take care of all the unpleasantries himself. That's only the beginning of his problems, if you ask me. I mean, how can you be King of the Western Lands if you can't even keep your own wife from running around as wild as a pack of greased weasels? I'm telling you, he needs to get rid of her and find a new enforcer or he's going to lose everything."

I blinked at her. That was the most intelligent, rational thing I'd heard her say yet. "The Vaults?" I asked. "You mean the underground portions of the city?"

"Yes, do you know it?" she inquired as she opened the double doors at the end of the hall that led to MacLeod's formal study.

"I've heard of Edinburgh's underground, but I've never seen it."

"Oh, you should go. There are lots of people. When I first got here Khalid took me into the city and left me to hunt with Old Bear. I don't know why they call him Old Bear. He doesn't look old. Maybe he's been a vampire for a very long time? And he's not big and hairy like a bear. He's kind of short and wiry and smells of peppermint. No, not like a bear at all, in fact, unless it was a very little bear. One who liked peppermint candies. But then he would be called Little Bear instead of Old Bear, don't you think? All I know is that he knows simply everything about everything. He's the one who showed me the Vaults and all the best places to hunt. It's very easy to drink in the Vaults. There are only poor people down there, and they seem willing to do anything for a coin. The smell is horrible, though. I mean really, how hard is it to bathe? I just don't know why people would choose to live like that . . ."

And that was the point I stopped listening again. It looked like I would be heading into town with

Michael and Devlin tonight. I needed blood, and if Bel was right and this Bear knew *simply everything about everything,* then he was someone we needed to talk to.

# CHAPTER 11

Nothing unusual was uncovered by any of us during the search of the house. That was frustrating in itself, but what truly had me on edge was the fact that all afternoon Michael had successfully resisted my subtle efforts to get him alone. At full dark he and Devlin had left for the Medical College without so much as a good-bye. Justine and I followed shortly thereafter, walking down Hanover and Princes streets to North Bridge, then crossing the High Street to South Bridge and the Cowgate. It would have been quicker to take a carriage, but I think Justine sensed that I needed the time and the fresh air to clear my head.

Drake had stayed behind in the shadows, watching the house and anyone who might come or go from it. My instincts told me that MacLeod had nothing to do with the attempt on Marrakesh's life, and I was having serious doubts as to whether or not Marrakesh herself was guilty of murder. Drake could believe all he wanted to in the *lex parsimoniae,* but we had murders, magic being performed in the royal residence, and a queen who was talking to people who weren't there and doing Goddess only knew what else. I didn't for a minute believe that these things were not related. But I had been wrong before, which is why Drake was staying behind to keep an eye on the house.

I fervently hoped that Michael would uncover some valuable information about the murders, or at least about the workings of the anatomy classes and the bodies that were being dissected there. This duty had fallen to him because he was the most suited to pass for a medical student. Drake looked like an aristocratic libertine and Devlin, well, Devlin was nearly six and a half feet tall and weighed over twenty stone. He looked like what he was, a warrior. He and Drake looked like men you would not want to meet in a dark alley. Michael, being five foot ten with a solid but lithe build, would blend in better and wouldn't attract any undue attention. The irony of that was that, of the three of them, Michael was the most dangerous. If it came down to a confrontation, you were better off facing Devlin. He would be reasonable and not offer you violence unless it was clear that you deserved it. With Michael, you sort of took your chances on his mood.

Devlin and I had been born into the aristocracy. He had been raised to command armies of men, and I to command armies of servants. We had both learned from an early age how to manage estates and tenants. Responsibility for other people's lives and well-being had been bred into us. Michael and Justine had both come from more meager beginnings. Their only responsibility had been the care and feeding of their families, and they had accomplished that by any means necessary. They'd both had to fight and scrape for everything they'd ever gotten. If backed into a corner, Devlin and I were more likely to talk and reason our way around it. It was our nature to see a problem, investigate all sides of the issue, and then hand down a fair and rational ultimatum on how said problem would best be resolved. Michael and Justine would just kick your ass and worry about the right or wrong of it later. It made them infinitely more dangerous. The two of them were rash and impetuous and passionate. It was one of the reasons Devlin and I loved them. They were wild and free in a way that we longed to be, but never would be. We were just too bloody English.

Justine walked beside me now, softly humming under her breath, but I could see her eyes watching the street in both directions as we made our way down South Bridge. She was itching for a fight tonight. I had obliged her by wearing the Craven Cross around my neck. Justine had plenty of fine jewelry, but the Craven Cross was quite a large, gaudy piece and would attract the attention she wanted. It was a Celtic cross wrought in gold and set with twenty-four large blood-red rubies and countless small diamonds; wearing the necklace in this part of town pretty much guaranteed that people would be standing in line to slit my throat for it. At least that was the reaction I was hoping for. Justine wanted a fight, so I'd worn the necklace. Never let it be said I'm not a good friend.

We were relatively safe north of Princes Street, where, in these modern times with the threat of invasion gone, those who could afford it had moved out of the cramped confines of the city walls. MacLeod's townhouse was in the fashionable New Town, an architectural marvel that was one of the reasons Edinburgh had earned the epithet *Athens of the North.* Down here in the Old Town, however, no human woman would be safe walking the streets with thousands of pounds' worth of jewelry around her neck. Here the poorer classes were crammed cheek-by-jowl into high-rise tenements and a rabbit warren of underground streets and chambers. Given the steady rise in population and the limited amount of space within the city walls, the residents had built up to the dizzying height of six to twelve stories. There were many places in Edinburgh's Old Town where you could walk down the street in broad daylight and never feel the sun on your skin. Combine that with a population of well over a hundred thousand people, and you had a vampire's paradise. And not only did they build up, but they also built down, creating whole underground cities in some places. It was in the underground vaults below South Bridge that Bel had said we would find Old Bear.

We were nearly to the Cowgate when a man stepped out of the shadowy entrance to one of the many narrow alleyways, dragging a scruffy young boy by the collar of his shirt. Justine and I paused as the man looked up and saw us. He gave us an assessing glare and then whispered to the child and shoved the boy in our direction. The child stumbled, then got his feet under him and made his way toward us. He was skinny and dirty, his ragged clothes hanging on his small frame. He looked to be about twelve, but was probably older than that. There was a touch of fear in his eyes but mostly he had that aged, weary look that so many poor children in the big cities have, like they have seen more horror than anyone should and are now completely desensitized. It's a look of hopelessness, a look that says that they aren't afraid of death because whatever it brings, it has to be better than this. I hated seeing that look on anyone's face, but to see it on a child's always broke my heart.

"Pardon, ladies," he said, snatching his cap off, "would ye be lookin' for a hot meal, then?"

"I beg your pardon?" I asked, not understanding what it was he wanted to know, or why.

The boy glanced back at the man, who I assumed was his father. The man scowled and motioned at the boy with his hands, as if to say *Get on with it*.

The boy looked back at us, wringing his cap between his hands. "I ken what ye are and I was wonderin' if ye'd be lookin' for a hot meal." He tapped his finger on the side of his neck. "Only cost tuppence a drink."

I jerked my head back and looked at Justine. "Is this what happens in MacLeod's city? Children selling their blood?"

"It is MacLeod's rule that if you drink from the poor, you must pay them," Justine said. "It is a good law, but every law is susceptible to exploitation, *non*?"

The boy seemed to get nervous at our exchange and the outrage in my voice.

"Och, miss, if ye'd like something a bit older then . . ." He turned to his father again, and the man barked out an order. Soon there was a shuffling sound from the shadowy recesses of the alley and a woman who could only be the boy's mother appeared, five children like stairsteps in tow. The mother looked no older than thirty, her carrot-red hair in disarray and a large purple bruise marring her right cheekbone. Her eyes were dead, vacant, but her hands clutched her oldest child, a girl of about fourteen, and her youngest, a little boy of maybe seven, in a death grip.

The father finally stepped forward, looking at me with a leering smile that made my skin crawl. "Any one ye want, ladies, tuppence a drink."

I clenched my fists until my nails had left deep furrows in my palms.

"Justine, do you have your purse with you?" I asked and glanced over at her with a wink.

*"Oui,"* she said. "I will take care of it."

Justine took the boy gently by the arm and led him over to his mother. I watched as she pried the woman's hand off her oldest child and placed what looked like a ten-pound note in it. It was probably close to what a housemaid would earn in a year.

"Take your children and go," she said. "Get away from this man who hurts you and sells your children like whores on the street. Go back to wherever you were the last time you were happy."

The mother stared at Justine for a long time, then looked dumbly at the money in her hand. She turned her head slowly to look at her husband. The man's face showed momentary shock, but as his wife's fist closed tightly over the note his countenance mottled with rage.

"That'll be mine. I'm the man of the house!" he said and started toward her.

She shrank back, instinctively moving her children behind her. Justine stepped in front of her just as I grabbed the man by the neck and jerked him back.

"You," I hissed in his ear, "are less than a man. Nothing they have belongs to you anymore. You won't hurt them, not ever again."

He struggled against me but he was only a human, and a pathetic one at that. I held him as effortlessly as one would hold a puppy as he cursed me, Justine, his wife, and his children in succession.

The mother turned back to Justine with wide eyes and whispered, "Who are you?"

"I am the Devil's Justice," she replied. "Now go."

The mother tucked the money into her bodice and looked once more at her husband. She shot him a glare that was angry, defiant, and triumphant, and it infuriated him even further. He lashed out at me, and I cuffed him on the side of the head hard enough to bring him to his knees. His wife smiled.

"Thank you," she said. She turned back to Justine and reached out, taking her hand. "Thank you. May God's grace forever shine on you."

Justine squeezed her hand. "Go. We'll take care of him."

The woman scooted her children off down the street, herding them like a mother hen. The boy who had approached us stopped and looked back at us in bewilderment, but his sister quickly snagged him by the shirt and pulled him along down the street.

The bastard at my feet groaned, and I pulled him to his feet. I was hungry and he was frightened, his blood pounding in his veins, calling to me.

"Normally I would bespell you so that you don't feel any pain, but I want to hurt you. I want you to feel it all. I want to taste your fear as you've tasted the fear of your family every time you've abused them. How many vampires have you sold those children to? Can you imagine how frightened they must have been?" I pulled him back against me so that my lips hovered just above the big vein that throbbed in his neck. "Doesn't matter," I hissed. "You will."

"You bitch!" he spat. "I'll kill you for this! And then I'll track down that faithless whore and kill her, too!"

I laughed. "You'll do nothing of the sort. You'll

bleed for me, and then you'll crawl back into whatever pit of hell you came from." I dug my nails into his arms. "And if you ever come near that woman or her children again, I will come for you in the dark of night. There will be nowhere you can run, nowhere you can hide. I will bleed you dry and revel in your screams as I do so."

Of course, I wouldn't, but I've found that when you're a vampire a little threat goes a long way. He stilled, finally realizing the trouble he was in. I looked over his shoulder and watched Justine approach. The man's heart beat like the wings of a hummingbird under my fingers, below my lips. My fangs lengthened and I sank them into the right side of his neck. He screamed as blood poured into my mouth. It had been years since I'd taken a human and not bespelled him. There were vampires who loved the screams, the fear, but I was not one of them. I felt a brief pang of regret that I hadn't put him under. And then the memories came.

When you feed from a human you get images, flashes of their thoughts or memories. It isn't like taking a stroll down memory lane with them, but you do get bits and pieces of whatever they happen to be thinking of at the time. I've learned to shield from this because I don't feed from blushing virgins who would give me images of skipping through fields of lavender in the sunshine. No, I generally feed from those who deserve to be used as food for the undead:

rapists, cutthroats, thieves, and wastrels. The kind of
men you'd find in a dark alley at night. I don't want
to know what they're thinking; it's usually the stuff
of nightmares. This man was no different. A few seconds of the horror those children had experienced at
his hands and I slammed that mental door firmly
shut. And then I bit harder.

The click of Justine's heels on the cobblestones
caught my attention. As I drank, I watched her come
to stand in front of us. She fisted her hands in the
man's shirt and then struck quickly and without hesitation. Both of us fed from him, one on each side of
his neck. When his heartbeat began to slow I pulled
back.

"Justine," I said.

She didn't move from him. I grabbed her by the
hair and pulled her away.

"Justine, stop. You'll kill him."

"He deserves it."

"Yes, he does," I said in a calm, rational voice.
"But his life is not ours to take."

It was illegal to kill humans, except under extenu-
ating circumstances. *He needed killing* was just not a
valid defense. The High King had decreed that we
must not kill humans, and that we must never inter-
fere in the affairs of their world. Since the vampire
had yet to be turned who could defeat the High King
in one-on-one combat, his word was law. Besides, it
was just common sense that you do not go around

extinguishing a renewable source of food. Not to mention that doing so would draw attention to our kind. True, we were stronger and faster than humans. One vampire could fight twenty of them and still come out victorious. But if you get enough humans together, armed with enough torches, eventually sheer numbers and firepower—quite literally—will win out. Humans liked a mob, and a mob was not the vampire's friend. Thus, no killing and no meddling. Even if they did have it coming.

Justine had to be reminded of this sometimes. She had a very strong sense of what was right and what was wrong. For someone who had lived for centuries she still had an almost child-like view of the world. Things were black or white to her. She and Michael both very rarely saw the gray that most of us learn to live with. And they were both hotheaded enough that if Devlin and I didn't keep an eye on them, *they* might end up being guilty of the crimes that we so often executed vampires for. I couldn't count the times over the years that I'd had to pull Justine back before she crossed that line. She often did not appreciate my efforts on her behalf. Such was the case this time.

She hissed at me and threw the man against a wall, where he crumpled like a discarded rag doll.

"Ah, shite, have you killed him then?" a male voice asked.

I spun, surprised that someone had managed to come up behind me without my sensing it. That didn't happen often. It meant that I was either getting sloppy or the vampire leaning against the wall was very old. I was betting on the latter.

He was about Michael's height, but he appeared smaller. His body didn't have the weight of Michael's muscle, and it gave him a lean, hungry look. His hair was dark and cut short, yet it still managed to look tousled, as if he'd been running his fingers through it. The short cut accentuated his hawkish features and the pair of round spectacles perched on his nose. He was dressed rather haphazardly in a brown vest with a small striped pattern that didn't quite match his brown trousers. His cream-colored shirt was open at the throat, and the sleeves were rolled up on his forearms. He looked like nothing more than a clerk who had been bent over his ledgers all day. It would fool most people.

"He'll live," I said cautiously, and hoped that I was right.

"Pity," the vampire replied. "I'd almost turn a blind eye if someone killed that one."

"You know him?"

He strolled over to the man on the ground and nudged him with one foot. The man groaned but didn't move. The vampire shrugged and turned back to me, taking his spectacles off and cleaning the lenses with a rumpled handkerchief that he'd fished out of the depths of his breast pocket. I wondered at the affectation. As a vampire he wouldn't need them to see clearly. Perhaps it was meant to lull the vampires he dealt with into a false sense of security. With the spectacles he looked like an unassuming clerk; without them he looked more like a man who might cut your throat for your purse.

"I try to keep the children away from us," he said, "but it's not easy. That one thinks a hard day's work would kill him. It's only a matter of time before he has his eldest girl working the streets so that he can sit on his lazy arse in the pub all day and night."

"Justine gave the mother some money. Hopefully she'll use it to get her children far away from here."

He walked up and stood very close to me. He looked at me, at my face, my hair, my neck. It wasn't a predatory look. It was more like he was memorizing every detail, from the freckle on my left cheekbone to the number of stones in my necklace. It was . . . disconcerting.

"Yes," he said, his voice dripping with sarcasm, "because women so often do what's best for them."

I caught a whiff of peppermint as he spoke. What was it Bel had said? *I don't know why they call him Old Bear. He doesn't look old. Maybe he's been a vampire for a very long time? And he's not big and hairy like a bear. He's kind of short and wiry and smells of peppermint.* I smiled.

"Mr. Bear," I said, in as professional a manner as I could muster, "my name is Cin Craven. I need to speak to you about some urgent matters regarding the queen."

I waited for a response, but he simply cocked his head to one side, his dark eyes assessing me. It was what a bird of prey must look like just before it swoops down and snatches up some unsuspecting field mouse. I took a step back and gathered my composure. By the gods, I was the Red Witch of the Righteous, and I would not be made to feel like a field mouse, especially by someone with such a ridiculous name.

"Mr. Bear," I began again, but he turned to Justine and spoke rapidly in French.

It was perfectly flawless, idiomatic French that loosely translated to something like, *Why does the daft woman keep calling me Mr. Bear?*

I stamped my foot and he turned his attention back to me. "You needn't speak to her as though I'm not here," I said. "I understand French perfectly. I've lived with her for the past thirteen years, after all. And I am not daft. I called you Mr. Bear because I was informed that there was a man whom I could find near the South Bridge Vaults who knows everything about everything that happens in Edinburgh, and his name is Old Bear."

He frowned and asked, "Who, exactly, told you that?"

"Belinda."

I got no response.

"Bel," I said again. "Small, dark hair, lavender eyes, dumb as a box of rocks."

The frown went away and he smiled. "Ah, yes, the extraordinarily lovely houseguest of the king and queen. She said my name was Old Bear?"

"Yes, she did."

He threw back his head and laughed. I looked at Justine and she just shrugged. Old Bear doubled over, his hands on his knees. It was a nice laugh, and was almost infectious. Almost. I crossed my arms and waited for him to finish. It took a while.

The spectacles and handkerchief reappeared out of his pocket. He dabbed his eyes and then put his spectacles back on. When he'd composed himself once more he said, "It's a good thing that she's beautiful because she doesn't have the wits God gave a dormouse. My name is not Old Bear, it's *Aubert,* Jacques Aubert. I am Chief Warden of the City of Edinburgh."

He extended his hand and I took it, shaking my head. "That woman is a menace," I muttered.

I introduced him to Justine, and they exchanged pleasantries in French.

"So, Monsieur Aubert, you're French?" I asked. When he'd first arrived his accent was definitely Scottish, but it lapsed back and forth into several English dialects as well. His French, however, was perfect.

"I am many things, Miss Craven, but yes, I came from France originally. I have, however, been in Edinburgh since Mary Stuart sat on the throne, and the fair Belinda is correct about one thing: I do know everything there is to know about what goes on in my city."

"Oh, good," I said, not quite liking his smug tone,

"then perhaps you can tell me who is killing humans on your watch."

He flinched. Oh, he covered it quickly enough, but I caught it.

"I know nothing about that. It's not a vampire problem."

"Someone tried to murder your queen last night," Justine said. "If that is not a vampire problem, then what is?"

He glared at Justine. "The king's household is his to protect. He has Khalid and Hashim, and they are more than equal to the task. What goes on inside the court is not my business. She asked about the murders, and I'm telling you that I don't think a vampire is responsible."

"Why?" I asked.

"Because the bodies are not being delivered by vampires, there are no puncture marks on them, and they are not drained of blood. If it were a vampire killing these people, why wouldn't they drink from them? If you're not going to feed, what's the point?"

I tended to agree with him, and I wondered if Michael would be able to verify MacLeod's and Aubert's assertions about the condition of the bodies when he returned from his visit to the Medical College tonight.

"Clarissa saw the queen herself deliver one of the bodies," I remarked.

"Aye, and Clarissa's dust now, isn't she?" he snapped.

"You're afraid," I muttered.

He nodded. "And you're a fool if you're not. I'm not afraid of anything I can fight, but something that can get past the king's lieutenants and murder a vampire in the court's holding cell without anyone seeing anything is not something I want to be involved with."

"Whatever, or whoever, is doing this, it's after your queen," I pointed out.

"Aye, well, and that's why you're here, is it not? You do your job, and I'll do mine."

"I'm trying to do my job, Aubert, but you're making it bloody difficult. You can lie to me and tell me that you don't know anything, but I think you probably know what goes on in this town down to the number of bottles of contraband whiskey that are smuggled in and out of here on a daily basis. Will you really let your queen die because you're afraid to talk to me?"

He raked his hand through his hair. "Ah, bollocks," he muttered and then snaked a hand out and pulled me up against him. I started to struggle, but then he was whispering in my ear and I froze. "I've seen men delivering the bodies to the college," he said, "and they're always human. Every vampire in town has heard rumors, but Clarissa was the only one who's ever claimed to have actually seen anything to associate the queen with these deaths."

"Do you know how they were killed?" I whispered.

"I've heard it's most likely suffocation," he replied.

"And if you're a vampire, why would you kill a human that way?"

"You wouldn't," I replied, "especially not if you're trying to make it look like another vampire has done the deed."

"Aye, the only way you'd kill someone like that is if you're human."

"Or if you're a vampire who's crazy."

Aubert pursed his lips. "I can assure you that if the Queen of the Western Lands had been running around Edinburgh murdering over a dozen people in the last year, someone other than Clarissa would have seen *something*."

"All right," I said and stepped back. "Can you tell me if anyone new has taken up residence in Edinburgh or the surrounding areas since the murders started?"

Aubert took a notepad out of his breast pocket and flicked through it. "Of course I can. Immigration control is one of my primary responsibilities. Other than court officials there are one hundred permanent resident vampires in Edinburgh and fifty places reserved for visitors. Visitors must apply for a vacant place and are only allowed to stay for six months before they are required to leave the city. It's a policy that's strictly enforced." He inclined his head toward us. "Emissaries of the High King have no need to apply for entrance, of course."

"So there are approximately one hundred fifty vampires in town?" Justine asked.

He cocked a brow at her. "There's no approximation about it, my dear girl. There are exactly fifty visiting vampires in town, none of whom has been here longer than six months. The court is made up of fifty permanent residents, but they've all decamped to Castle Darkness, so that just leaves the fifty residents who are not attached to the court. Add in the five of you, the king and queen themselves, Khalid and Hashim, myself, and my four captains and there are exactly one hundred fourteen vampires in Edinburgh."

Justine and I looked at each other. "That's . . . amazing," I said. "What do you do if someone moves in without permission?"

"I'd know of it within an hour and they would be given twenty-four hours to depart or I am within my rights as Chief Warden to have them thrown into the street at high noon."

That would certainly be a very effective way of enforcing the law. "And what about Bel?" I asked. "When did she arrive, exactly?"

Aubert flipped through his notebook. "She made port in Leith four months ago."

I nodded. Of all the residents in the king's household, she was the only one we could reasonably exclude as a suspect.

My attention was caught by the sound of someone running down the street. A young man came racing out of the darkness like the very hounds of hell were after him. He skidded to a halt in front of Aubert.

*"Wächter, eine gruppe von zehn vampiren ist gerade ohne genehmigung in die stadt eingedrungen."*

Aubert nodded and replied, *"Danke,* Fritz. *Ich werde mich darum kümmern."*

He turned back to us. "You'll have to excuse me, ladies. I have a situation that requires my attention."

Justine smiled. "What you have is a rather large group of vampires trespassing in your city, Warden. Would you care for some help with that?"

"You speak German as well." He smiled and inclined his head. "A woman of many talents. *Merci beaucoup, mademoiselle,* but I can handle this."

He kissed both our hands in a very courtly manner and then bid us *adieu.*

As I watched him disappear down the cobbled street, the young German lad trailing behind, Justine came up beside me and put her hand on my arm.

"What did he say to you?" she asked.

I looked around, wondering just who it was that Aubert had worried would overhear him. I linked my arm with hers and said, "Let's go find our boys, and I'll tell you on the way."

# CHAPTER 12

"So what do you think?" I asked Justine.

"I think Jacques is correct. It's hardly likely that the queen has killed a dozen people without anyone seeing anything."

"Anyone but Clarissa, that is."

She shrugged. "I think this town is probably crawling with Aubert's spies. He wouldn't be a good Warden if it was not. If anyone other than a human was committing these murders, he would know it."

I shook my head. "That's what I don't understand. Why would a vampire kill multiple people without drinking from them? A feral vampire will always drink. We have seen it often enough."

"And why sell the bodies to a human to sell to the Medical College? There's no logical reason to it." She waved a hand. *"Il est fou."*

"Yes, it is crazy," I replied. "Then again, perhaps that's what we're meant to believe."

At that moment we both saw two familiar figures

turn onto South Bridge from Infirmary Street a block
ahead of us. Justine and I paused as we watched our
men make their way up the street in front of us. I
loved the way Michael walked, full of masculine
grace with just a touch of a swagger. Justine giggled
and nudged me.

"Stop drooling. *Mon Dieu,* you two are like bun-
nies," she quipped.

"Us two? Don't try to tell me that you aren't throwing Devlin's clothes off every chance you get. I live
with the two of you. I know."

She gave me that coquettish smile. "Well, he is
particularly lovely without his clothes on."

I laughed. We could have called out to them, but
for the moment we simply followed them up the
road, enjoying the view.

"You were saying?" Justine asked.

"Was I?" I murmured, thinking of nothing more
than what I would like to be doing with Michael
right now.

"That we were meant to believe the queen is mad?"

"Oh, yes," I said, getting my mind back on the
matter at hand. "I think we've walked into the middle of a coup."

"Truly? Then why not go after MacLeod instead
of Marrakesh? If she is executed, he is still king."

"But for how long? In case you hadn't noticed, I
don't think the man *does* anything. She's the one
everyone fears. She's the one who metes out the

punishment. He seems to be little more than a figurehead. If you want to take a throne, you take down the power behind the throne first."

Justine shook her head. "It may be true, but I think you vastly underestimate MacLeod. He was given his kingdom by the High King himself. I doubt that such an honor would be bestowed to a man who was not worthy."

I shrugged. "He may well have been. But how many centuries ago was that? Perhaps he truly is a force to be reckoned with. How would anyone know? It seems that Marrakesh has been running the city here for quite some time. Either way, I don't think that it necessarily matters what the truth is, but what the murderer *believes*."

"So we take her away. Either the murderer will go after MacLeod's throne, or he will come after her. In either case, we draw him out into the open."

"And if she truly is crazy and running about killing people, if we can get her out of town and isolated, we'll know that, too."

Justine nodded. "*Oui,* it is a good plan."

I was about to call out to Michael and Devlin when I saw something that stopped me cold.

They were walking down the street, talking earnestly to each other, much as Justine and I had been, when they passed a prostitute lounging against the pole of one of the gaslights. From a distance her features were indiscernible, but she did have an incredibly impressive bosom that filled the bodice of what passed as a gown to overflowing. And Michael looked. Devlin walked past her without blinking an eye, but Michael, *my Michael,* turned and looked.

I stopped and stared. He kept walking without a word to her, but that appreciative glance made me feel like someone had just punched me in the stomach.

It took Justine several steps to realize that I wasn't beside her anymore. She turned and came back to me. She'd seen it, too, and for some reason that made it sting even worse.

"He looked," I said, my voice sounding hollow even to me.

"Of course he did, *chérie.* He is a man."

I shook my head. "Devlin didn't look."

She snorted. "Devlin caught my scent the moment they turned onto South Bridge." She shrugged. "It is the new perfume I bought in Paris."

"It's lovely," I murmured, because it seemed like the thing to say.

Justine touched my cheek and turned my face, making me look at her. "*Chérie,* it means nothing. They are vampires, true, but they are still just men. A man will look at a whore with her breasts hanging out of the front of her gown. Of course he will look, but it is just a glance. Why do you anger yourself over such a trifle? You know that Michael loves you with all his heart."

"I know," I whispered. "It's just that I've never seen him look at another woman like that before. I'm not mad, I just . . . I need to walk."

If I stayed with Justine we would catch up to Devlin and Michael in a few minutes, and I didn't particularly want to see Michael just now. My pride was wounded, and if I didn't get some perspective I would say something spiteful to him that I would probably regret later.

I turned and started down Hunter Square behind the Tron Kirk.

"Cin! Wait!" Justine called.

I raised a hand and waved her off. "I'll meet you back at the house. I'm fine."

But I wasn't fine. Oh, I didn't worry over some prostitute that he glanced at on the street, not really. I'd be the worst sort of hypocrite if that had upset me, for hadn't I looked at Drake with similar appreciation recently? What bothered me was that I'd seen Michael gaze at me that way, thousands of times, but I'd never seen that look directed at another woman.

I thought of the night Fiona and I had talked of her husband's travels in India. Was this what she'd meant by karma? Was this my punishment for enjoying Drake's flirtatious banter a little too much? Already it had caused a rift between Michael and me, and now this.

I picked up my pace, cutting down Bank Street, past the rather impressive new Bank of Scotland. When I got to the park that lay in the shadow of Edinburgh Castle I picked up my skirts and ran. The park wasn't nearly big enough. I could run for miles without tiring, and right now it felt as if I could run for days. When I got to the far side of the park I stopped and leaned against the iron fence, staring at the traffic moving along Princes Street. It was just a glance. I knew it didn't mean anything, but in light of the argument we'd had earlier, I felt as though my world was beginning to unravel.

# CHAPTER 13

I was nearly back at the townhouse when I heard movement behind me. I turned and found Drake standing in the shadows, watching me.

"Trouble in paradise, my dear?" he asked as he walked to me slowly.

I looked up into his green eyes. "I don't know what you're talking about."

"Of course you do," he said softly, leaning toward me until his lips were nearly touching mine. I repressed the urge to back up and stood my ground. We would have this out now, Drake and I.

He inhaled. "You smell of discontent. The boy's made you angry."

"It's nothing," I said shortly. "Just a bad night."

My body tensed as his fingers came up and caressed my cheek, slowly trailing down to my jawline, my neck.

"Would you care to repay him for hurting you? You can let all that anger loose with me. I promise you a night that you'll never forget."

His fingers kept moving down, down, and I grabbed his wrist and squeezed. "You must stop this, Drake," I snapped. "I know you have a history with Michael and you only say these things to even a score with him. I dislike being used in such a manner."

Drake shook his head. "Is that what you think? I will admit that it pleases me to see him mad with jealousy, but, Cin, you are a woman worth risking any consort's displeasure over," he said, and a strange sort of tenderness crept over his features. It was a look I'd never seen in Drake's eyes before and I almost believed that he meant what he said. "All that crimson hair and pale skin—you're like fire and ice, my dear. I'll wager every man you meet wonders what it would be like to have you."

I laid my hand on his chest, and said softly, "I'm sorry, Drake. No one but Michael will ever have me."

His expression grew cold and that fleeting bit of tenderness was suddenly gone, as if he'd firmly slammed the door on such a vulnerable emotion. "You're so young," Drake laughed in that bitter, humorless way of his. "Justine warned me to stay away from you. She said that Michael was the only lover you'd ever had and that you weren't up to playing my games. You don't know what you're missing, my dear."

I shoved him away from me. It made me angry that Justine would say something like that to him. Justine and I were best friends, but sometimes she acted as if I was unable to care for myself without her guidance.

How long would it be before she stopped seeing me as a newly turned fledgling she had to cosset and protect?

"Let me explain something to you, Drake," I said harshly. "You may be a handsome devil, but you hold no interest for me. I feel nothing for you, and you feel nothing for me other than the possibility of getting one over on Michael for whatever happened between the two of you in the past. Michael is my heart and my soul, and if you think I would jeopardize that just to sample your charms, then you're as crazy as the queen."

He looked down at me and smiled, giving me such a condescending expression that I wanted to smite him with a ball of fire right there on the sidewalk.

I shook my head sadly. "You stand there with that look on your face, mocking me for my youth and inexperience. Has it really been so long since you were in love?" I asked. "It doesn't matter. If you cannot understand my reasoning, then let me put it in terms a jaded womanizer such as yourself will comprehend." I grabbed the lapels of his frock coat, pulling him down so that I could whisper in his ear. "Unless you can give me ten orgasms in an hour, as he can, then you have nothing whatsoever to offer me."

I turned him loose and strode across the street. I was angry. Angry at Michael for sleeping with that trollop all those years ago and putting me in this position in the first place, and at myself for perhaps allowing things with Drake to go too far, but mostly I was angry at Drake for his callous disregard of the impact his games were causing in my life.

I took the steps to the townhouse two at a time, and then slammed the door behind me. Khalid came out of one of the drawing rooms, a disapproving scowl on his face, and opened his mouth to say something.

"Where is he?" I snapped.

"The king?" Khalid asked.

"Yes, the king. Where is he?"

"In his study," Khalid replied, his disapproving look turning to one of bewilderment. It probably wasn't often that he saw an angry woman storming through the royal residence. Something had occurred to me, though, as I was crossing the street after leaving Drake with his mouth open on the sidewalk. MacLeod was being less than forthcoming with us, and tonight I was in just a foul enough mood to force some answers from him.

# CHAPTER 14

I threw open the doors to MacLeod's study. He was sitting at his desk, polishing a rather lovely basket-hilted claymore, which he promptly dropped as I slammed the doors behind me. He rose to his feet and we stared at each other across the desk.

"Where do they live?" I asked.

"Who?"

"Your court. I talked to Jacques Aubert tonight. He said there are fifty vampires in your court who are now at Castle Darkness. There aren't enough bedchambers in this house to accommodate them all. When they're in town, where do they live?"

He looked at me with a puzzled expression, like he couldn't grasp the significance. Maybe he hadn't yet, but he would. "They live in the other townhouses."

"What," I said slowly, "other townhouses?"

"I own the two townhouses on either side of this one. They've been converted to house the court."

"And you didn't think that it was important to tell us this, oh, say, *while we were searching this house*?"

He shrugged. "I didn't think it was relevant."

I closed my eyes and took a steadying breath. I had to, or I was going to explode. "You didn't think it was relevant that the person who is working magic against your queen is quite possibly doing it from a room directly on the other side of the wall from your bedchamber? That didn't seem relevant to you? Are you stupid? Or are you *trying* to get her killed?"

His eyes narrowed and I could feel the anger rising in him. It probably hadn't been wise to push him like that, but I was about at the end of my tether tonight and I was tired of trying to convince everyone that MacLeod was innocent when he was making himself look guilty at every turn.

He braced his fists on the desk and leaned across it. "You will not speak to me like that, madam. I am king here, not you."

I braced my hands on the opposite side of the desk and leaned toward him. "Then why don't you get off your ass and start acting like it!"

"I beg your pardon?"

"Someone is trying for your throne, MacLeod, and they're using Marrakesh to get it. From what I've seen she's the monarch here, not you. She's the one everyone is afraid of."

"I have more important matters to concern myself with than the policing of a handful of vampires in this city. I am King of the Western Lands, duly appointed by the High King himself. Do you think that the whole of western Europe just runs itself?"

I cocked my head to one side. "How did you get to be King of the Western Lands, anyway?"

He looked surprised, as if no one had ever asked him that before. "I was there when the High King was fighting all comers for his right to rule."

"So you acquitted yourself well in battle with him?" I asked.

"No, actually Drake and I were the only ones who declined to take up arms against him. He gave us our kingdoms because we had the wisdom not to fight a battle we could not win. He said that he needed kings who possessed the wisdom to keep a level head and would not get so caught up in the thrill of battle that they didn't know when they were headed for disaster."

He seemed proud of that fact, but his story only added to my growing frustration. "So you got your throne by not fighting, and you keep it by letting your queen fight for you?"

It was perhaps the wrong thing to say.

In one blink of an eye he was no longer standing on the other side of the desk. I'd never seen a vampire move that fast. My eyes couldn't even track him. When I turned to see where he had gone, the tip of the claymore that had been on his desk pressed into my cheek. I took a steadying breath and held very still.

"Let me explain something to you, little girl," he ground out, his voice low and vibrating with barely restrained anger. "I am probably the oldest vampire you will ever meet. I was leading men into battle when Rome was still an empire. I have spilled enough blood to fill the Trevi Fountain. I can assure you that I do not fear death or battle. There are reasons that Marrakesh is my enforcer, reasons that you cannot begin to understand, and I don't feel the need to justify them to you."

I moved a step to the left. When the blade didn't follow, I took another step and turned. Standing there with that sword in his hand, he looked like the king that he should be.

"Well, maybe you should explain it to me," I said softly, "because right now I'm just about the only one who doesn't think you're guilty of something here, and the more you keep from us the more guilty you look."

He lowered the sword to his side, the tip of it tapping against his boot to mark his irritation. "I am not keeping anything from you, Miss Craven. The houses are locked and the only keys to them are in my safe. Only Marrakesh and I have the combination."

"And there are no hidden passages in either of these houses?"

He smiled. "Yes, there are passages to be used as escape routes in case of fire, but they are all locked and bolted from the inside."

"And it's impossible that someone might have broken in by way of a window?"

"All the ground-floor windows are sealed, and as of this evening all windowpanes are intact."

I sighed. He wasn't purposely trying to undermine our efforts; he really didn't understand what he was up against.

"MacLeod, a good witch or wizard doesn't need your keys to open those houses. There isn't a lock made that I can't break with magic, and you'd never know if I had done so or not."

He looked embarrassed. "I had no idea," he said finally.

"That's the problem. You have no idea what you're dealing with here. You need to be straight with me and, by the gods, you need to help us instead of hindering us, and let us do our jobs before it's too late."

"She's right."

I turned to see Marrakesh standing in the doorway. I wondered just exactly how much of our exchange she'd overheard. Given the sensitivity of a vampire's hearing and the volume at which we'd been shouting at each other, I was betting she'd heard most of it.

She stepped back and pushed the door wide. "Come, Miss Craven," she said and gestured to the hallway. "I believe it's time you and I had a talk."

# CHAPTER 15

I followed Marrakesh silently up the stairs to her chamber, feeling a bit like a schoolgirl being called to the headmistress's office. Except no headmistress ever looked like Marrakesh. Her long golden hair was unbound and the white dress she wore clung to her curves, its train flowing behind her on a whisper. The sleeves were long and belled and partially obscured the white gloves on her hands. All she needed was a conical hat with a scarf floating from it, and she would look like everyone's idea of a medieval princess.

Her bedchamber was warm, a roaring fire in the hearth providing plenty of heat and light. Hashim was bent over the table between the two Roman couches. He jerked upright when he heard us enter the room, as if he'd been caught doing something he ought not be doing. I glanced behind him to see what he'd been so busy with, and found an ornate silver tea service on the table. He saw me looking at it and scowled. The big Arab hadn't liked me catching him delivering tea to the queen. With the shortage of servants in the house someone had to do it, and I assumed that he thought that such a task was beneath him. I smiled at him in what I hoped was a friendly, encouraging manner but he just scowled harder, if that was possible. Truly, the man did not like me. I wondered, not for the first time, if it was just me or if he had an aversion to all women.

Hashim bowed to Marrakesh. "I will be just outside if you need me, my queen."

She inclined her head to him. "Thank you, Hashim."

Marrakesh sat on one of the couches and motioned for me to sit next to her. The big double doors closed with a solid thump, a little more forcefully than necessary, as I took a seat. Marrakesh winced.

"You'll have to forgive him," she said. "He worries."

I smiled at her tightly.

"Go ahead and say it," she said. "You certainly held nothing back with MacLeod a few minutes ago."

I chuckled. "I was merely thinking that he worries unnecessarily. If I wished you harm, I would have let you burn this morning."

Her eyebrows raised and she stared at me a moment. Then she laughed. "*Touché,* Miss Craven. Chocolate?" she asked, pouring the rich, dark liquid into a dainty Sèvres cup.

I inhaled the aroma. "Mmmm. English or Swiss?"

She smiled. "Dutch, actually. It's made with a new process. Have a taste."

She handed me the cup and saucer and I took it, being very careful not to touch her in any way as I did so. I blew across the rim of the cup, watching her, and waited as she poured another for herself. Taking a sip, I let the drink roll around on my tongue before I swallowed.

"Dear Goddess, this has to be the best chocolate I've ever tasted."

"Isn't it lovely? I'll package some up for you when your work here is done."

I thanked her. She took an appreciative sip herself then settled against one end of the couch. I settled against the other and we regarded each other over the white-and-gold Sèvres cups while I waited for her to open the conversation.

"I hear that I owe you a large debt, Miss Craven. MacLeod tells me that you saved my life this morning."

I shook my head. "It would please me if you would call me Cin," I said. "And you owe me nothing, Highness, truly. I'm just glad that we found you before the dawn did."

"As am I," she replied.

"Are you feeling better?" I asked.

"Whatever is ailing me, it comes and goes. I assure you that I am perfectly lucid at the moment." She took a long sip of her chocolate, and I had to repress the urge to shift uncomfortably under her gaze. "So tell me, did you save me just so that you and Devlin can kill me later, or lock me up in Castle Tara like a madwoman?"

I was silent for a moment and then said, truthfully, "I don't know yet."

She laughed. "Well, I thank you for being honest, anyway. It gives me hope that you'll keep an open mind. I know Devlin and Justine, and I know them to be fair. I have faith that you'll catch whoever is trying to make me look guilty of these murders. I can't believe anyone truly imagines that I'm running around Edinburgh killing people and selling their bodies. It's ridiculous."

I didn't tell her that we had all pretty much come to the same conclusion. I was hoping that if she was motivated to prove her innocence, then she might let something slip that could actually be useful to us.

"I'm happy to have help in figuring this out, though," she said. "It's obvious from what happened last night that whoever is responsible is working some nasty magic against me."

"You think someone is working magic against you?" I asked.

"I've been losing time, a few hours here and there at first, now sometimes it's days. Yesterday, for example—one minute I'm sitting in that chair in front of the fire, trying to make it through Mrs. Radcliffe's *Gaston de Blondeville,* and the next I'm chained to

the gazebo on the roof, apparently. I don't even remember being there."

"So you don't recall seeing or hearing anything
unusual while you were reading? Even if it seems
unimportant, it might be helpful."

She shook her head. "No, nothing."

Well, that was disheartening. Now we had someone who could not only work magic but also defy a
vampire's keen sense of hearing.

"What about food or drink?" I asked. "Did you
have anything to eat or drink just prior to . . . the incident?"

She narrowed her eyes. "You think someone
drugged me?"

I shrugged. "Or managed to slip a magic potion
into your food."

I looked down at my cup of chocolate, and she
looked at hers. Marrakesh gingerly set hers down on
the tray, and I did the same with mine. It clattered
more than I would have liked. My mind flashed on the
image of Hashim bent over the tray when we came in,
of the guilty look on his face when he stood up. My
stomach clenched and I had to tear my gaze away
from the silver teapot when Marrakesh answered.

"No," she said, "I hadn't had anything since Khalid
brought a young man to me at about nine o'clock."

"Do you have regular people that you drink from?"
I asked. It wasn't uncommon for vampires to have
veritable harems of willing donors. Many vamps

didn't like to drink from strangers, and I'd found that the vampires of the higher classes, regents and their courts, usually didn't go out and hunt. They had people who brought their meals to them. Some habits even death doesn't change.

Marrakesh surprised me, though. "No," she said. "Khalid brings MacLeod and me someone fresh every night. It's too easy for humans to get addicted to feeding us, no matter how willing they think they are."

She was right. Drinking blood from a human is a very sensual thing, whether you wish it to be or not. It's why most vampires will generally only drink from the opposite sex, unless their sexual tastes run to the same gender to begin with. The process can be painful, it can be downright erotic, or the human can walk away without remembering a thing. It all depends on what degree of control the vampire doing the drinking wields. To do it painlessly, or with pleasure, you have to bespell them. It's a form of mind control that vampires acquire with age. Often a human who has been drunk from on a regular basis will come to crave it, as one would crave a drug or a lover's touch. The feelings aren't real, though. They're not built on anything more substantial than vampire magic.

Also, once you drink from humans they are essentially yours. A strong vampire can crawl inside their heads and bend them to his or her will. If they're not drunk from again, the hold will wear off eventually, but it could take weeks, months, or years, depending on the age and strength of the vampire in question. The possibilities for abusing that power are staggering. It's illegal by the laws of the Dark Council, but it's a very hard thing to prove, and it's done with far more regularity than the High King would like.

"MacLeod told me what I said last night on the roof," the queen said, pulling me from my thoughts. "And that you saw the tattoos on my back."

I schooled my features and replied, "Yes, though I'm surprised that he would tell you."

She held her gloved hands out, palms up, and said, "It is my gift, or my curse. He can keep nothing from me. The gloves offer protection from my ability but there are times, with him, when I do not wear them."

Of course. Anytime she touched him she would be able to see whatever she wanted in his mind. There were moments, like tonight, when I wished that I could tell what Michael was thinking as easily as that.

Marrakesh shook her head. "I don't even have to touch you to know what you're thinking now. Do not ever envy me this ability. It has been a strain on my relationship with MacLeod from the very beginning. We love each other with everything we have, but there are some parts of yourself that you should be able to keep private, even from your lover. Do you have any idea how strong a man he is, to be able to hold absolutely nothing back from me in order to be my husband? Can you even begin to imagine what it would be like to have your lover know every thought or feeling that ever tripped through your mind?"

I considered that for a moment. The things I had been thinking about Drake in the carriage flashed through my head, and I thought about how mortified I would be if Michael ever knew that I'd had those thoughts. And did I really want to know what had run through his mind when he'd been ogling that prostitute's breasts tonight?

Marrakesh smiled. "I see you understand."

"So," I said slowly, "you would know if MacLeod were in any way connected to what's happening to you?"

She snorted. "I would know if MacLeod thought my dress was unattractive. I can assure you that he is not plotting to kill me."

I nodded and then something occurred to me. "Marrakesh!" I exclaimed, almost slapping my forehead that I hadn't thought of it sooner. "You can solve this! Touch them; that's all you have to do. Then you would know . . ." But she was already shaking her head. "Why not?"

"This ability that I have has no filter, Cin. I can't just pick and choose what I see. When I touch someone, I see it all. I know them inside and out. It is not a parlor trick. It's a weapon. There are things that we all bury deeply, and they should be allowed to stay there. Hashim, in particular, has a fear of me touching him."

"But don't you see? That's the very reason that

you should do this. You're powerful, Highness, and at the moment someone else is pulling your strings like a puppeteer. If you have the ability to stop it, but you won't do it because your lieutenants are squeamish . . ."

"I will not force such humiliation upon my friends, especially not when I know in my heart that they are innocent."

"But you can't be certain of that."

"Of course I can. I know because . . ." She paused for a long moment as if gathering her thoughts, then smiled a bitter smile and said, "After what you heard and saw last night you have me at a bit of a disadvantage. No one living knows what you do now, except MacLeod, Khalid, and Hashim."

I almost reached out and touched her hand. Almost. "If I could take back the knowing of it, I would, Highness. It's not my right to know such things, and I want to assure you that anything you said while under the influence of . . . whatever that was . . . will never go any farther than that rooftop."

She nodded. "I thank you for that. However, now that you know half of the story, you might as well hear the rest. Then you will understand why I would no more suspect Khalid or Hashim of trying to harm me than I would MacLeod. Trust is not one of my virtues, nor is it something that I give lightly. There are the only three people in this world that I trust. We have a bond, Khalid, Hashim, MacLeod, and I, one that has been forged with pain and blood."

"I can't imagine the horror you must have felt on that beach," I said.

"If that had been the end of it, then maybe I wouldn't be so . . . damaged," she said. "But that was only the beginning."

# CHAPTER 16

She leaned back, looking not at me but at the fire in the hearth, until I thought that she had forgotten I was there at all. When she spoke, her voice was detached, as if she were telling a story she had no part in. Perhaps that was how she had to tell it, to get through it.

"Magnus took me off that beach. He avenged my honor as I had asked, and in return I showed him where the gold and valuables were hidden. He was a man of his word, an honorable man, and he married me within a month. I don't know that I could say that I was happy, necessarily. I don't know that I *could* have been happy at that point in my life, but I was content. Magnus treated me like a queen and the next year I gave him a son." She closed her eyes and smiled bitterly at the memory. "Magnus was so proud of him. He doted on that baby, and nothing was too good for either of us. Erik was ten months old when his father was killed on a raid. No one saw it happen, but I know that he was stabbed in the back by his nephew. Gunnar had always been Magnus's heir, and then I came along and gave him a strong, healthy child. He hated us both with the fire of a thousand suns. I would pray at night that Gunnar would be killed in battle, or that at least Magnus would live long enough for his son to grow into manhood, so that he could protect himself. When they brought Magnus's body home to me I knew that my son and I would soon be dead. There was no place for me to go, no one who could protect us from Gunnar."

"What happened?" I whispered.

A tear slipped down her cheek. "That black-hearted bastard, may his soul be damned for eternity, drowned my baby and sold me to the slavers. He stood on the dock and told me that I was nothing more than a whore his uncle had dressed up as a queen, and that now I would once again be what I was meant to be."

My heart ached for her. I couldn't imagine how she had lived through those years.

She took a deep, shuddering breath. "I ended up in Algiers. Darius was a vampire of . . . varied appetites. He had a harem of a hundred women, but it wasn't just the women who fed his needs. Men, boys, young girls, it didn't matter to Darius. Sometimes he participated, and sometimes he just liked to watch. A concubine who became pregnant by one his human slaves was rewarded, and Darius was gifted with another soul to destroy as he willed. Needless to say, I lived in fear of becoming pregnant. Khalid and Hashim were particu-

lar favorites of his. Their mother had died in child-
birth, and I took them under my wing. I tried to protect them but Darius was fascinated by the fact that
they were twins. You cannot imagine the horrors they
endured growing up."

I blew out a breath, thinking that all my new theories were unraveling before me. Khalid and Hashim
were not just soldiers to her, they were her children.

"Darius didn't just keep concubines for his own
entertainment. The ones who were . . . particularly
skilled . . . he prostituted for gold, or land, or information. I had been there for a little over a year,
Khalid and Hashim were just babies, when Darius
came to me and said that he was going to present me
as a gift to the Caliph of Cordoba, and that I was to
get the information he wanted or he would have
Khalid and Hashim killed. I'd just lost my own son a
few years earlier and I couldn't bear to lose those two
precious babies as well. So I went with him to Cordoba, where the caliph found himself quite taken
with me. He also had a tendency to talk too much
while he was making love." She shrugged. "When I
got the information Darius required, he stole me out
of the palace and took me back to Algiers. He said
that he was so pleased with me that he couldn't bear
to lose my beauty to the ravages of time. He turned
me into a vampire, as he did with a few of his favorite
concubines."

For the first time she turned her face from the fire

and looked at me. "I had longed for the day when my beauty would fade and he would have no more interest in me. Sometimes he killed his humans when their faces and bodies no longer pleased him, but the ones who had been obedient he often set free." She laughed. "Not that I had anywhere to go if he had set me free, but a slave rarely thinks that far ahead. So instead of earning my freedom, I was forced into another three hundred years of slavery to Darius's greed, twisted appetites, and frivolous whims."

I swallowed. I had thought that I wanted to know this, but now I wasn't so sure. I searched for some safe thing to comment on, anything that would take that look of painful remembrance out of her eyes.

"And the tattoos?" I asked. "I assume that they're tied to your gift somehow. They're all symbols of knowledge, prophecy, or protection."

"Darius had an Irish priest as one of his prisoners. He never harmed him, would never drink from him or force him to do the things the rest of had to do to survive. I think he served as a mirror for Darius. The more shocked the priest was by Darius's perversions, the more Darius liked it. The tattoos were at one time nothing more than paint. I used to have to lie still for days at a time while the priest painted me like an illuminated manuscript before Darius gifted me to one king or another. He thought the markings on my body would intrigue a man. The priest drew symbols of knowledge in the hope that I would be successful in my mission, and not be punished by Darius for failing to acquire whatever it was he wanted. After Cordoba, Darius had me painted again before he turned me. When I woke as a vampire the markings were permanent . . . and I had the ability to see into a man's soul simply by touching him."

"It's an amazing gift. I've never heard of anything like it before." And I hadn't. Usually, other than your standard vampire magic, a vampire's abilities were a magnification of the abilities they'd had as humans. Marrakesh's clairvoyance was completely new after her change. I wondered how much of that was due to the heavy symbolism of the tattoos on her back.

She shrugged. "It was, and still is, a blessing and a curse. On the one hand, after Darius realized what had happened, he never touched me again. On the other, I was now of infinite value to him and he would never let me go. I was given a suite of rooms and I never again had to endure what the other concubines did. It made me bold. We tried to escape once when Khalid and Hashim were twenty. Darius caught us and I spent the next five years in a windowless cell drinking stale blood from a pitcher, and that was only when someone bothered to remember I was down there. When I was released and I saw how much Khalid and Hashim had suffered—" She closed her eyes and shook her head. "My God, Cin, the scars they have, both inside and out. And Darius had turned them, because he knew it would hurt me. Leaving them human was the only thing I'd ever asked of him."

"How did you end up here?" I asked.

"In 1250 a young man issued a summons for one, and all to come and challenge him for the right to rule the world's vampires. The date of the combat was set for July 1, 1260, because it would take years for the news to travel throughout Europe, central Asia, and northern Africa. Darius laughed it off, as did most in the beginning. As the time of the challenge grew nearer, however, more and more vampires made arrangements to attend. After all, if someone was going to be king of us all, then you'd much rather it be you and not your neighbor. They went in droves, and when the dust settled the High King had won the right to rule, and MacLeod had won the Western Lands while Drake had won the East."

"Did Darius attend the challenge?"

"No," she said. "No, he didn't, and he refused to accept the High King's authority or sign his name in the Book of Souls. MacLeod came to him and gave him two choices: Either Darius could swear fealty to the High King, or he would face an army that would take everything he had, including his life."

I raised my eyebrows. "I'm surprised MacLeod would make that trip. Now it's our responsibility to go to the High King."

She shrugged. "Things were different in the beginning. When the two kingdoms were new there were many concessions extended to the older vampires in an effort to bring them peaceably under the

High King's dominion. Now that our rule has long been established, such compromises are no longer made."

"So MacLeod saw you when he went to visit Darius?" I imagined him meeting her and instantly falling in love.

"He did. We had moved from Algiers to Marrakesh by then. MacLeod came to bring Darius to heel . . . and he left with me."

"Darius gave you up?"

She laughed. "No," she said with a mischievous glint in her eye. "MacLeod stole me. Khalid and Hashim came to his chamber one night and begged him to take me away. They told him that I would make him a fine queen. Darius sealed his own fate when he got greedy and sent me to MacLeod, ordering me to use my skills and my gift to find out everything I could about the king—his plans, his weaknesses, everything."

"Did you?" I asked when she paused and didn't continue.

She smiled and her eyes took on a dreamy, faraway look. I was happy that she was finally remembering something pleasant. She had the look of a woman in love, and it sat much better on her than the pain I had seen on her face until now.

"I found out everything I needed to know," she said. "I found out that he was a good man, a warrior of incredible skill, and a wise leader. I also found more pleasure in his bed in one night than I had experienced in my entire life. But Darius would not give me up; I was too valuable to him. For days his men watched us like hawks. MacLeod had only a handful of soldiers with him, not enough to take Darius's army. When we finally made our move, Khalid and Hashim went west, MacLeod's men went east, and MacLeod and I went north to Tangier. Darius's men had to split up to search for us. We kept off the roads so we wouldn't be spotted. When we couldn't find shelter for the day, we buried ourselves in the sand so that we wouldn't burn. Pray to whatever god you worship that you never have to know what that feels like. It was weeks of pure hell before we reached the port in Tangier." She was quiet for a moment and then she said, "That's why I love Edinburgh so much. It's green, and it rains often, and I never have to feel the sand against my skin again."

"What happened to Khalid and Hashim? Did they follow you here?"

"They went west, leading a portion of Darius's men away from MacLeod and me. They made it to the eastern capital at Vienna—"

"I thought the eastern capital was in Saint Petersburg?"

"It was in Vienna when Drake was king. The new queen moved it to Saint Petersburg in the last century. They say she and Peter the Great were lovers, you know."

I chuckled inwardly. It still amused me how the older vampires threw around words like *new* and *old*. The "new" Queen of the Eastern Lands had sat on her throne since Drake had been deposed in the 1680s.

"At any rate, Darius's men caught up with them in Vienna. Khalid and Hashim assumed that MacLeod and I were either safe or recaptured and there was no reason to continue leading the soldiers on a wild goose chase. They let the soldiers catch up with them in a field outside of town. They fought, and Khalid and Hashim killed them all. Drake heard of this and whatever else he is, he is a . . . practical man. He had a new kingdom to establish and he is a diplomat, not a warrior. He offered Khalid and Hashim Darius's head in exchange for two hundred years of service."

"Did they take the offer?"

"Oh, yes. It was a small price to pay for vengeance."

"But how did he do it? If Drake's kingdom was so young, how did he muster enough soldiers to take Darius's palace? I'm assuming such a place would be nearly impregnable."

She smiled wickedly. "Oh, it is. Drake, as I said, is a very practical man. Why send an army when one soldier will do?"

"*One* soldier?"

"The palace may not have had weaknesses, but Darius certainly did. Alecto was young then and very eager to prove herself to her new king."

I threw back my head and laughed. Alecto was one of three sisters, the Furies, who were The Righteous's counterpart in the eastern kingdom. "So she killed him?"

"Yes, and sent his ashes to me with her compliments."

I fell silent, thinking. Not only had Khalid and Hashim grown up with Marrakesh as a mother-figure, they had escaped being prisoners of one master just to turn around and indenture themselves to another, all to keep her safe.

"Understanding now your . . . history," I said softly, "I have to wonder why you would take the name *Marrakesh*?"

"I did it so that I would never forget where I came from. So that I would never get pampered and comfortable with my position here and forget that I had once been a slave."

"I would think that would be something you would want to put behind you and try to forget," I pointed out.

She shook her head. "No, never. As long as I remember the pain, I'll never allow it to happen again. There is nothing more important than the power to control your own destiny." She took a ragged breath and leaned forward. "That's why you have to find whoever is doing this to me. I will not go willingly into another prison, Cin. I'd rather be staked than locked away in the bowels of Castle Tara. I know they tell you that the old ones sometimes go mad. They may even point to Drake when they say it. But Drake went mad when the love of his life died. I am here with my lover. I love my life, Cin, and I am happy. If three hundred years with Darius didn't break me, I can assure you that I didn't just wake up crazy one day, with no rhyme or reason for it. Someone is doing this to me. Do you believe that?"

"Yes," I whispered.

"And will you help me?"

"Yes, I'll help you," I said. "But you have to help yourself as well. You have an awesome weapon at your disposal, Marrakesh. Use it. I may believe that MacLeod and Khalid and Hashim are devoted to you, but the others have their doubts. If you can positively clear everyone in this household, then we can move on and look elsewhere. The only other option is to remove you from the city in order to flush out whoever is doing this."

She shook her head. "A queen does not abandon her capital in a time of war. It will be seen as a sign of weakness."

"Marrakesh, we have no leads. We don't even have any solid theories about who could be behind this."

"Other than those in my household, you mean." I didn't reply. I just watched her as she thought it through. Finally, she nodded. "I'll do it, but only if they come to me willingly. I will not have such a thing commanded of them, do you understand?"

"I understand," I said. "I'll go tell MacLeod now."

"Cin," she said as I reached the door. "Thank you."

I shook my head. "Don't thank me yet. I have a feeling this is going to get worse before it gets better."

# CHAPTER 17

I left the room and ran directly into MacLeod's rather impressive chest.

"Umph," I grunted and stepped around him. "Isn't it a little unseemly for a king to be hovering in the hall, eavesdropping?"

He crossed his arms over his chest. "Do you understand now why she is the way she is? Why our lives run as they do?"

I leaned back against the wall. "She has an understandable need to be in control of everything around her, because she wasn't in control of anything for so very long."

"Yes, but it's more than that," he said. "I made her a queen, and I stand in the background because twice in her life she has lost a husband and lost her place in the world because of it. I love her too much to see that happen to her again. She is my enforcer because if something should happen to her, regardless of what *you* might think, I would still be king. If, however, something should happen to me, then I need her to be strong enough to hold this kingdom without me."

My heart melted just a little. "Then help me now," I said. "She's agreed to use her gift to rule out anyone in this house as a suspect."

He looked surprised, and then he nodded. "All right."

"Khalid and Hashim look guilty. Devlin and the others are never going to believe that they're not involved without proof. This is the fastest way I know to get it and give us the freedom to look elsewhere. Marrakesh refuses to force anyone to submit to this, so I don't care what you have to do but you make sure they come *willingly,* do you understand?"

He nodded. "It will be done."

# CHAPTER 18

True to his word, MacLeod gathered everyone in his chamber. Marrakesh was dressed in a stunning gown of green silk that perfectly matched her eyes—eyes that kept darting nervously over at both of her lieutenants. I watched them as well, to make sure that they at least appeared to be here of their own free will. Khalid looked resigned and as stoic as a statue. Hashim looked like he might become violently ill at any moment. Bel just looked confused, as usual. Devlin had decided that Marrakesh should touch Bel also. Since she had been living in the house for several months, Bel may have seen or heard any number of things that may not seem out of the ordinary to her, but might to the queen.

"Shall we begin?" I asked.

"Is this really necessary?" Hashim asked, and the tension between his eyes said that the question meant more to him than his emotionless tone implied.

Drake came up and put his hand on the Arab's shoulder. "I'm afraid it is, old friend."

Hashim nodded once and then glared at me as if it was all my fault, which I suppose it was.

"Will it hurt?" Bel asked, her bottom lip trembling charmingly.

"No, it shouldn't," Marrakesh assured her. "I will start with the king and perhaps that will put everyone at ease."

She took off her gloves, which were exactly the same shade of green as her gown, and laid them over the back of the Roman couch. Without any direction everyone in the room seemed to have separated themselves into two lines. Drake, Devlin, Justine, Michael, and I stood facing the others, waiting. I frowned and moved around to Michael's other side, but that position was no better. From where I was standing I wouldn't be able to see Marrakesh's face. I wanted to gauge her reaction as she read each of them, so, drawing as little attention to myself as possible, I moved over to MacLeod's desk and leaned against it. This was much better. From here her back was no longer to me, and I could see both of them in profile.

I watched as she approached MacLeod and held her hands out, palms up. He smiled down at her and placed his hands in hers. She closed her eyes and breathed deeply. I expected to feel something similar to what I sensed when another witch called her power, but, whatever the source of Marrakesh's gift was, it was not the same as mine. There was a vibration in the air, almost like that of an approaching storm, but nothing that smacked of a witch's magic.

I don't know what Marrakesh saw or felt, but when she opened her eyes she smiled up at her husband and leaned up to place a chaste kiss on his lips.

"I love you," she whispered and I smiled with her.

When she took her hands from MacLeod's, the vibration stopped. She moved to Khalid next.

"Do you do this willingly?" she asked.

He looked down at her for a moment, then nodded gravely. She held her hands out, and his came up to hover reluctantly just above hers. I held my breath, hoping that he wouldn't back out at the last moment and ruin everything. When Marrakesh took a step back before he touched her hands, I almost cursed aloud in frustration. Had his hesitation made her pull back? I watched as she frowned and put her hands to her head. She took another step, shaking her head. MacLeod moved toward her with his hand out, but before he could reach her, the queen's head snapped up and she lunged toward Khalid. The big man staggered backward in fear, careening into the couch behind him. Before anyone could get over their shock and react, Marrakesh pulled Khalid's scimitar from the scabbard at his waist. She swung the blade around in a wide arc, forcing MacLeod to jump back out of her reach. And then she turned and looked directly at me.

Madness filled her eyes as she screamed and ran at me, the scimitar raised in her right hand. I scurried around the desk, partly from instinct and partly because putting the big piece of furniture between us would give me the precious seconds I needed to call my magic. MacLeod was faster, though, and grabbed her around the waist, swinging her off her feet. The scimitar fell from her hands, clattering across the wooden floor. The queen screamed her frustration and started raking her nails across her husband's arms in an effort to get free. Khalid had regained his composure and intervened, grabbing her wrists. Marrakesh was screaming and thrashing as MacLeod swung her around to pin her between himself and the back of the couch.

"The gloves!" he shouted. "Get the gloves on her!"

A look of horror crossed Drake's face and he ran to help, snatching the gloves off the back of the couch. What I had seen of Marrakesh's gift had seemed rather benign, but it was apparent from the look on Drake's face that it wasn't always so. I was betting that he knew her well enough to know that, in this state, her ability could cause some serious damage. Drake and Khalid were wrestling her into the gloves while Bel cowered behind Hashim. It was only then that I noticed that sometime during the fray Michael had put himself between me and the queen, his sword drawn. Devlin and Justine stood in front of him. With the immediate threat to my continued health and well-being gone, I began to notice other things as well—like the smell of sulfur and wormwood. I spun around and stared at the wall behind MacLeod's desk. That horrible stench seemed to be emanating from it. I placed my hand on the paneling.

Whoever he was, he was in the townhouse next door, spinning spells to make the queen mad before she found out anything that would incriminate him or his accomplice.

"He's here!" I shouted and moved around Michael, grabbing his shirtsleeve. "Come on, he's here!"

I practically dragged Michael from the room. He, of course, had no idea what I was talking about or where wc were going, but he followed me anyway. As we raced down the stairs, Devlin and Justine on our heels, I explained. "MacLeod neglected to tell us that the two townhouses that flank this one are used as the residences of the court. He didn't seem to think it was important since they're empty and locked."

We flew out the front door and raced up the steps of the townhouse next door. Devlin put his shoulder into the door. It cracked and groaned, but held fast.

"MacLeod's an ass," he grunted, backing up to try again.

I put my hand on his chest and held him back. "No, he just didn't realize that any witch worth her magic can do this."

I put my hand on the lock. My blood was racing with the excitement that we might just catch this treasonous bastard, and my magic flew into the lock with such force that not only did the lock give, but the whole door flew inward and banged against the wall like a crack of lightning. Well, so much for stealth.

Devlin and Michael took the stairs two at a time, weapons drawn. I followed behind. I had no blade but I did have my magic, and I was hoping that was enough. Justine was at my back with more weaponry at hand than I would have thought she could hide under that dress. The room we were looking for would be at the end of the hall on the third floor. I was betting it would be a mirror image of MacLeod's suite.

Devlin kicked the door open and we all spilled into the room with a good deal less caution than I would have advised, if I hadn't been so flush with the excitement that we might actually catch this fiend in the act. The smell of sulfur and wormwood choked me. It was a large suite, much like MacLeod's, but it was empty. I spun around, and Justine was so close behind me that the tip of her sword nearly sliced open my shirt.

"Careful!" I said, clutching my breasts and scowling at her.

She gave me a look and took a step back.

"Damn it all to hell!" Devlin shouted in frustration. He wrenched open the doors of the great wardrobe, which stood against the wall opposite the foot of the bed. There were clothes in it but little else. Growling, he stalked from the room, throwing open doors left and right as he moved down the hall.

"Go with him and help him search the house," I said.

Justine nodded and walked out, but Michael stayed by my side.

"If you think I'm going to leave you alone in here, you're addled."

I smiled at his concern, especially since he had been so very upset with me earlier in the night. "All right," I said, "but stay very still and let me do this."

He nodded and stepped back.

I closed my eyes and reached out with my senses and my magic. I could hear three sets of footsteps coming up the stairs. I heard Devlin speak to Drake and Hashim. Bel was chirping away about something. They were telling Devlin that none of them had seen anyone come out of the house after we'd gone in. I tuned them out and turned my attention back to this room. I held my hands up in front of me, pushing my magic out, feeling it form a circle around me like a mist of sparkling golden light. I moved through the room, hoping that the magic would find something that it liked, something equally magical that the wizard, or whatever he was, had used to cast his spells. Magic was like that sometimes, as if it were a living thing that sensed a kindred spirit. It moved over Michael, settling around him, calm and still. My magic reacted that way to the undead. Humans pulsed with energy and vitality, like the beating of a heart. Vampires gave off the glassy stillness of a perfectly peaceful lake under the moonlight. I walked around him like a sleepwalker, still hoping that my magic would pick up on anything that would give us a clue as to what had been wrought here, but I wasn't feeling anything out of the ordinary. That changed when I got to the door. There was something there, something I had never felt before.

My magic spilled outward in a rush, moving like curious fingers over a foreign object. I opened my eyes and I could see it surrounding something human-sized—except there was nothing there. It settled around the nothing, but whatever it was, it was neither human nor vampire. It seemed to have the characteristics of both. I hadn't seen anything like it since I was human. It reminded me of the shimmering of the horizon on a hot day, dead and living, warm and still. The shape moved quickly toward the door, and I pulled my magic back.

"What the hell was that?" Michael breathed.

I sank down in the nearest chair, its holland covers flying up in a soft *poof*. "I don't think MacLeod needs a slayer," I said. "I think he needs a priest."

# CHAPTER 19

"How the bloody hell can I have a ghost?" MacLeod demanded. "It's a new house. No one has died here!"

"Except Clarissa," Bel grumbled.

I pursed my lips and looked around the room. Everyone was looking at me, expecting that I would have all the answers. I glanced over at Marrakesh, still as death in her bed. MacLeod had said that she had collapsed after we left the room, and he could not wake her. Seeing her lying there like that made me wish I really did have all the answers.

I held my hands up in supplication. "All I know is what I saw."

It was all I had to offer, and it wasn't nearly enough.

At dawn Michael and I fell into bed, exhausted. He was lying with his hands folded behind his head and I was curled up against his side. Normally he would have put his arm around me and pulled me close, but this morning he did neither. I looked up at him. He was staring at the ceiling, his face so blank I couldn't read his thoughts.

"Justine informed me that I'd upset you tonight," he said, finally.

"I wasn't angry with you," I replied softly.

"Were you not?" he said, as if he didn't believe me. "I rushed back here to apologize to you and I saw you . . . with Drake."

I was quiet for a moment, wondering whether or not I should tell him the unvarnished truth. "I won't lie to you, Michael. He was trying to get me into his bed."

"I noticed."

"And I told him in no uncertain terms that I was not interested, that I love you, and that he would never have me."

"Really," he said icily.

I sat up and looked down at him. "What do you think? That I was so angry because you ogled some prostitute that I came directly back here and tried to seduce Drake on the street?"

"That's certainly what it looked like from where I was standing," he replied.

I narrowed my eyes. "You *ass*," I spat and threw back the covers. "I have never given you a reason not to trust me and yet ever since we arrived in Edinburgh you've treated me like I was some trollop, ready to hop into Drake's bed at the first opportunity." I snatched my dressing gown up and angrily shoved my arms into it. "I do not deserve that, Michael."

The door made a satisfyingly loud bang as I slammed it on my way out.

I stood in the hallway, uncertain of what to do next. There were other bedrooms I could use but I was too angry to sleep. Instead I wandered down to the library and stared blankly at the shelves for a long time. MacLeod's tastes ran heavily to histories, treatises on warfare, and poetry. There wasn't a gothic novel in the lot. Finally I moved the ladder that allowed access to the upper shelves and climbed up to retrieve a book of poetry. I flopped down on the leather sofa and thumbed through the pages. Every few minutes I glanced over at the library door, expecting that Michael would walk in at any moment.

I didn't understand what was happening between us. There had been many vampires over the years who had tried to seduce either Michael or myself, to entice one of us away from the other, and we'd always laughed at such attempts. The very idea that anyone would think it could be done had been amusing to us. What had changed since Drake's arrival? The cold, unreasonable man upstairs was not the Michael I knew.

Sometime near dusk I fell asleep with the book of poetry open on my lap. I dozed fitfully until I heard the door softly click shut. *Michael,* I thought, sitting up. But it wasn't Michael. I blew out an irritated breath as Drake strolled into the room.

"So you and the boy had a fight, did you? The

whole household heard your bedroom door slam. I must say, my dear, that I'm surprised to find you here. A woman should always throw the man out, not the other way around."

"He did not throw me out," I grumbled, disappointed that the entire day had passed and Michael hadn't bothered to seek me out to make amends for his abominable behavior. "And I wish you'd leave. It wouldn't help matters if Michael were to find us in here alone together."

Drake plucked the volume titled *Kentish Poets* from my lap and glanced down at the poem I'd been reading when I fell asleep. "Ah, Thomas Wyatt."

I rolled my eyes and snatched the book back. "If you won't leave, then I will."

I walked over to the shelves. Drake followed me and leaned against the bookshelf, his hot gaze traveling up the length of my body.

"Whoso list to hunt, I know where is an hind," he quoted from the poem.

I looked down at him from the top of the ladder and replied, "Who list her hunt, I put him out of doubt, / As well as I, may spend his time in vain. / And graven with diamonds in letters plain, / There is written her fair neck round about, / 'Noli me tangere,' for Caesar's I am, / And wild for to hold, though I seem tame.' "

I had just reshelved the book when the ladder shifted sharply to the right and I lost my balance. I tumbled backward . . . and landed in Drake's arms.

"I'll wager you would be a wild thing," he murmured.

"Well, isn't this a pretty picture?"

I shoved at Drake and turned to find Michael standing in the doorway. He was not pleased.

"Michael," I whispered.

He stared at me and then turned on his heel and walked away.

"You did that on purpose," I snarled at Drake before rushing after Michael. I caught up to him in the foyer. "Michael, it's not what you think."

He turned swiftly and grasped my upper arms. "Why is it that every time I come to apologize to you I find you in that bastard's arms?"

I shook my head. "I was on the top rung of the ladder replacing a book and I fell. He caught me before I hit the ground. It was nothing more than that."

Michael shook his head and pushed me away. "You always have a ready explanation for everything," he said as he moved past me.

"Did you ever stop to consider that's because it's the truth?"

I winced as the front door slammed shut behind him.

I prowled around the house all night like a caged animal. Michael had yet to come back, and it did not escape anyone's notice that Bel was also missing. I knew in my head that Michael wouldn't stray, not with Bel and not out of spite, but telling that to my heart was a different matter entirely. To make matters worse, all night everyone looked at me with quiet pity in their eyes. Except for Hashim—he actually smiled for the very first time. Drake hovered about, I suppose expecting that my wounded pride would propel me into his bed, but he finally gave up and retired to his room.

Sometime after three o'clock I allowed Devlin and Justine to talk me into playing *vingt-et-un* with them. I grudgingly agreed to deal but refused to play against either of them, as they were both quite adept at counting cards. They made a concerted effort to be amusing and tried to keep my mind off the fact that my consort had walked out on me, but their witty banter only served to remind me how solid their relationship was and how mine was falling apart. I should have never let Michael leave. I should have made him stay and fight with me until we'd sorted the whole mess out. It's what Justine would have done. She and Devlin often raged at each other like a hurricane—a brutal tempest that was quickly spent and soon gave way to the peaceful calm after the storm. Perhaps I should have learned from their example. Michael and I had certainly had our disagreements over the years, but nothing like this had ever come between us and I had no idea how to handle it.

Near dawn I pleaded exhaustion, and Devlin and Justine retired to their rooms. I looked at the clock and miserably decided that wherever Michael and Bel were, it was almost too late for them to make it home before sunrise. I'd just reached the first landing on the stairwell when something large and solid hit the front door. I whirled around and heard someone fumbling with a key in the lock. A moment later Michael and Bel tumbled into the house, giggling. Giggling? What the—

"You're drunk," I spat accusingly.

They both straightened, looking sheepishly up at me, and I could smell the gin and whiskey all the way across the room. It took an amazing amount of liquor to get a vampire drunk, and the two of them smelled as if they'd bathed in the stuff. They stood there, waiting for my reaction. It must have surprised them when I turned my back and continued up the stairs to my room. I wanted to march down those stairs and confront them, but I was so angry that my hands were shaking and I was afraid that if I didn't put some distance between us I might just kill them both.

# CHAPTER 20

I locked my bedroom door and leaned against it. Unbidden, the candles in the room flared to life and the fire in the hearth burned brighter, as if in answer. Already I could feel it, the darkness within me that rose with my temper. Bad things were going to happen if I didn't get control of my emotions quickly. I closed my eyes, took a shaky breath, and thought of Venice.

Ten years ago Devlin, Justine, Michael, and I had gone there for a holiday. When I was human I'd longed to experience a romantic gondola ride down those famous canals, and Michael had finally made good on his promise to take me there. It had been a wonderful trip until the four of us had been abducted by a coven of evil witches. Their leader, an Englishman named Edmund Gage, had planned to use the executions of The Righteous and my own conversion to the dark side of magic as his instrument of vengeance against the local regent. I was young then and, despite my aunt Maggie's training, my magic was still wild and almost uncontrollable. If the goddess Morrigan—the creator of vampires and all supernatural things that hunt the night—hadn't intervened, Gage would have killed us all. She showed me how to harness my power, how to fight Gage and win. I didn't realize at the time what the cost would be.

In one last act of defiance Gage had infected me with his dark magic. It had consumed me, burning through me from the inside out, and I had done unspeakable things. I was responsible for the deaths of a dozen humans, and Devlin, Justine, and Michael hadn't been able to stop me, not while I was flush with Gage's power. Even though Gage and his coven were evil, had murdered countless innocents in a quest for blood to feed their black magic, they were still human. I'd killed rogue vampires for less than what I'd done that night. Morrigan, however, had seemed pleased. She'd acquitted me of any guilt in the matter, but that hadn't eased my conscience or stopped the nightmares that still woke me on occasion. She'd also cleansed Gage's dark magic from my body.

At least that's what we'd all thought at the time. It didn't take long for me to learn the truth. I could still feel the remnants of that black magic, deep inside. The darkness liked me. It liked the blood I drank and the violence that was so often a part of my life. I could feel that darkness within me now, fairly pleading with me to turn it loose. My anger fed it and it wanted blood and pain and vengeance. I thought of the looks of horror and pity on my friends' faces all those years ago when I'd finally come to my senses and realized what I'd done. I thought of Michael and how, regardless of our current problems, I still loved him with all my heart. Those things, as always, helped me push Gage's power down until it came to rest in some dark, secret corner of my soul.

Feeling more in control of myself, I walked over and sat on the edge of the bed. I was still sitting there several minutes later, staring blankly at the locked door and wondering what to do next, when the knob turned and a soft curse came from the other side. I crossed the room and jerked the door open to find Michael standing in the hall looking disheveled and apologetic and reeking of whiskey.

"I love you," he said, weaving slightly on his feet.

"I know," I replied and crossed my arms over my chest. "But you've bloody well lost your mind if you think I'm going to let you into my bed after you've spent all night out drinking with that tramp."

He closed his eyes and swayed to one side so sharply that I had to reach out and steady him before he fell. Swallowing hard, he looked at me and said, "I swear by all that's holy, Cin, nothing happened."

I cocked a brow at him. "And that might carry more weight with me if you'd believed me when I said the same thing to you about Drake," I replied, and then I stepped back and shut the door in his face.

I leaned my head against the wood and listened to him on the other side. He was still out there; I could hear him breathing. Suddenly a loud *thud* from the hallway made me jump. I pulled open the door and peered out. Michael was lying sprawled on the floor, unconscious.

"Oh, for the love of Danu," I muttered.

While I was still trying to decide whether to drag him inside or leave him exactly where he was, Bel appeared at the top of the stairs. She glanced at Michael's inert form and then raised her beautiful lavender eyes to mine.

"I could assure you that I have not poached on your preserves," she said, "but I doubt that you would believe me right now."

She continued down the hall to her room and I watched her go, taking in the way her glossy black curls bounced with the sway of her hips as she walked. With a low curse I snatched a blanket off the bed and tossed it over Michael's sleeping body.

Then I slammed the door and locked it.

# CHAPTER 21

What followed were two grueling weeks that left me at the end of my emotional tether. Michael and I lived like strangers in the same house, neither of us willing to give in and admit that we were wrong. I knew that I was partially to blame for what had happened with Drake. I had treated him like any other man who flirted innocently with me. But there was nothing innocent about what Drake was doing, and I should have realized it sooner than I had and put a stop to it. Michael, however, had grossly overreacted to the whole situation. I could have quietly forgiven that, but I refused to sweep under the rug the fact that he'd stayed out all night drinking with another woman. Only groveling would fix that and Michael, stubborn fool that he was, had not yet begged for my forgiveness. The fact that he hadn't made me question all of my actions thus far, wondering what I'd done that would make him think that I should be the first one to apologize.

And if those thoughts weren't enough to drive me mad, it seemed that the whole town was conspiring to make me doubt myself. After I'd revealed my belief that we were dealing with a ghost, MacLeod had paraded an assortment of priests and ministers through all three townhouses. He even brought in old ladies who had reputations for being able to communicate with the dead. He actually went so far as to get the Right Reverend Daniel Sanford, Bishop of Edinburgh, to come bless the house. We all tried to stay clear of the bishop during this process. Crosses and holy water are only effective if wielded by a true believer, and even then they will only burn if the vampire they are being used against means harm to the human. Still, you can never be too careful. Every one of them, from the bishop himself to old Mrs. Munro, pronounced that the houses were spirit-free. I didn't tell any of them exactly what I had been doing when I saw the ghost—the mob hadn't burned a witch in Scotland in a 106 years, though again, you can never be too careful—but they all pretty much patted me on the hand and mumbled something about "the vapors" or "the fancies of young ladies these days." It was enough to make me want to bite every one of them, including the bishop.

In addition to half the clergy in Edinburgh thinking that I was nothing more than a high-strung twenty-two-year-old girl with an overactive imagination, every vampire in the house was starting to doubt what

I had seen as well. Michael believed me, because he had seen it, too, but the others were beginning to voice their skepticism. Sometimes I almost doubted myself, but I knew that whatever it was, it had not been entirely human, and it had not been entirely dead. And what was there between the two, and invisible, other than a ghost? Damned if I knew.

Marrakesh was still in a coma. Khalid and Hashim glared at me every time we passed in the hall, as if I were somehow to blame. Drake had suggested that Khalid was responsible for her condition, but I had felt her power when she had touched MacLeod and I knew that Khalid had never touched his skin to hers. Of course, after the ghost debacle I'm not sure how much credence anyone put in my opinion anymore. So it remained that the queen could not be woken and was being force-fed blood to keep her strength up. Blood not tapped directly from a vein loses a lot of its potency, but getting her to swallow from a cup was the best we had managed to do for her.

I'd found out from Devlin that Michael's visit to the Medical College had confirmed MacLeod and Aubert's information that the bodies had been pristine, and that they had not died of a vampire bite. The night Michael had been there Dr. Knox had been performing an autopsy on a young man who had caused quite a stir among the students. It seemed that he had been a beggar known as Daft Jamie, a well-known figure in town. Michael said that when Jamie had been recognized by several students, Dr. Knox had begun the autopsy by disfiguring the boy's face so that his body would no longer be identifiable.

There was talk in town, among the humans, about the bodies that had been used in Knox's dissecting room in recent months, but no criminal activity could be proven. Drake, arguing that the deaths were vampire-related, had pointed out that a human would be foolish to kill someone as well known as this beggar and that a vampire would be far less likely to realize that his, or her, victim would be so recognizable. Devlin had pointed out that we must never underestimate the stupidity humans were capable of.

Whoever was responsible, he was not stupid. It was as though he had realized the likelihood of getting caught, now that we were all hunting him, and was laying low, waiting for us to get frustrated and leave. Or perhaps he was waiting for us to decide that the queen truly was guilty, because there had been no new murders in town since she had become incapacitated. If it hadn't been for me and my utter certainty that someone was working deadly magic against Marrakesh, she would have been locked up in Castle Tara by now. But I knew that there was someone else out there. Until he made his next move all we could do was wait.

# CHAPTER 22

I was on my way to my room with a book of spells I had purchased in town when MacLeod hailed me from the doorway of his study.

"Miss Craven, a word, please?" he asked.

"Certainly, sire," I agreed, fervently hoping he wasn't planning to ask me yet more questions I didn't know the answers to.

I was surprised to find Jacques Aubert seated in one of the leather chairs facing the king's desk. We exchanged greetings, and the king resumed his seat while I occupied the chair next to Aubert.

"Jacques," MacLeod said. "I think that perhaps Miss Craven and her companions might be of assistance in this matter."

"I'm sure we would be happy to help," I replied, and looked at Aubert questioningly. "What is it you need?"

"Normally I would not have to ask," Aubert said, "but several of my Wardens are with the court at Darkness Castle and three others are . . . elsewhere tonight liberating six cases of whiskey for His Highness. If I thought this could wait until tomorrow night, I would gladly do so."

"What is the problem?" I asked.

"Do you remember the night we first met? The group of ten vampires that Fritz came to warn me about?"

"Yes. I don't speak German but Justine translated for me. She said you had a large group of vampires that had entered the city illegally."

"Aye, well, we threw them out on their arses that night, but it seems that they're back now, and they've brought friends."

MacLeod tapped his letter opener absently on his desk. "They know we're short of Wardens?"

"Aye, and rumors abound that the queen is either ill or dead."

The *click-click-click* of the letter opener grew more rapid. "So they think they can come into my capital as they please, without fear of punishment?"

Aubert swallowed hard and glanced at me briefly before answering, "It would seem so, Your Highness. There are some who believe that the queen's disappearance has weakened your hold on the city."

"Then I will go with you," MacLeod said.

Aubert's eyes widened. "But . . . er, yes, of course, Your Highness."

It was apparent from Aubert's reaction that MacLeod did not often go out on such expeditions.

"Your Highness," I said, "The Righteous and I can take care of this problem."

MacLeod stood. He walked around the desk until he was so close that I had to look up into his dark eyes. "Someone reminded me recently that my people no longer fear me. I believe it is time I remedied that."

I nodded gravely and waited until MacLeod had left the room and was out of earshot before I asked Aubert, "You looked nervous just now. Can he fight?"

Aubert glanced down the empty hall. "Aye, he fights like nothing you've ever seen."

"So why the look?"

"Well, for all that His Highness generally stays out of a fray, he does love a good fight. The problem is that he throws himself into it with little consideration of what's around him. He's an old warrior, used to fighting armies on the field of battle, not skirmishing in the middle of his own city. The last time I took him on a raid was back in 1700."

"And?" I asked.

Aubert shrugged. "He lit several vampires on fire and ended up burning Edinburgh from the Cowgate to the High Street."

I stepped back and surveyed my reflection in the mirror, smiling. Now was the time to look like an assassin, and I'd certainly accomplished that. I had wonderful tailors and boot makers in London and

Paris who happily overcharged me in exchange for
their discretion and the marvelous men's clothing
they made for me. Tonight I wore a tight-fitting brown
leather vest over a cream shirt. Wrist sheaths on both
of my forearms held a set of balanced throwing daggers. My legs were encased in supple brown leather
breeches, and another set of throwing daggers was
strapped to my thighs, hidden in the tops of my tall
leather boots. I sighed and stretched one leg out. I
loved these boots. They were modeled after some
riding boots that Devlin had had since Elizabeth was
queen. He'd had them remade in the 1600s when
heels became fashionable. Mine had a two-inch heel,
high enough to please my vanity, but thick enough
that I could still run in them.

I adjusted the shoulder straps on the sheath that hid
a short sword along my spine and slid my basket-
hilted claymore into the scabbard at my hip. I tied my
hair back tightly with a ribbon—not that it would survive the fight. Justine seemed to be able to come out
of just about any confrontation with perfectly coiffed
hair, but my red curls had lost more pins and ribbons
than I could even begin to count. I took off my diamond earrings and necklace and gently placed them
in the cloisonné jewelry box that Michael had bought
for me in Rome. As if conjured by my thoughts he
came into the room.

I watched him in the mirror as his gaze moved over
me, hot with lust. I smiled, pleased that things were

not so far gone between us that I could still inspire such a reaction from him.

"Watch your back tonight," he said, finally.

"Why? I mean, other than the obvious reasons?"

"MacLeod is bringing Khalid and Hashim with him. The help will undoubtedly be useful, but I don't entirely trust either one of them."

"Who is staying with Marrakesh?"

"Drake and Bel."

I nodded. I didn't particularly like the thought of Khalid or Hashim at my back, but I liked the thought of them alone here with Marrakesh even less. I still didn't really believe that they were involved in whatever was happening here, but the evidence was certainly beginning to pile up against them. Like everyone else, I found it rather suspicious that Marrakesh went stark raving mad and then fell into a coma moments before she could ascertain for sure whether or not they were involved. I knew that Marrakesh and MacLeod believed that the twins would never harm either of them, but the whole episode was just a little too convenient for my taste. I donned a russet-colored cloak trimmed in red fox, which served to hide the arsenal of weapons I carried, and Michael and I went to meet the others in the front hall.

# CHAPTER 23

It took three carriages to take us all into the Old Town. The king, Khalid, Hashim, and Aubert rode in the first carriage. Devlin, Justine, Michael, and I followed in our own coach, and two of Aubert's Wardens, Wallace and Ross, came behind us in the third. We disembarked at the end of the Cowgate near Grassmarket, making our way on foot toward South Bridge in the hope that we would find the group of rogues, or they would find us. Aubert's human drivers followed behind with the carriages at a discreet distance. As we walked down the street I wondered what our little group looked like to the humans. Glancing around at Justine and the men surrounding me, I could only guess.

Michael was silent and brooding at my side, so I slowed my pace until I fell in step next to MacLeod.

"Are you all right?" I asked him.

"Of course," he replied, glancing at me suspiciously. "Why do you ask?"

"I was just wondering. That's the fourth time

you've shifted your shoulders like that in the last half of a block. Is there . . . something in your shirt?"

He mumbled a reply. I turned around, walking backward so that I could look him in the eye.

"I'm sorry, what did you say?"

Khalid coughed and averted his gaze. MacLeod glared at me, and then reached out and grabbed my hand, raising it up and placing it on his chest.

I stumbled and nearly fell. "Is that—"

"Yes," he hissed before I could get out the word *armor*.

"Why?" I asked, puzzled.

"Marrakesh makes me wear the breastplate, to protect my heart, anytime I go on a raid or anyplace where I might be in danger. I hate the bloody thing, but she would . . . she would know if I said I wore it and didn't."

He was an important man, the King of the Western Lands. If anyone deserved to have a little added protection, it was him.

I smiled at him. "Yes, well, we're women. We always know when you're lying to us. Unfortunately, you just happen to live with a woman who can prove it."

He chuckled. "Aye, well, it's no great hardship if it means she doesn't worry so much," he said, scowling and shifting his shoulders again. "But I think this used to fit better. Bloody thing feels like I've been shoved into a whiskey barrel."

I laughed and patted his very solid chest. "Try wearing a corset sometime," I said.

Before he could reply a soft *whoosh* rent the air above our heads. We all turned and stared at the arrow that pierced the door to my right.

"Move!" Devlin shouted.

We rushed forward, only to be blocked by another arrow that missed Devlin by scant inches.

"Into the alley!" someone yelled.

Michael rushed toward me, grabbed my hand, and we all spilled down the steps into one of the narrow alleys Edinburgh was famous for.

This one unfortunately did not open onto the other side of the block as many of them did. It ended with a seven-story tenement. On either side of us the stone walls of the buildings were seven to ten stories straight up with no balconies or ledges. I could make two, possibly three stories in a leap, but not seven. Since it went without saying that none of us was willing to burst into a human tenement with a group of rogue vampires on our heels, we were trapped. The only way out was through the group of vamps headed our way down the alley.

I could have reached out and smacked Aubert. When he'd said that the original gang of ten had returned with friends, he'd neglected to mention exactly how many. There had to be fifty vampires descending on us. I didn't like five-to-one odds as a general rule. On the bright side, the alley was so narrow it would

keep them from rushing us all at once, and if they had
to come at us a few at a time we'd be fine. On the not-
so-bright side, at least one of these idiots had a crossbow, and I was betting he wasn't going to be on the
front line.

I pulled the short sword from my spine sheath and
held it in my left hand, the claymore in my right.
Aubert had moved to stand in front of our group,
Wallace and Ross on either side of him. Khalid and
Hashim were at their backs. The twins had maneu-
vered their king behind them, but MacLeod quickly
pushed his way between them. Khalid turned to say
something to the king, but MacLeod snapped, "I
didn't get all dressed up just to stand in the back of
the line." Devlin and Justine flanked the king's party
to the left, Michael and I to the right. Michael looked
over at Devlin and made a few quick motions with
his hand. Devlin nodded back. When you've fought
side by side for over eighty years, few words are necessary. The three of them often moved through a
fight like a choreographed dance. It was one I was still
learning.

"What was that?" I asked.

Michael leaned down and whispered in my ear, "If
they engage us, we let the king's men take the brunt
and we go around the sides and take out their bow-
man. That's more of a danger than their numbers."

"Yes, flying death is never good," I mumbled.

The rogues came to a stop no more than twenty

feet in front of us, and I'd rarely seen a more ragtag group of vampires. They looked like common gutter trash and carried rusty swords, axes, and stakes. I even saw one pitchfork. It looked as though they they'd armed themselves with whatever they could steal off the street. The good news was that there appeared to be only one man with a crossbow. The bad news was that he was at the very back of the group, standing on the steps that led down into the alley, giving him a perfect vantage point to shoot at us over the heads of his comrades. The crossbow was raised and ready to fire, and I wondered which of us he was aiming for.

Aubert took a step forward, his ever-present spectacles perched on his nose. When he spoke his accent was that of an English aristocrat, and I marveled again at how easily he slipped from one dialect to another.

"Gentlemen, you are in flagrant violation of the immigration laws of the City of Edinburgh. For some of you, this is not your first offense." He looked pointedly at the barrel-chested vampire standing at the front of the group. The man's clothes were unkempt, his black hair was shaggy, and the greasy mustache he sported made my skin crawl. "I warned you, Simon, that a second violation was punishable by death."

The big vampire regarded Aubert for a moment, then spat on the ground, rocked back on his heels, and crossed his arms over his chest. "Little man, in case you ain't noticed there are fifty of us, and only eight of you."

Devlin chuckled and called out, "Aubert, are you sure you explained the laws to him in small words that even he can understand? The man can't even count."

Simon straightened to his full height, his shoulders stiff and his fist flexing in anger. "I can count fine. I just ain't countin' the two doxies," he sneered.

Michael bristled with anger. "You'll watch your tongue when you address my consort, or I'll be cutting it out shortly."

"Perhaps," Devlin said, "what we need here are introductions all around. Gentlemen, we are The Righteous. We are the defenders of the innocent."

Justine added, "We are the hand of justice."

Michael pulled his great claymore from its scabbard. "We are the sword of vengeance."

I looked Simon in the eye and said slowly, "We are what evil fears."

A few of the rogues shifted uneasily, and I saw one vampire toward the back slip up the stairs and disappear into the darkness. Simon's eyes showed confusion for a moment, but soon that arrogant bravado was back. He was young, and either he'd been turned by another young vampire, or the vamp who had turned him had abandoned him to learn on his own. The older vampires told stories of The Righteous to keep the young ones in line, but Simon had obviously not heard of us. I almost felt sorry for him. Ah, well. If he lived, he'd learn.

Simon shrugged. "The queen is the only vampire who scares me, and rumor has it she's dead. So it seems to me that the only thing standing in the way of our taking this city is the ten of you. Not very good odds, if you ask me."

"You speak of treason," Aubert hissed.

"It's only treason if the puppy tries to take my land without first fighting me in one-on-one combat, and winning," MacLeod said, stepping forward to address Simon. "I am MacLeod, King of the Western Lands, and you are trespassing in my territory. You want my city? Come and fight me for it, if you have the balls."

Simon shifted his weight and regarded MacLeod. The rogue had the dangerous quality of a street fighter, but MacLeod was a warrior and he had the confidence and commanding presence of a king. I would not have wanted to stand against him.

"The king himself, eh? You hear that, Brodie?" Simon called to one of the men behind him.

My gaze moved over the crowd, trying to figure out who Brodie was. Too late I heard the whoosh of an arrow slice through the air, and Khalid's roar of outrage. MacLeod was surrounded by his men and none of them had gotten in front of the arrow fast enough. The king stood in the middle of our group with a crossbow bolt embedded in his chest, directly over his heart.

# CHAPTER 24

We all stared. He should have been dust. MacLeod looked down at his chest in shock and then a slow, menacing smile formed on his lips. I rushed forward as the king grasped the arrow and snapped it off. The sharp, tangy scent of pine filled my nostrils. It appeared that the whole gang of rogues was as young as Simon. Not just any type of wood through the heart would kill a vampire, and any vamp with any age to him should know that. There were ten sacred trees whose wood was lethal to vampires, and pine was not one of them. If you staked a vampire with any common wood, the pain would be excruciating and it would give you the time you needed to take the vampire's head. If he survived being staked, the wound would not heal quickly. Wood through the heart healed slowly, like a human wound, but only a stake made of wood from a sacred tree would kill a vampire outright. It was sheer luck that these brigands didn't seem to have the experience to know that yet.

The arrow MacLeod held was mostly intact, having been stopped by the breastplate. MacLeod held the arrow up to show that it was missing no more of the shaft than just the tip, and a rousing cheer fell over us from above. As a whole, everyone in the alley looked up.

What appeared to be the entire vampire population of Edinburgh perched, like gargoyles, on the rooftops surrounding the alley. Those of us below stared up at them, waiting to see if they would move to defend their king. It appeared that they were impressed that MacLeod seemed impervious to the arrow, yet not one of them came to our aid.

"Are they here to help us, or hinder us?" I whispered.

MacLeod surveyed the rooftops one more time, and then turned to me. "They are here to see whether or not I am still worthy of my crown."

"Still, a little help would be nice," I grumbled.

"Very impressive, Your Highness," Simon sneered, "but you're still outnumbered and your people ain't makin' a move to save you. It's sad, really, that you're all gonna die in this alley. Me and my boys are gonna feast tonight, ain't we, boys?" Emboldened by the shouts of approval and encouragement that rang out among the men behind him, Simon continued on, "No more rules, no more laws. We're gonna drain this city dry, ain't we, b—"

Simon's speech was cut short when MacLeod drew

back and threw the arrow he held, impaling it in the rogue's throat. Simon clutched at the arrow, panicking, and tried to pull it free.

"I grow tired of listening to you," MacLeod said as he drew his sword. "You have two choices, puppy: I will grant everyone here immunity if you leave this city now and never show your face in it again, or you can die. Make your decision."

Simon worked the shaft free of his throat, and blood poured down his neck from the open wound. He held his hand out, and the man next to him put a sword in it. Aubert sighed audibly and we all looked over at him. He made a great show of removing his spectacles and placing them carefully in his breast pocket. When he was finished, he looked up at Simon. It was amazing to watch that indefinable *something* change within him. Jacques Aubert used his appearance the same way he used his many accents: to keep the vampires he dealt with off balance. Gone was the unassuming civil servant, and in his place stood a man who looked like a killer. I wondered if it unnerved the rogues as much as it did me.

MacLeod nodded. "Let us finish this."

Simon hefted his sword and came at MacLeod with all the grace of a charging bull. Until one of the other rogues made a move, we would stand back and let MacLeod fight him one-on-one, as a challenge to his throne was meant to be received. MacLeod allowed Simon a few good blows, but it was clear to us all that the king was merely toying with him. I felt

confident enough in his abilities to look away from
the fight, keeping my eyes on Brodie and the crossbow. Michael and I slowly moved toward the far side
of the alley, trying to make it appear as if we were
stepping aside to give the combatants room to maneuver. I glanced across the alley to see Justine and
Devlin doing the same. The clang of Simon and
MacLeod's swords rang in my ears, and when I was
sure that Michael's attention was fixed on Brodie, I
allowed myself a glance to my left to see how the
fight was progressing.

Simon and MacLeod were locked blade-to-blade,
chest-to-chest. The king was smiling, his whole body
humming with the thrill of battle. Simon shoved forward, throwing his weight into MacLeod, and the
two separated, MacLeod stumbling backward. Simon
lifted his sword and brought it down in an arc that was
meant to take the king's head. MacLeod blocked the
blow, sparks flying from their blades, and in a move
that was as graceful as any I'd seen danced on stage at
the Paris Opera, MacLeod spun around and brought
his sword up to slice cleanly through Simon's neck. I
cringed and looked away as his head rolled to the
ground and his body collapsed. I hated killing the
young ones. The magic that animated a vampire's
body died when the head or heart was taken, leaving
the body in whatever state of decomposition would
be natural if the person hadn't been made a vampire.
The older ones turned nicely to dust and bones. The
younger ones were just decomposing bodies.

There was a murmur of approval from the vampires above as MacLeod raised his sword in victory.

"Your leader has challenged me and lost," MacLeod addressed the crowd. "I tell you again, leave this city now and you may live. Stay, and you will die."

There was a moment of silence as we waited to see whether they would run or fight, and then Brodie spoke up from the back. "Kill them all and the city is ours!" he cried.

Warden Ross had moved up behind me. "What do you think? Can you turn them all into toads?" he whispered.

"Not likely," I muttered.

I doubted my ability to turn nearly fifty vampires into toads, but I did have magic that would help us. Devlin didn't like for me to use my magic in a fight, though, unless it was absolutely necessary. He'd never said so, but I always felt that he was of the opinion that it was dishonorable to use magic against those who didn't have any of their own to call. Of course, he didn't complain when it saved us from getting killed. I glanced up again at the vampires lining the rooftops. My using magic against the rogues would do nothing to cement MacLeod's position as king. Unless things took a turn for the worse, we would have to fight this battle with blades and fists.

I tensed as the vampire who had handed Simon the sword reached down and picked it up from where it lay in a cooling pool of his leader's blood. The rogues were waiting, watching to see what this man would do. It was obvious that he, and not Brodie, was Simon's second in command. I prayed that he would have a care for his men, and take them and leave. He looked down at the bloody sword for a long moment, and when he looked up I could see the anger in his eyes. I groaned and shifted my stance as he raised the sword, shouted to his men, and four dozen vampires rushed us.

While it was true that the rogues couldn't surround us in so confined a space, it didn't stop them from battering us like a wave against a cliff. We were forced to fall back into three lines because the width of the alley was such that any more of us abreast hampered our movements. Even so, it wasn't long before swords were sheathed and knives and fists came into play. There simply wasn't enough room to swing a sword.

As Michael tried to maneuver us around the edge of the melee, keeping our backs to the alley wall, Warden Ross grabbed my arm.

"Get behind me," he shouted.

I shook my head. "He is my consort. My place is at his side."

Ross regarded me for no longer than the blink of an eye, then nodded. "I'll guard your back as well as I can."

I nodded and followed Michael as we pushed and

fought to get to Brodie. I'd had to sheath the claymore but I still had my short sword. It was well bloodied, and my hands and shirt were splattered with red.

The rogues had pushed the king's men to the far end of the alley. They fell to our blades, but there were so many of them that they continued to come, pressing our men back. As far as I could ascertain the king and his men were bloodied, but still standing. I could see the top of Devlin's head on the far side of the alley, simply because he was so much taller than anyone else around him. He and Justine hadn't made it as far around the edge of the throng as we had. They were only a few feet in front of MacLeod and his men. I glanced behind me and could no longer see Ross at all.

My inattention was rewarded with a knife blade slicing across my arm. I didn't waste time looking down. It was a deep enough cut that I could already feel blood running down my arm. I dropped my sword arm and drove the blade up through the ribs and into the heart of the vampire who had cut me. I hadn't even pulled the blade out when another rogue grabbed me by the hair, jerking me around the vampire I'd just impaled and pulling me into the middle of the throng. I shouted in frustration as my sword slipped from my hand.

Fingers clawed at me from all sides, and before I could reach for the knives that were sheathed at my wrists I found myself in the grasp of at least three vampires, one with his arm around my neck and the other two holding each of my wrists. Michael growled in outrage and pulled his great claymore from its scabbard. He came through the crowd like an avenging angel, and blood flew as one vampire after another fell to his wrath. Unconcerned that the rogues could now surround him, his only focus was reaching me. I saw blades slice at him, rogues with weapons raised coming at him from behind, and then the vampires holding me spun me around and I lost sight of him entirely. Instead I looked over the heads of a dozen rogues to see Brodie aiming his weapon directly at my heart.

He smiled as the arrow shot from the crossbow. It seemed as if I had all the time in the world to watch it fly toward me. I braced myself for the impact, knowing it would hurt worse than any wound I had ever suffered in battle, but the instant before it hit, Michael threw himself in front of me. I cringed in horror at the meaty sound of the arrow slicing into his chest. He turned to me, the bolt piercing his heart, with a look of surprise on his face.

"I'm not dead," he said, his hand reaching up to touch my face, and then I watched the man I loved fall to the ground in front of me.

I screamed and kicked backward at the vampire who held me, connecting solidly with his leg just below the knee. I heard the snap of bone as either the leg broke or the knee dislocated. He released his hold on my neck with a strangled cry and, to my surprise, the men holding my wrists let me go as well. That was a mistake.

I dropped to my knees and rolled Michael over, sending up a silent prayer of thanks that he was alive. He winced and reached for my hand.

*"Mo ghraidh,"* he whispered in a ragged voice, "pull it out. Please."

My stomach clenched at the thought, but I nodded. Grasping the arrow, I pulled it out of his chest in one quick movement. His body bowed in pain and then his blue eyes fluttered closed, and he was still in my arms. I pulled open his shirt, popping buttons off until I could see his bare chest. He was breathing. Blood flowed from the wound and I pressed my hand over it to stanch the bleeding. The sounds of the fight around me receded until all I heard was my own ragged breathing, and the sound of my voice saying over and over, "You'll be fine. You have to be fine."

Then hands were reaching for me again, pulling at my shoulders and my hair, trying to drag me off Michael. We were surrounded by our enemies, too far away for any of our allies to reach us in time. They were going to kill us both. I tried to hang on to Michael as the rogues pulled me back, but my fingers, slick with blood, slipped from his wrist. I watched his hand fall lifelessly to the ground, and something snapped inside me.

Rage, fury, the thirst for vengeance—it all fed that little bit of dark magic that Morrigan had left within me. I felt it stir and build, gaining momentum until it threatened to choke me, and for the first time in ten years I didn't push it down.

I set it free.

# CHAPTER 25

The darkness that filled me erupted like a volcano. If light could be black, then that's what poured from my body. I stood, and the vampires who were reaching for me flew backward. The dark magic surrounded me, forming a protective circle around me and Michael, and shot into the air above me like a beacon. The fighting stopped, and all eyes turned to me.

I held my hands out and my skin glowed like polished ivory. I knew without being told that my whiskey-colored eyes had turned black with the magic that filled me. I turned slowly to Brodie, and smiled a wholly evil smile. He nocked another arrow. I spread my arms wide, giving him a perfect target.

"Take your best shot," I called to him.

The arrow hit the protective circle around me, and exploded into splinters. Two more arrows followed, each meeting the same fate. Brodie threw down his crossbow, his face mottled with rage, and shouted, "Kill her! Kill her!"

The rogues who were still standing, twenty-five or

thirty in all, rushed me. I laughed as the smell of burning flesh filled my nostrils, and the screams of the vampires rang in my ears. I turned in a circle, watching them try for me and fail. My magic was strong, the heady rush of power coursing through my body. It felt as though I could hold this circle forever, and no one short of the Goddess herself could break it. But that wasn't what the magic wanted. It wanted blood.

I turned back to Brodie, and whatever he saw on my face made his eyes widen in panic. He tried to run but I reached out, pouring my magic through my fingertips, imagining those fingers curling around his neck. He stopped and turned back to me, his eyes wide, his fingers clawing at the invisible hand that was gripping his throat.

"Your leader has challenged the King of the Western Lands and died in honorable combat," I called out. "You were given the opportunity to live, and yet you chose to stay and commit treason. Your life and the lives of all you command are now forfeit."

"Mercy," Brodie cried in a strangled voice. Several of his followers dropped to their knees in front of me and made a similar appeal.

Mercy. It was a plea that would have swayed me if I hadn't been flush with black magic that had lain dormant inside me for a decade. Evil knows nothing of mercy, and it was the darkness that was in control now.

I laughed, and some part of me that was still me

cringed at the sound. I looked down at Michael's unconscious body, then back up at Brodie, making sure he saw the fury in my eyes. I wanted him to know that his death had little to do with treason, and everything to do with the arrow he'd shot into my beloved's heart.

"The king offered you mercy," I said. "I will grant you none."

I raised my hands and let the dark magic ride me. I couldn't control it and I had no wish to do so. It was wild magic, and it knew what it wanted. All I had to do was hold on. I watched the dark light surround Brodie and he thrashed and tried to wipe it off with flailing hands. It swirled around him from the ground up, and when he opened his mouth to scream, the darkness spilled inside him. It filled him and, through its connection to me, I could feel it literally sucking the life out of him. Dark magic, black magic, is fueled by blood and death, and this magic had been hungry for so very long.

I watched, partly in horror, but mostly in triumph, as Brodie's skin withered until he looked like an old man. His mouth still screamed, though no sound came from it, and his body jerked violently, arching upward as if pulled by strings. Then he fell forward, down the steps, and when he landed his body exploded into fine dust. And I smiled at the rush of it all.

For about five seconds even a human could have heard a pin drop in that alley, and then all hell broke loose. The rogues ran for the stairs, scattering the ashes of their fallen comrade. The magic welled up around them and blocked their retreat, surrounding them and boxing them in. I threw back my head and reveled in the power that poured into me as the darkness sucked their lives from them, just as it had sucked Brodie's. I felt more than a twinge of regret when the power began to ebb. The dark light slunk back over the cobblestones, returning to me.

"Cin?"

I looked down to see Michael blinking up at me. The smooth expanse of his chest was flawless and perfect again. Unconsciously my hand reached up to touch the gash across my arm. It, too, was healed. It was then that I noticed there was no longer any blood on my hands. My skin was as clean as if I'd just emerged from a bath. Michael ran a hand over his heart, as if to make sure he was truly whole, then rose to his feet. He cupped my face and looked into my eyes.

*"M'anam,"* he said, *my soul,* and there was such pain and regret in those two words.

I looked up at him, confused. I didn't understand the look on his face. It was as if he hurt for me, the way you would hurt for someone you loved if they were in pain. But I wasn't in pain. I felt wonderful, my body humming with magic. I was healed and, more importantly, Michael was healed. The magic had healed us as it had . . .

I stood very still, only my eyes darting to the left and right. There were piles of dust and ash in the alley, piles that had once been people. I closed my eyes, and I could hear Devlin and Justine whispering behind me, the king and his men as well, all wondering what they should say or do. I opened my eyes and looked up, watching as the city's vampires melted into the night. Only one shadow was left on the rooftops, the figure of a woman with long black hair, wearing a cloak made of raven feathers. With a flourish of that cloak she bowed low to me, and then simply vanished.

I took a deep breath, pushing every bit of magic I had, both dark and light, as far down as it would go. Now that the rush was gone, my body started to shake with fear and fatigue. I looked back up into Michael's eyes, and I could see the strain on his face as he gathered me against him.

"What have I become?" I whispered and collapsed into his arms.

# CHAPTER 26

I was dimly aware of Michael scooping me up and carrying me quickly up the stairs and out of the alley. He hailed one of our carriages, shouting orders to Fritz, the driver, to take us back to the townhouse. I slipped in and out of consciousness on the ride there, waking every few minutes to find myself cradled in Michael's arms, his hands stroking my hair as he whispered to me in the darkness. When we arrived I assured him that I could make it in under my own power, but he would hear none of it, swinging me out of the carriage and carrying me up the steps. Drake was waiting by the door, and he opened it before Michael gained the landing.

"What happened?" Drake asked. "Where are the others?"

"Everyone's alive," Michael snapped at him as he swept through the door.

Bel was standing on the bottom step, a worried frown marring her otherwise perfect features. "What's wrong with her?" she asked.

"Nothing's wrong with her," Michael said. I heard the edge to his voice and tensed in his arms. He sighed, and made an effort to sound more reasonable. "She's fine. She just needs rest."

I laid my head in the crook of his neck, breathing in the scent of him. As he carried me up to our room I took the time to enjoy the feel of his arms around me, because I knew that the peace of this moment wouldn't last. Silently I cursed Edmund Gage for tainting me with his magic, and Morrigan herself for not taking it all when she performed the cleansing. It may have saved our lives tonight, but would it destroy our love? I'd kept this from Michael for the past ten years. It would not be any easy thing to forgive under normal circumstances, and right now our relationship was far from normal.

Michael laid me gently on the bed, and then turned to the whiskey decanter on the dressing table. He poured us each a generous serving and sat on the edge of the bed, staring into his glass as he swirled the dark liquid in circles. I took a large sip, closing my eyes and taking comfort in the familiar burn as the whiskey settled in my stomach.

"Are you all right?" he asked.

I sighed. "You probably want to know what happened back there."

"If I'd wanted to know what happened, that's what I would have asked. All I want to know right now is if you're all right."

I looked into his eyes, and the full weight of what

I'd done came crashing down on me. I had betrayed his trust, and all he was concerned about was my welfare. For a decade I'd lied to him, and to my friends, about something that obviously had deadly consequences, and even so my safety was still his first concern. Truly, I did not deserve him.

I felt tears well up in my eyes. "Oh, Michael, what have I done?"

Over the years I had become adept at suppressing the black magic, tamping it down whenever I lost my temper and felt it stirring within me. I had become arrogant, believing that as long as I didn't use it, I could pretend that it wasn't truly a part of me. Tonight it had gotten the better of me, and men had died because of it.

The strained look left his face and his features softened as he gathered me in his arms and let me cry. I laid my head on his chest and he stroked my hair, whispering comforting words to me in Gaelic.

"Is anything hurting, lass?" he asked.

"Only my conscience. Michael, I killed those men."

"Aye, you did at that. Men, I'd like to remind you, who were traitors to their king and guilty of high treason. I know it must have been difficult, but they were dead men anyway, Cin, and they would have killed the both of us, and who knows how many others, if you hadn't killed them first."

"That's just it, Michael," I whispered. "It wasn't difficult. It was . . . so very easy. Taking someone's life shouldn't be that easy. I can close my eyes and see the face of every vampire whose head I've taken. I know when I execute someone that I am taking their life and I feel the burden of it. Tonight, and a decade ago with Gage and his coven, all I felt was the power, the thrill of the kill. When I was taking those lives, it meant nothing to me, Michael, and it *should*. Every life we take, no matter how deserved the execution is, should mean something. Am I evil, Michael? That I could do something as horrible as that, and feel nothing?"

"Of course you're not, lass. You feel the loss of every life we take more keenly than any of us. Your tender heart is one of the things that I love about you. Evil knows no guilt, no remorse. You are not evil, the black magic is. I just don't understand how you came to be in possession of so much of it."

I sighed and told him everything, starting with the first time I'd realized that Morrigan hadn't gotten all of Gage's magic when she'd done the cleansing. I nearly faltered when I saw the look on his face as he realized that tonight's fireworks had not been some sort of spell gone wrong, but the result of magic that I'd been secretly carrying for a decade. Surprise, disbelief, hurt, anger, they all warred with one another as I told my tale. When I was finished he said nothing for several minutes. Then he stood abruptly and began pacing the room, never looking directly at me.

"Why would you hide this from me? What have

you been thinking all these years? That I would love you less because of something that you had no control over? Because of something that happened to you while you were trying to save my life, and the lives of our friends? Is that the kind of man you think I am?"

"No, of course not. Will you let me explain?"

He continued pacing, but now he was running one hand through his hair. It was a nervous gesture he'd picked up from Devlin over the years. "If you could possibly have a rational explanation for this, I'd love to hear it."

In as calm a voice as I could muster I said, "It wasn't because I doubted your love for me that I kept this from you, Michael. I know you love me, and I knew that this would worry you. I didn't tell you because I didn't want to spend the last ten years with you looking at me the way you did tonight."

"And how was that?" he asked with a bitter edge to his voice.

"Like you hurt for me," I said softly. "And I heard Devlin and Justine whispering to each other tonight. They're afraid of me now. I could hear it in their voices. I kept this from the three of you because I didn't want them to be afraid, and because I didn't want you to worry about something you can do absolutely nothing about. Was it so wrong of me to have saved us all a decade of hurt and worry by not telling you?"

He stared down at me and shook his head sadly. "I wish we'd never come here."

I felt a moment of panic as he crossed the room to the door. "Where are you going?" I asked.

He paused with his hand on the doorknob. "I have to tell Devlin and Justine about this."

"I should be the one to tell them."

"I think it would be better coming from me right now," he replied. "You stay here and rest."

"Michael? Will you be back?"

He turned. "I'll be here when you wake up," he said, but there was such a look of defeat in his eyes that I almost didn't believe him.

When the door clicked shut I lay back and closed my eyes, listening to the rain that had begun to fall gently on the roof. I'd been wrong to have kept such a secret from Michael, but in the beginning I'd been so afraid that it would change things between us, and by the time the initial panic had subsided . . . well, there hadn't seemed to be a proper time and place to confess. I'd just wanted to move forward and pretend that none of it had ever happened.

Deep down I'd known that I couldn't hide the black magic forever, and I'd envisioned having this conversation with him a thousand times over the years. This was not how I'd thought it would go. I'd imagined that one day I would tell him the truth. He would be hurt and angry. I would cry and beg his forgiveness, and because he loves me he would give it. And if it hadn't been for Drake and Bel that's how it probably would have happened.

I felt a tear roll down my cheek and brushed it

away. When Michael had caught me in Drake's arms I had told him that I'd never given him a reason not to trust me. Now I had . . . and I wondered if things would ever be the same between us again.

# CHAPTER 27

Perhaps it was the cold that woke me. Shivering, I sat up and noticed that the fire had gone out. The clock on the mantel chimed softly and I realized that Michael had been gone for over an hour. Surely it didn't take that long to explain what I'd done to Devlin and Justine. I got out of bed, still wearing the clothes I'd had on earlier, and walked downstairs. The house was dark and quiet except for a light coming from the library. I could hear Justine's voice as I crossed the foyer.

"You know I'm right, Michael," she said.

Michael sighed. "I know."

"Then why don't you go upstairs to her?"

There was a moment of silence and finally he said, "Because I don't know how I can face her now."

My breath seized and fresh tears gathered in my eyes. *Has it come to this?* I thought. *This man who once loved me to the depths of his soul now can't even stand to be in the same room with me?* The walls seemed to close in as panic overtook me. Someone had discarded a cloak on the hall table, and I snatched it up and ran out the front door.

The rain had stopped and the sidewalks were wet and shiny under the fall of light from the gas lamps. Dawn was still an hour or so away, and the sky was a moonless inky black. I walked aimlessly, my mind racing with dark thoughts. Michael and I had been together for thirteen years, and before tonight it had honestly never occurred to me that I might lose him one day.

Time moves differently for vampires. When you don't see the effects of each passing year every time you look in a mirror, when you don't have to worry about growing old or dying, it's easy to lose track of the years. With the possibility of eternity stretched out before me, thirteen years was nothing. We were still like newlyweds, and something tightened in my chest at the realization that it might not always be so. For the first time I thought, *What if I lose him? What if he no longer loves me?* It was more than I could bear.

If I had still been human I would have married someone I liked and respected, but I probably would not have been in love with him. I would have done my duty in the marriage bed, but I didn't imagine that my husband would have made love to me every night until I begged him to stop and let me rest. He would have been handsome, perhaps, but I doubt he would have inspired the wild lustful images that flashed through my mind every time Michael walked into a room. The most excitement my life would have had to offer would have been attending a grand ball, or an appearance at court—not the thrill of hunting down a rogue vampire, or the rush of the fight that followed.

I glanced up at the rows of darkened houses as I passed. The people in those houses, their lives had always seemed so mundane to me, so unexciting, even back when that had been my life as well. I had chosen to become a vampire and I had never regretted the decision, even in the face of all of the things I truly did miss about being human. I had always felt incredibly lucky to have been given the gift that Michael had given me when he turned me. I watched a carriage pass on the street and wondered for the first time if these people with their dull, ordinary lives hadn't gotten the better deal. To have been given everything that I had, and then to think that it might one day be taken from me . . . it would have been better to have not known, to have blithely gone about my life in society, thinking that money and a good marriage match and a grand title were the best the world had to offer.

And what would become of me if he left me? I didn't even know who I was anymore without him and The Righteous, and the work that we did. That fact probably should have bothered me more, but it didn't. All I seemed to be able to think of was the gut-clenching prospect of one day not having him in my arms and my heart and my bed.

As I glanced to my right before crossing Queen Street I caught sight of a woman standing under one of the gaslights on the opposite corner, watching me. Her black dress proclaimed her a widow, but she was young and quite strikingly beautiful. I wondered what she was doing out here alone in the middle of the night. It was an affluent neighborhood, but still . . .

As I gained the opposite sidewalk I froze. I suddenly realized that I had seen her before, thirteen years ago in London. The night that I had faced Kali and Sebastian for the first time as a vampire, I had seen that woman standing across the street from my cousin Thomas's townhouse. She had been just standing there, watching me. I'd thought it was odd at the time, but then again at the time I'd had other things to worry about, and I hadn't thought of it again. It *was* her, though. I could still see her in my mind, so incredibly lovely. I hadn't forgotten the glossy black hair, the high cheekbones, or the full lips on her almost aggressively beautiful face. And she hadn't aged a day in thirteen years.

I whirled around but, just as before, the woman was gone. The light from the lamp fell in an empty pool on the sidewalk. I scanned the street in both directions, but she had vanished.

"Damn," I muttered and turned.

And then I screamed.

There she was, right in front of me. She had disappeared from the opposite street corner and materialized behind me in the time it had taken me to turn

around. Even vampires don't move that fast. *What
are you* almost came out of my mouth, but before I
could speak the words I noticed her hair. It was pulled
up high on her head, accentuating her sharp cheekbones, and falling in glossy waves across her shoulders to her waist. Up close it wasn't just black, it was
the shiny black of a raven's wing, shimmering with
purple and green highlights. I had seen that before,
too, in Venice. I looked up to meet her black eyes.

"Morrigan," I said.

She inclined her head and without a word turned
and walked off down the street, back toward
MacLeod's townhouse. I stared after her for a moment, then ran to catch up. Morrigan, the Great Phan-
tom Queen, was a goddess of war, life, and death.
Vampires, werewolves, things that hunt the night—
we were all her creatures. And she seemed to have a
particular interest in me. She had once informed me
that she had created me to be one of her greatest
weapons. A weapon against what, I had no clue and
she wouldn't say. Back then her cloak had hidden her
features from me, but I recognized her now. She had
been watching me almost since the moment of my
turning, if not before.

"You must remedy this," Morrigan said. "You've
become so consumed with it that you've lost sight of
why you came here in the first place. You do not see
what is right in front of you."

"I know that," I replied. "Marrakesh needs our
help, I have not forgotten. I just . . . I cannot concen-

trate on anything else when all that fills my head is the fear that I've lost his love."

"Did I not tell you once that I had handpicked Michael to be your mate?" she asked, impatiently. "Did I not tell you that I created all of you with the capacity to love one person for centuries? Do not let what's happened make you doubt that. He's a man, so he'll bollocks it up from time to time." She shrugged. "Then again, so will you." She stopped walking and turned to me. Her hand reached out to me, and I eyed her long, shiny black fingernails with caution. She cupped my cheek, very much as my mother had when I was a child, and said, "It's a precious gift I've given you, Cin, but what you do with it is up to you. Look at the larger picture. If you were staked tomorrow, would any of these troubles truly matter?"

Chills went through me. Morrigan was a harbinger of death. She was the Washer at the Ford who decided which warriors lived, and which died.

"Am I going to get staked tomorrow?" I asked in a small voice that sounded frightened even to my own ears.

She snorted. "If you did, I would be very put out. I've invested a lot in you, more than you know."

"Is that why you're here now?"

"Let's just say I'm interested to see how things will turn out."

I glanced at her. "I don't suppose you'd like to tell me who's behind the attacks on the queen?"

She arched a brow at me. "My dear, if I had the

time to do your job I wouldn't need you, now would I? I will tell you this: No one in that house is truly as they seem to you now."

Well, that was . . . vastly unhelpful.

"I saw you tonight, up on the roof," I stated.

"I know you did," she replied and continued walking, never looking back to see whether I followed or not.

"So you saw what happened, what I did?"

She nodded.

"The cleansing you performed on me in Venice didn't work, Morrigan, not entirely. Perhaps if you tried again—"

"No," she said tersely.

I blinked. "What do you mean *no*?"

She closed her eyes and took a deep breath. "Truly, you are the most exhausting of all my creatures. Did it never occur to you that I did not make a mistake by leaving a bit of the darkness within you?"

"Well . . . no, actually it didn't. Why would you do that?"

"Because you are now, *potentially,* everything I need you to be."

"But that's not who I am," I pleaded. "The dark magic, it's not the sort of witch that I am."

"You're young, child. You don't yet understand what you are."

I opened my mouth to argue with her but before I could get the first word out she simply vanished, leaving me staring at an empty street. I sank down on the steps of a darkened townhouse and put my head in my hands.

She was partially right. I didn't understand what she wanted me to become . . . but I did know who I was. Quite suddenly everything seemed very clear to me, and I stood and continued down the sidewalk, my stride long and determined.

Yes, by the gods, I knew exactly who I was.

# CHAPTER 28

I strode into the house as dawn was breaking and took the stairs two at a time. When I opened the door to our bedroom Michael was pacing in front of the fire, a haggard expression on his face. He crossed the room to stand before me, looking me over for any signs of injury.

"Where the devil have you been?" he demanded. "It's dawn and I was worried that you'd—"

I grabbed the front of his shirt and spun him around, slamming his back into the door. "I'm yours," I said fiercely.

He blinked down at me. "What?"

"I am yours," I reiterated, slowly and emphatically. "You knew I was a witch when you turned me and I will not let you leave me now just because my magic has gotten a little frightening. You promised to love me until we were both dust and bones and I fully intend to make you live up to that bargain."

"Cin, I am not going to leave you," he said softly.

"I heard you talking to Justine in the library. You told her you couldn't even face me now. I'm sorry I lied to you, Michael, but I was scared and our love was still so new. I did what I thought was best at the time."

"I know," he said, looking down at me with tenderness and understanding in his eyes. It was an expression I hadn't seen on his face in weeks.

I released my hold on his shirt, confused. "You do?"

He smiled at me. "You obviously didn't hear *all* of the conversation while you were eavesdropping. Justine made me realize that, at that time, you were so young and we'd thrown you into a world you weren't prepared to deal with on your own. I understand if you were frightened that I—that we—might leave you alone in the world with no home you could go back to. That would never have happened, Cin, and I wish you'd trusted more in my love for you."

"I did, Michael. I do. What Justine said, that may have been part of it, but it wasn't the only reason. That night . . . you all looked at me as though I'd been damaged beyond repair, and I wanted more than anything for you to believe that I was exactly as I had been before we'd come to Venice. And perhaps I thought that if I didn't say it out loud I could believe it, too."

"I understand the reasons you didn't want to tell me, Cin, but the fact that you've borne this burden alone all these years hurts me far worse than anything you were trying to spare me. I love you more than my life, and I wish you hadn't hidden this from me."

"I was wrong and I'm sorry, Michael, more sorry than you know." I looked at him with all the regret I felt showing in my eyes. "Can you possibly forgive me?"

He took my face in his hands and tilted my lips up to meet his. "You are my heart and my soul. I think I could forgive you almost anything. If you can forgive me as well."

I looked down, unable to meet his eyes. "I know in my heart that nothing happened between you and Bel," I said, "but it would be nice to hear you say it when you're sober."

"Nothing happened," he assured me. "I was sitting in a tavern, drinking and feeling sorry for myself, and she just showed up. I tried to politely get rid of her but you know how she is. The bottles of gin and whiskey kept appearing on the table and the next thing I knew it was nearly dawn and we were both spectacularly drunk."

"Did she try to seduce you?" I asked, my imagination running wild.

"No. In fact, she told me I was behaving like an ass."

I laughed at that. "As long as we're confessing all of our sins tonight, do you want to tell me what bothers you so much about Drake?"

Michael glanced away. "Oh, hell, Cin, I don't

think the queen is the only one going crazy in this house."

"That's a distinct possibility," I replied. "But it's not an answer. Michael, I'd be lying if I said that Drake wasn't appealing in a dark and dangerous sort of way, but then most vampires are. I've had more than my share of admirers over the years, but none of them has ever sparked this sort of jealousy in you, not the way Drake has, and I've come to realize that this really has nothing to do with me at all. What is it about that man that disturbs you so?"

Michael raked one hand through his hair and walked to the fireplace. I stood and watched the tension in his shoulders as he stared into the flames and gathered his thoughts. Then I quietly sat down on the bed and waited for him to speak.

"We all found ourselves in Christiania, Norway, in the winter of 1790. Karin and Drake were lovers, but he didn't seem bothered when she left his bed for mine. I . . . cared for her," he said and turned to me. "I didn't love her. You're the only woman I've ever loved. She and I . . . we were friends and I thought we enjoyed each other's company."

"What happened?" I asked softly.

He shrugged. "When Drake left town she went with him. She left without so much as a farewell. I guess he could offer her something I couldn't."

"And you . . . what? Thought that Drake would crook his little finger and I would just run away with him?" I asked, incredulously.

"No. Maybe. Hell, I don't know, Cin."

I smiled sadly at the frustration evident in his voice. "Michael, look at me," I said. "I don't know why any woman would be foolish enough to willingly leave your bed, but I'm very grateful that she did because I cannot imagine living my life without you. No other man will ever make me burn the way you do. You are mine, and if I know nothing else about myself I do know that I am yours, now and forever."

He swallowed hard and then turned away. It wasn't the reaction I'd been hoping for.

# CHAPTER 29

I watched in confusion as he walked to his trunk, which rested against the far wall, and rummaged around in it until he'd piled all of his clothes to one side. He reached into his boot and pulled out a dagger. The *sgian dubh* was the same blade he'd used to open a vein the night I'd drunk his blood and become a vampire. I heard the sound of fabric ripping as he cut open a seam in the lining of the trunk and pulled out a small velvet pouch, weighing it in his hand. Tossing the *sgian dubh* onto the pile of clothes, he turned and came back to the bed.

Kneeling in front of me, he opened the pouch and spilled a large ruby ring into his hand. As he held it up, I marveled at its beauty. Set in gold, the dark red stone was oval, large enough to cover my finger to the knuckle, and surrounded by small diamonds. I had a particular love of rubies, and Michael certainly knew my taste in jewels.

"Do you know what this is?" he asked.

"Other than stunning?"

I reached out to touch it, but he pulled his hand back. Lettling out an exasperated breath, I clasped my hands in my lap and turned my full attention to him.

"This is the stone that Morrigan gave you in Venice."

"You had it cut and set."

"Messrs. Garrard in London had that honor. It's made of our blood, Cin, yours and mine, and fashioned by a goddess who chose us for each other. I cannot think of any greater symbol of our love and commitment. I've lived a long time, a hundred and eleven years, but until I met you I have never been in love. I wanted to give you time before I asked this of you—because you're very young and I wanted to make sure that this is what you truly desired as well—but you are the last thing I think of before I sleep and the first thing I reach for when I wake up. I want your love to warm me, your heart to inspire me, your humor to cheer me, and your beauty to tempt me for the rest of eternity." He took my hand in his and slid the ring onto my finger. "Cin Craven, will you marry me?"

I stared down at the ring, unable to believe this was truly happening. Vampires do not get married as humans do, in a church with a priest, but there is a bonding ceremony that any king or regent can perform. Michael and I had been consorts—the term vampires use to describe a committed couple—since the moment of my turning, but he'd never mentioned marriage. Over the years I'd told myself that it wasn't important—after all, Devlin and Justine had been blissfully happy for over 150 years and they weren't married. Until this moment, though, I hadn't realized how very much I'd wanted him to ask me.

Tears fell freely down my cheeks as I threw myself into his arms and we tumbled backward onto the floor. "Yes!" I cried. "I would be so proud to be your wife."

For a long time he held me as if he would never let me go. I wept in his arms, unashamedly, and by the ragged sound of his breathing I wondered if he cried as well. For weeks now it had seemed that I would lose him, but finally we were in each other's arms again and all was right with the world.

Eventually I pulled away and looked into his blue eyes. "How soon can we do it?" I asked.

Michael chuckled. "When we've sorted things out here MacLeod can perform the ritual, or if you'd rather wait until—"

"No," I said, grinning like an idiot, "I don't want to wait."

He ran his hands up my sides and then down across my back and over my butt, pulling me down to him so that my body was flush with his. I ran my tongue along the edge of his ear and then sucked his lobe into my mouth. He groaned and his fingers squeezed me harder.

"Michael," I said as I trailed kisses down his neck, stopping to linger in the hollow of his throat. "How did Messrs. Garrard get my ruby when it was stolen several years ago, along with a good portion of my jewelry, from our hotel room in Amsterdam?"

His hands stilled and I smiled into his neck.

"Ah, well . . ."

I felt my canines lengthen and I ran the sharp tips of them over the big vein in his neck. He shuddered underneath me. "Go ahead and say it."

"I robbed you," he confessed.

I looked up at him and arched a brow. "Obviously. And my grandmother's pearls, and my mother's diamond bracelet, and the gold bracelet you bought for me in Madrid? Where are they?"

"They're all safely tucked away in the Bank of England," he replied.

I rolled my eyes. "I'll be getting those back the next time we travel through London. Do you have any idea how distraught I was to have lost them?"

"I know. I'm sorry," he said, as he ran his hands over my hips. His thumbs pressed against the front of my breeches, moving slowly from the juncture of my thighs to the bottom button of my leather vest. "I wanted your ring to be a surprise, though. Was it worth it?"

I watched his hands unbutton my vest with slow precision, and I nearly forgot the question. I glanced down at the huge ruby with its little round diamonds sparkling around it. "Oh, yes," I whispered.

He sat up, pushing the vest from my shoulders. His lips were just a breath away. "Yes, what?" he asked.

"Yes, it was worth it." I smiled wickedly, and then ran my tongue along his lower lip. "And yes to anything else you want tonight. It's been a long time, you know."

He fell back onto his elbows with a mischievous look on his face. "Yes, it has. You know, I was thinking that since we've gone this long without making love perhaps we should do this properly and wait until we're married. After all, I wouldn't want to cheat you out of your wedding night."

I didn't bother pointing out that we'd slept together every night for the past thirteen years. If he wanted to play this game, we'd play.

"If that's what you want," I replied, as if it didn't matter to me one way or the other. I pulled my blouse off over my head and his gaze fell to my bare breasts. My nipples tightened as he watched, and I stood, resting one booted foot on his thigh. "Will you help me off with my boots?"

He grasped my ankle and looked up the length of my body. Hunger was raw on his face as I slipped my leg out of the boot and then stretched the other leg out. His fingers played over the back of my knee and then trailed down my calf. When my boots were in a pile on the floor, I modestly turned my back to him. Unfastening the buttons on my breeches, I bent over as I slowly slid the leather down my thighs. I deposited the breeches onto the pile of clothes and walked past him to the wooden steps at the side of the bed. I heard a strangled moan from behind me as I climbed them, and then crawled across the bed with the sinuous grace of a cat.

I laughed as he landed on top of me, his body pressing me down into the mattress. That certainly hadn't taken long.

"I thought you wanted to wait?" I asked innocently.

"Ah, lass," he said against the back of my neck as he slid his hand between my thighs, "you're so wet. What sort of a man would I be to leave you in such a state?"

I groaned as his fingertips moved slowly back and forth across my flesh. "Not the sort of man I'd marry."

I arched back against him. Wanting him to slip that finger inside me, but he continued to tease me, stroking me until I thought I would cry in frustration and pleasure. The muscles in my stomach quivered and I grasped a handful of pillow. Michael ran his tongue slowly up my spine before he finally slid one finger inside me at the same time he gently bit me on the back of the neck. I cried out as he moved inside me.

"Come for me," he whispered in my ear, and I was so hot that my body exploded. I arched my back and cried out as his hand stilled, splayed against me, and tremors rocked my body. "That's my girl."

When I was spent I rolled over, smiling, and pushed Michael onto his back.

"And what would you have of me, lass?" he asked, as I straddled him.

"Everything," I replied, and slowly went to work on the buttons of his shirt. When his boots joined mine on the floor I sat back on my heels and surveyed the beauty of his body. From the swell of his chest, to the lean ripples of his stomach, to the powerful muscles of his thighs, he was a symphony of strong, graceful lines. He folded his hands behind his head, watching me watch him, and I licked my lips at the sight of the muscles bunching in his arms and shoulders. Unable to resist any longer, I had to touch him.

I ran my hands up his legs and followed with my tongue, licking a line up the inside of his left thigh. I saw the muscles in his stomach clench as I blew my breath out over the heavy weight of his balls. I teased him as he had teased me, barely grazing my lips over them and then licking, ever so softly. He arched his hips and I slipped my hands under them, pulling him up to my mouth. I slipped one soft globe into my mouth, rolling my tongue across it and then sucking gently as he moaned in pleasure. His shaft was throbbing and I grasped it, stroking him until he was glistening. I moved slowly up the length of him, his own wetness mingling with my moist tongue as I circled the head of his shaft. One hand reached out and grasped a fistful of my hair, and I knew what he wanted. I sucked the length of him into my mouth, slowly at first, and then harder and faster. I loved to have him in my mouth, and I could do this all day. I splayed one hand against his stomach so that I could feel his muscles clench and quiver when I found a stroke that he particularly liked. With the other hand I ran my fingertips lightly over his balls, enjoying the feel of the velvet sac tightening when his release was near. With a shout, Michael arched his hips, spilling into my mouth as I drank him down.

He sat up, growling that inhuman sound that is unique among vampires and large jungle cats, and grasped my hips. He pulled me up the length of his body until I was on my knees with my legs spread wide on either side of his shoulders. I looked down into his blue eyes as he smiled wickedly and lay back against the pillows, pulling me down to his mouth. I clutched the headboard of the bed as Michael feasted on the most intimate parts of me, licking and sucking until I was throbbing in his mouth. I threw my head back as my body shook with its second release of the night. He didn't stop, though, continuing on until he'd brought me to climax once again.

"I want you inside me," I said, sliding down his body until I could rub my slick core against his erection.

He grabbed my wrists and rolled with me until he was on top. "But that's only three times," he teased. "Surely we can do better than that."

"We will," I assured him. "Later."

I wiggled around until he was once more pressed against me. I was frantic to feel him inside me, and I moved until I felt the tip of him at my center. He pushed slowly forward, stopping with perhaps just an inch of his length inside me. He stayed there, not moving, until I was shaking and quivering around him, wanting more. And then he slowly pulled out of me. I growled in frustration and Michael pinned my wrists to the bed.

"Not so fast, *mo ghraidh,*" he said. "I want you to come for me many, many more times first."

He punctuated each word with a kiss, moving from my lips to my neck to the taut, pink peaks of my breasts. For the next hour we teased each other, kissing, licking, sucking, biting, driving each other to the edge of pleasure and beyond. When I didn't think I could possibly have the strength for one more orgasm, he knelt between my thighs and I reached out and guided him to me. The feel of him finally pushing into me, fighting for every inch even though I was so very hot and wet, was almost more than I could bear. When he'd impaled me to the hilt he paused for a moment and the feel of him, not moving, just filling me with the thick throbbing heat of him, nearly sent me over the edge. I held on as he began to move, stroking in and out of me in a rhythm that had been perfected over many years, and many passionate nights.

"Now, lass," he said in a ragged whisper, as his movements became less controlled. "Please now."

His fingers bit into my hips as he thrust one last time, burying himself as far as he could as he spilled inside me. I felt the hot pulse of his release and I let go, falling with him over the edge and into the sparkly, weightless wonder beyond.

Tonight I had wrought magic powerful enough to have drawn the attention of a goddess. In that moment, though, I was certain of one thing: Of all the magic I possessed, none of it could begin to compare to the magic he and I created together.

# CHAPTER 30

I woke to find Michael propped up on one elbow, staring down at me. I smiled back at him and stretched, glancing at the clock. Dusk was a few hours away.

"Would you like me to get you a pot of chocolate?" he asked.

"I would love that."

He leaned down and kissed me swiftly on the lips, then bounded out of bed. As I watched him dress, I almost called him back. It was such a shame to cover that luscious body. When he had gone, I crawled out of bed, feeling the muscles in my body protesting against any sort of movement. I shrugged into my dressing gown and was admiring the way my new ring matched the red silk when someone knocked softly on my door. I crossed the room and opened it, surprised to find Devlin standing.

"I collected your weapons after the fight," he said.

"Thank you, Devlin," I replied, motioning him in. "Would you lay them on the trunk?"

It was a testament to how worried Michael was

about me that he'd left his great claymore behind. The sword was older than he was, and his prized possession. Devlin laid our swords and knives gently on the trunk lid and turned to me.

"I cleaned them for you," he said.

"I appreciate that," I replied and walked over to him, intending to give him a quick kiss on the cheek.

He backed up a step before he caught himself and stopped. I froze. He was afraid of me now. How was I supposed to handle this? He was the leader of our group, and it was imperative that I make things right between us. I decided that the best course of action would be to act as if nothing had changed, to make him see that I was still me, the same girl he'd known and shared a life with for all these years.

I put my hands on my hips. "Oh, for the love of Danu, Devlin, I won't bite."

He looked startled and then let out a nervous laugh, raking a hand through his black hair as he paced the room and settled against the mantel. He leaned back against it and crossed his arms over his wide chest. Nodding toward my hand, he said, "I see the boy finally came up to scratch. It's about time."

I glanced down at the ring and smiled. "You knew about this?"

"We all knew. It took all three of us to organize that bit of thievery."

I smiled and we lapsed into silence again. It was a weighty, uncomfortable silence that had never occurred between us before.

Finally, he said, "It's a great and terrible thing you did last night, Cin."

"I know," I replied softly.

He nodded. "If this is something we're all going to have to live with, then I need to understand something, Cin."

"If I can explain I will, Devlin," I said.

"It's apparent that you've had control over this dark magic for a long time. What went wrong last night?"

I sighed and shook my head. "Michael did. When I saw him lying there with that arrow sticking out of his chest, I lost it. Black magic feeds on all your darkest emotions. Gage's magic seems to like my temper. Most of the time I don't feel it inside me but it rises when I get angry, and last night I was very angry. I could have kept it bottled up if I'd tried, but I didn't want to try. If that arrow had been made of oak or rowan, any of the sacred woods, he'd have been killed. I set the magic free on purpose. At the time I didn't know what it would do and I didn't care. Now I know, and I'll never set it free again." I paused and looked up at him. "If it had been Justine lying at your feet and you'd had the power, you would have done the same thing."

He nodded. "You're probably right. I don't have that power, though, and I didn't think you did, either. I never thought I'd see your eyes turn black like that again."

"I hoped you wouldn't, either, Devlin. I never

wanted any of you to look at me the way you just did when you walked into this room. I'm no different than I was yesterday, or the day before that, or the month before that. This has been a part of me for a long time now and it seems that, as long as no one stakes my lover through the heart, I can control it."

Devlin chuckled. "I don't envy Michael. Trust that boy to fall in love with a redhead who has powerful dark magic tied to her temper."

I smiled back at him and the tension between us eased.

"I saw her last night," he remarked. "Up on the roof."

"Morrigan?" I asked. I'd wondered if I was the only one who had seen her.

"She looked . . . pleased."

"She is pleased, damn her. Devlin, I didn't ask for this and if I could make it go away, I would. But Morrigan says that it's a weapon I'll need, and who am I to argue with a goddess?"

Devlin frowned. "I'm a Christian man, Cin. It was a hard enough leap of faith for me to accept that Morrigan actually existed. She may be a deity but she is not God Almighty, and I don't believe that she is infallible. She is, however, the guardian and the fountainhead of our race, and I've heard from her own lips that we vampires are meant to fight some great battle. If she believes that the dark magic will help us all get through it alive, then I will trust her judgment. But, Cin, if this causes you to become a danger to yourself or others I will lock you up in Castle Tara myself, and Morrigan and I will have a reckoning."

"I accept that as your responsibility, Devlin. If I ever do become a danger, though, you'd better summon Morrigan before you try to take me. After what I felt last night, I don't think there's a witch alive who could bind my powers."

Whatever he was going to say to that was lost as our attention was drawn by the shouting of men's voices from one of the lower floors, followed by the sound of someone running up the stairs. Devlin, even after everything he'd seen last night, pushed me behind him and grabbed Michael's claymore from the top of the trunk. The bedroom door swung open and Justine burst in.

"You need to come quickly," she said, looking at me.

"What is it?" I asked.

She opened her mouth, then snapped it shut, shaking her head. "He's asking for you and if you don't come quickly someone is going to get killed."

Justine turned and rushed out of the room. Devlin and I caught up to her on the stairs.

"Who is asking for me? Michael?"

Already I could hear a male voice shouting, "I'm Drum Murray and I'm telling you, mate, I'm not leaving here until I see her."

As we reached the first floor, Justine motioned toward the front door. "Not Michael. Him."

I looked across the foyer into a face I never thought

I'd see again, and tripped down the last two steps. Only Devlin's hand snaking out to catch my arm prevented me from falling on my face. All eyes in the foyer turned to me, expectantly.

I cocked my head to one side and said, "What the bloody hell are you doing here?"

# CHAPTER 31

A wolfish grin was my reply, which I suppose was proper considering that he was a werewolf. Khalid and Hashim, who had apparently been trying to throw him out the door, fell blessedly silent as the werewolf and I stared at each other across the marble expanse of the foyer. Michael, who was holding a tea tray and wearing a perplexed look on his face, gently set the service down on the Chippendale hall table and walked to stand beside me.

"Darling, who is he?" he whispered.

I'd met the werewolf exactly twice. The first time was in London the night I'd woken as a vampire, the night I had fought for the first time as one of The Righteous. While Michael, Devlin, and Justine had been brawling with a rogue master and his followers, I had freed a man whom I'd thought to be a human prisoner. In my youth and inexperience I hadn't realized that the chains binding him were solid silver. When the man had promptly escaped by leaping from a window two stories up, I'd realized my mistake.

The second time I'd seen him was after I had fought Kali and won. He had followed me to Stonehenge and, in werewolf form, saved me from Kali's lieutenant, Sebastian. The debt of honor he owed me for rescuing him had been repaid and I'd never thought to see the man again.

"He's the werewolf who held Sebastian at bay until you arrived," I whispered back. "I don't even know his name."

"My name is Drummond Murray," the werewolf said as he crossed the foyer. Khalid and Hashim moved to block his path. "I need a word with you in private, Miss Craven."

I regarded the werewolf for a moment, then glanced at Khalid and Hashim and nodded. They did not look pleased, but they stepped back and let him pass.

I motioned toward the drawing room. "Please make yourself comfortable," I said. "I'll only be a moment." I watched Drummond walk through the open door, and then I turned to Michael. "I think you'd better come with me."

He glanced down at me and nodded, following after Drummond.

Justine gave me a confused look, and I shrugged as I closed the drawing room doors. Drummond Murray was standing by the hearth with a grim expression on his face. He was perhaps six feet tall with the sort of raw, earthy masculinity that you'd expect from a werewolf. The liberal strands of silver that ran through his long black hair belied the fact that he appeared to be only in his thirties. He'd been very lean when I had freed him from captivity, but the intervening years had added an impressive amount of muscle to his frame. Other than that, he looked exactly the same as he had when I had last seen him, thirteen years ago. Were werewolves virtually immortal, like vampires? I had no idea. Drummond was the only werewolf I'd ever met.

"Drummond, this is Michael, my consort. Anything you have to say to me you can say in front of him."

"I remember," Drummond said as he extended a hand in greeting. "I damn sure wouldn't ever want to cross swords with you, mate."

Michael grinned at him. After the tension of the last few weeks it was nice to see that smile again.

"What brings you to Edinburgh?" Michael asked.

Drummond nodded in my direction. "She does. Her cousin sent me here."

I looked at him, confused. "Lorie?"

"Actually her daughter Raina sent me. The girl wouldn't leave me be until I came here to warn you."

Michael stiffened. "Warn her about what?"

"Mary Margaret Macgregor is on her way here," he said grimly, "and you need to get out of town."

I collapsed onto the sofa. "Aunt Maggie is coming here?" I asked breathlessly. "Why? And how do you know that?"

"I work for your aunt as her gamekeeper," Drummond explained. "I lived near Glen Gregor when I was human, and after you freed me I wanted nothing more than to go back to the Highlands."

I narrowed my eyes at him. "You don't sound Scottish."

"I was held captive by an English vampire, may he rot in hell, for several centuries. I lost my brogue long ago," he explained.

I still didn't believe it was a coincidence the werewolf just happened to be employed by my aunt, but at the moment it was the least of my concerns.

"How does Maggie know I'm here?" I asked skeptically.

"She didn't," he replied, "but I expect she does by now. She went to Ravenworth because she said you're always there this time of year. Neither Raina nor I knew exactly where Ravenworth was so Raina cast a location spell. Imagine our surprise when instead of pointing in the vicinity of London, it said you were in Edinburgh."

"Lorie's daughter cast a location spell? She can't be any more than sixteen years old," I said, surprised. I hadn't come into my magic until I was twenty-two.

"Why is Maggie coming here?" Michael asked impatiently.

Drummond looked at me, and from his expression I wasn't certain I wanted to hear the answer.

"She's coming to bind your powers," he said. "And Raina says we must stop her."

# CHAPTER 32

I set down the whiskey decanter and pointed the tumbler I held at Michael. "I told you she thought I was evil."

And that was even before what happened in Venice. Unlike Fiona and Mrs. Mackenzie, Aunt Maggie had never come to terms with the fact that I was a vampire. After I'd been turned she had reluctantly agreed to spend some time with me every summer in Inverness, teaching me how to control my magic.

I had been taught from childhood that I would one day come into my powers and be a true witch. I hadn't been prepared for the awesome surge of magic that had filled me the night my mother had died in a carriage accident on the way home from a neighbor's ball. As I had explained it to Michael at the time, it was like spending your life reading about swordsmanship and then one day having someone put a claymore in your hand. In your head you understood how it worked, but having never wielded the weapon, you were bound to be inept. I'd been more than inept. I'd been a disaster waiting to happen.

In my mother's absence, Maggie had trained me. She had coldly taught me what I needed to know, but the closeness that we had shared when I'd been human was gone. In a way I didn't blame her for being wary of me, once I'd been turned, but it hurt all the same. I hadn't gone back to Inverness after Venice. I had learned to control my power, and I no longer needed her guidance. In all honesty, though, the real reason I had stayed away was that I was afraid she would take one look at me and *know* what darkness was buried deep inside.

Michael was still questioning Drummond, asking all the things I wasn't truly certain I wanted to hear the answers to. "How long do we have until she arrives?"

"She would have made it Ravenworth by now, and found out that you aren't there. I'd guess that she would rest for a couple days and then drive down to London and take a ship to Edinburgh. I think that would be easier on her than a trip overland by carriage."

Good, I thought. I probably had a week, a week and a half at most, to get out of town. I just hoped it was enough time.

"And she wants to bind Cin's powers? Why now? And whatever for?"

I smiled at him. After what I'd done to those vampires tonight I didn't think I deserved the amount of incredulity in his voice.

"She said she needed to do it now, before she got too old to travel such long distances. As to the why, I've heard her say that Cin's magic is unnatural and dangerous."

It was an old argument that Maggie and I had had many times. It was true that my magic was not the same as the other witches in my family. It was not a tool I used; it was a living part of me. I required no ritual, no spellcraft to call my magic. It was always there, ready to rise and do my bidding. The Macgregor women had always needed sacred circles, ceremony, and the paraphernalia of our craft to call and focus their magic. That I did not had always worried my aunt. She wholeheartedly believed that wielding the kind of power I had without the counterbalance of blessing and sacrifice would one day consume and destroy me. I tended, however, to believe that Morrigan would not have given me such power if she didn't trust that I could carry the burden.

"You said you came here to stop her," I said. "Why?"

"Because Raina is in possession of a journal that belonged to one of your ancestors, the first Macgregor witch of your line, and she firmly believes there's a passage that specifically refers to you."

"What does it say?" I asked, intrigued. Lorraina Macgregor, who was called Rainy by her family, was the first witch of our line, and the firstborn female of every generation was named for her. She was also believed by some to have possessed the second sight.

Drummond pulled a piece of paper from his pocket. "I made her write it down for me. It says, 'One day there will come a red witch, beloved of the Goddess, to our line. Danger surrounds her, but she must be protected at all costs, for she will restore what was taken from you, and she will save our world.' This is where Raina and your aunt have a fundamental difference of opinion. Maggie is certain that the passage refers to your great-grandmother Charlotte, who married Lord Robert right before Culloden and, because he was English and her lands passed to him, saved Glen Gregor from Butcher Cumberland."

I frowned. "It's generally assumed that Rainy's journal entries were actually letters to her husband. If that's true, then when she says this witch will 're-store what was taken from you,' one can assume that the 'you' she is addressing is her husband. As far as I know, great-grandmother Charlotte didn't restore anything that was taken specifically from John Mac-gregor, way back in the mid-1600s. And if this prophesy does refer to me, how exactly am I sup-posed to restore something to a man who's been dead for nearly three hundred years?"

"I don't know," Drummond said, handing me the piece of paper. "I suppose you'll figure it out eventually. What I do know is that they call you the

Red Witch of The Righteous, and that you did once save the world. Raina is adamant that you need to be protected, even if it is from your own aunt, and that's why she sent me to warn you. Luckily I made it here before Maggie so you should have plenty of time to board a fast ship and be on the Continent before she arrives."

Michael and I looked at each other. "It's a little more complicated than that," I said.

Drummond narrowed his eyes. "How complicated can it be?"

I laughed harshly at that. When I'd explained to him why we were here, he sat down and blew out a frustrated breath.

"Is there anything I can do to help?" he asked.

"Actually, I have a spell that might do us some good, but I need a few things from the market. Obviously none of us can go out in the daylight—but you can."

Michael glanced sharply at me. I knew what he was thinking. Spellcraft was not my forte, but we were running out of options. Nothing had happened in two weeks, no more bodies, no more attacks. We needed to flush the villains out and we needed to do it quickly—not only because the queen was unwell and my very powerful aunt was coming to bind my magic, but also because Michael and I had finally sorted out our problems and I wanted to put as much distance between us and Edinburgh as possible before anything else went wrong. It was past time to end this, and if I could manage to work this one spell properly then we might be able to be on a Calais-bound ship in two days' time.

The werewolf nodded. "If it will speed things along I'm happy to be of assistance. I promised Raina I would see you safe and I think it goes without saying that I'd rather not be here when your aunt arrives."

I shook my head, baffled. Aunt Maggie had nearly run mad when she'd found out that I had let Michael turn me into a vampire. I wondered what she would do if she knew she was harboring a werewolf on her estate.

# CHAPTER 33

MacLeod's study door was slightly ajar, and a shaft of light spilled out into the dark hallway. I paused with my hand on the knob when I heard muffled sobs and a female voice from within.

"I don't understand it," I heard Bel ask. "Am I not pretty?"

"You know you're beautiful, lass," MacLeod said.

"Then what's wrong with me? Why doesn't he love me anymore?" she cried.

"Whoever he was, he was a fool to let you get away," MacLeod replied in the sort of tone a father would use with his child.

I certainly wouldn't have been able to stand her for more than a month, but men often have different criteria when choosing a mate. I would have thought that a woman as beautiful as Bel would leave a string of broken hearts behind her, not the other way around.

Bel sniffled. "Yes, he was. And I was so good to him," she said softly, her voice taking on a seductive timbre. "You have no idea how very good I can be."

I cleared my throat and pushed open the door. MacLeod looked up from where he was leaning against his desk. He seemed surprised but didn't look the least bit guilty. Bel, however, looked ready to scratch my eyes out. She was standing mere inches from the king with one delicate hand placed gently on his chest.

"If you'll excuse us, Bel, I need a word with His Majesty," I said.

She gathered her composure and nodded to me coolly. When she'd gone I closed the door and gave MacLeod an arch look.

"Things ended badly with her former lover," he explained.

"Does she cry on your shoulder often?"

He shrugged. "I think she sees me as something of a father-figure."

I laughed. "I highly doubt that."

MacLeod seemed inclined to drop the matter. "What was it you wished to talk to me about?" he asked.

"How is the queen?" I asked.

"There's been no change," he replied glumly, "and I don't know how much longer she can continue on like this."

"Actually, that's what I wanted to speak with you about. I'm going to attempt a spell this evening. If it works, it should allow us to see the ghost that's doing this to her."

"What sort of spell?" he asked.

"If it works correctly, and I'm not guaranteeing anything, it should allow us to see the unseen."

"Such as the ghost you believe is in my town-house?"

"Whatever the entity is, this should allow us to see it."

"Do you have any plans for what we're going to do if we actually see this ghost?" MacLeod asked.

I blew out a breath. The spellbook I had contained several banishing spells, which might be helpful if I could work them properly, but I was reluctant to use them quite yet. I wasn't certain what would happen to Marrakesh if I exorcised the ghost before it reversed whatever it was doing to keep her unconscious. I didn't tell MacLeod, but in light of our villain's recent inactivity, I was sincerely praying that all the blessings we'd had performed on these two houses over the last few weeks hadn't driven the ghost away and condemned the queen. At this point I would be happy just to be able to see what I was dealing with.

"We'll cross that bridge when we come to it," I answered. "If we know for certain what *it* is, then we can figure out a way to fight it."

MacLeod nodded. "All right. Is there anything I can do?"

"I'm asking that everyone gather downstairs at midnight. I should be finished by then, and we'll be able to see if the spell worked or not."

The king nodded. "I'll be there."

I turned to go and then remembered the other reason I had sought him out. "Your Highness, do you know where I might find Jacques Aubert this evening? I need to ask him to keep an eye on the harbor for me."

"The harbor?"

"Yes," I said with a frown. "My aunt is coming to Edinburgh, and if we don't get things here settled in time for me to get out of town before she arrives . . . well, let's just say that I'd like as much warning as possible before she shows up on our doorstep."

MacLeod cocked his head to one side. "Are you afraid of her?"

I shrugged. "Not afraid, particularly. She's just one of those people who makes you feel like an awkward child, no matter how old you are."

He looked at me expectantly, but I didn't elaborate. There was no way to describe Aunt Maggie without sounding as if you were either a frightened child or vastly overreacting. Since I didn't wish to appear as either to the king, I simply let it be.

"Aubert generally begins his rounds near Greyfriars and moves east from there."

I nodded. "Thank you," I said and laid a hand on MacLeod's sleeve. "We will figure this out and we will bring her back."

"I hope you're right, Cin, because she is the world to me."

# CHAPTER 34

I sat alone, surrounded by a circle of candles, in one of the empty drawing rooms. A bowl filled with peppermint, vervain, saffron, lavender, yarrow, cinnamon, and cloves rested before me. I picked up a sprig of wormwood and lit the tip of it in the flame of one of the candles. Dipping the burning stick into the bowl, I held it there long enough for the herbs to ignite, then pulled it out and drew the stick to my lips, extinguishing the flame with a small puff of breath. The smoldering stick and the slowly burning bowl of herbs gave off a very pungent odor, which was starting to make my nose itch and my eyes water. Still, everything seemed to be progressing as the book said it should. I took a deep breath and closed my eyes.

"We seek what is hidden to be displayed/Goddess, bring light unto the shade/Clear the veil that blinds our eyes/Reveal that which the spirits would disguise!"

My power rose up as I said the words of the spell.

I could feel it swirling around me and cracked my eyes open to see what I had wrought. I was enveloped in a golden cloud of magic, and I watched in fascination as it pulled away from me and condensed into a tight, pulsing ball of energy that hovered over the bowl. Slowly it sank down and melted into the bowl of herbs. And nothing happened.

I sighed. I should never have given in to temptation and opened my eyes. This was why I was bad at spell-casting. Aunt Maggie had always said that working spells required discipline and concentration. She'd often complained that she'd had puppies who could sit still and focus their attention better than I did.

I leaned over and peered into the bowl at the smoldering herbs. Suddenly there was a loud *pop* and a blinding flash of light shot out of the bowl.

"Oh, bugger," I cursed as I jerked backward, falling onto my butt. I squeezed my eyes shut and saw nothing but sparkles lighting the insides of my eyelids. "This is why I hate spells," I muttered.

When I could see again I picked up the bowl and looked inside. It was smeared with what appeared to be nothing more interesting than ash from the burned herbs. The spell had said that we should apply the ash to our eyelids and it would allow us to see the spirit world. It hadn't said anything about a small explosion. I picked up the bowl and headed for the door.

"Let's hope this works."

\* \* \*

I smeared the ash from the bowl onto my eyelids. We all looked like ghouls, with the black ash coloring our lids. There were eight of us going on this mission: me, Michael, Devlin, Justine, Drake, MacLeod, Bel, and Drummond. Khalid had gone out hours ago to procure blood for the queen and hadn't returned yet. MacLeod had decreed that Hashim would stay with the queen until we returned, but I wasn't particularly pleased with the idea. I would have much rather left Drake with her, not only because I didn't want him around but also because Hashim and his brother were both suspects, in my opinion. However, as Michael had pointed out, if they'd wanted her dead they'd had plenty of opportunities to accomplish the task before now.

We split up in groups of four to search the townhouses on either side of the king's residence. Drake, Devlin, Bel, and MacLeod took one while Michael, Justine, Drummond, and I took the other. I made sure that my group got the townhouse that shared a wall with the king's bedchamber. I was certain that our villain was there. I had seen *something* in that room, and no one was going to convince me that I hadn't.

My heart sank as I stood in the doorway to the bedroom. The noxious odor of sulfur and wormwood still lingered in the air, but if the spell was working I couldn't see anything. I reached out with my magic, as I had before, but whatever had been in the room then was not here now. Turning, I glanced behind me as Michael came out of the last room on the hall.

"Nothing," he stated, shaking his head.

Justine and Drummond came up the stairs, followed by Bel.

"I'm to tell you the other townhouse is empty," she said, and wandered off down the hall, peeking into the bedrooms.

"What do we do now?" Justine asked.

I opened my mouth to reply but was interrupted when Bel exclaimed, "Oh, my God!" from the doorway of one of the bedrooms.

I glanced sharply at Michael.

"There was nothing there a moment ago," he said.

We all rushed down the hall, expecting to see a spirit. What we saw as we gathered around Bel was something almost as incredible.

Shelving with glass-fronted drawers lined the walls of the large bedroom and marched in several rows down its center. Hatboxes were stacked neatly on top of the shelves next to hundreds of pairs of exquisitely crafted shoes in a rainbow of colors. Bel, Justine, and I entered the room like moths to a flame. We walked down the aisles, pulling out drawer after drawer to reveal dresses of all colors and fabrics, their styles spanning centuries.

"What is this place?" I asked, running my fingers along a row of neatly folded silk corsets.

"Heaven," Bel whispered.

I pulled open the next drawer, which was filled with pressed and folded handkerchiefs. All of them bore a delicately embroidered C in one corner. Could this be the wardrobe of the slain vampire Clarissa? The thought made rifling through her things somewhat less appealing and I silently closed the drawer.

Justine walked to the far side of the room to take a closer look at sixteenth-century farthingales and eighteenth-century panniers that hung on the wall. "Sometimes I miss panniers," she said with a sigh.

Bel nodded in agreement, and I looked at both of them as if they were mad. "Why?" I asked, incredulously. "I can't imagine what it was like trying to fit through doors in those wide skirts."

Justine shrugged. "Palaces have rather large doors."

"Or you just turned sideways," Bel added.

I shuddered. "I much prefer the fashions at the turn of this century. There are a lot of nasty things to be said about Napoleon, but Josephine was a woman of style."

Bel crinkled her nose. "What style? Those weren't dresses, they were scraps of cloth. You could practically fold them up and put them in a man's coat pocket."

"I know," I said as I glanced at Michael. He smiled back at me in a way that made it clear we were both remembering how scandalously fun those dresses had been. "Fashion has definitely taken a turn for the worse since Josephine died and I became a vampire," I lamented.

Bel snorted. "The dresses these days are not worth the fabric they're made from. Have you seen the fashions the ladies are wearing? They all look like dowdy milkmaids."

"Ladies," Drummond interrupted, "I hate to disturb your fun but obviously the spell has not worked. Cin, did you have an alternative plan, or was this it?"

I sighed and returned a pair of yellow brocaded silk heels with what appeared to diamond buckles to their place on the shelf. "Actually," I said, "I don't know whether the spell didn't work or there just doesn't happen to be anything to see at the moment. I think it would be wise if Michael and I stayed here through the day tomorrow. Justine, you and Devlin can guard the other townhouse. This place reeks of magic, and since we can't seem to catch anyone going in or coming out, perhaps we will find what we're searching for if we're just patient and wait."

"Sounds rather tedious to me," Bel chimed in.

"I'd prefer it if you were on a ship by tomorrow," Drummond complained.

I nodded. "Give it one more day. If we've found nothing by then, Michael and I will take the king and queen and retire to Castle Darkness. That should flush out whoever is behind this one way or the other. Either he'll come after the queen or he'll try to take the city."

Drummond nodded.

"It's a good plan," Michael said. "I've grown tired of waiting for him to make his move."

"Yes," Bel said as she poked through a drawer filled with ribbons. "I've been thinking that it's time to leave town as well. The capital has not proven to be as . . . empowering . . . as I had hoped it would be."

I frowned at her choice of words, but Drummond drew my attention. "Out of curiosity, how do you vampires manage to travel long distances by ship? Won't someone notice if you start draining blood from the passengers or the crew?" he asked.

"Actually, we have our own shipping line that caters to our kind. They operate under the name Macmillan Parties, Privateer."

"Owned by a vampire named Macmillan, I gather?"

I frowned. "Actually, the line is run by a vampire named Christian Sinclair. I met him once. He was the captain on the Blood Cross ship *Falcon* that took us from London to Barcelona the year I was turned."

"Blood Cross?" Drummond asked.

"That's what we call the Macmillan line," I replied. "Because they fly a black flag bearing a red Templar cross."

"The line is owned by The Templar himself," Bel asserted.

I rolled my eyes. "That's nothing more than a centuries-old legend."

"Ah, but what a romantic legend it is," Bel said with a sigh, turning her attention to Drummond. "Rumor has it that the French king, Phillip the Fair, talked in his sleep and that's how one of his mistresses found out that he was planning to arrest all the Knights Templar. The mistress was in love with

one of the Templars, even though the knight had
made a vow of celibacy and she knew he could never
be hers. Still, she warned him of the king's treachery,
and the day before the arrests were made, eighteen
Templar ships sailed out of La Rochelle, never to be
seen again."

"How did they come to be vampire ships?" Drummond asked.

Bel laughed. "The mistress was a vampire. To
avoid King Phillip's retaliation for her betrayal, she
sailed away with her Templar knight. They fell in
love and, because he couldn't face the prospect of
ever dying and leaving her side, she made him a
vampire so they would always be together. It's said
that they settled on an island in the Caribbean and
that the crews who man the Blood Cross ships today
are the human descendants of the crewmen on the
original eighteen ships."

"The truth," Michael insisted, "is that The Templar
is a myth. I asked Devlin once, since he's the oldest
of us, and he says he's never met a vampire who's
ever laid eyes on him."

"I've met him," Bel said softly.

We all turned to her, but she suddenly became un-
characteristically silent. Ignoring our inquiring ex-
pressions, she began sifting through a box of jewels.
Justine and I glanced at each other and shook our
heads. The Templar was a nothing more than a myth,
and Bel was one blade short of a sharp edge. She'd

believe any lie a handsome man told her. I almost felt sorry for her.

Drummond noticed the look Justine and I exchanged and wisely did not ask Bel to elaborate. "If the Blood Cross fleet is reputed to be owned by The Templar and is run by a vampire named Sinclair . . . then who the devil are the Macmillan Parties?"

I frowned and looked at Justine, who shook her head and shrugged.

"I have no idea," I replied.

"Ladies," Michael interrupted, "as much as I hate to interrupt your fun, we should get back to the house and speak with the king."

We were leaving the house when Drummond said, "Isn't that one of the king's guards?"

"Yes, it is. Hello, Khalid!" Bel called out.

I looked up at the man walking toward us. He was a block away, carrying a sack under one arm, and had his hat pulled down low on his brow to repel the misty rain that had begun to fall. I knew it was Khalid because even at this distance I could see the gold hoop earring in his right ear.

"Who is the boy he's with?" Drummond asked.

We all glanced at Drummond in confusion and then looked back at Khalid. "What boy?" I asked.

Drummond waved a hand in Khalid's direction. "The young man he was walking with. The dark-haired boy who just turned off down Frederick Street."

I looked at Michael, eyes wide. "I didn't see any-one with him, did you?"

"No," Michael said tersely.

Without another word we all rushed down the sidewalk toward Khalid.

# CHAPTER 35

Khalid stopped short with a look of shock on his face, unsure what to make of several vampires and a werewolf running toward him. When we reached the end of the block we came to a halt and looked to Drummond for direction.

"The street's empty," he said. "I don't see him anywhere."

I turned to Khalid. "Who was he?" I demanded.

The lieutenant seemed genuinely confused. "Who are you talking about?" he asked, looking at us like we'd all gone mad. "It's three in the morning. I haven't seen anyone on the street in several blocks and I think I'd bloody well know if someone was walking right beside me!"

"The spell worked," Justine said in awe. "Drummond saw a ghost."

"Then why didn't we see it?" Michael asked.

"Because we're dead," she replied with a nod to the werewolf, "and he isn't."

"That very well could be," I reluctantly agreed,

though it didn't seem fair that it was my spell and I hadn't seen a thing. "The fact that we're no longer truly among the living could have interfered with a spell created to allow humans to see the dead. I hadn't considered that. But was the ghost Drummond saw *our* ghost?"

Khalid snorted. "Edinburgh is an ancient city and likely full of restless spirits, if one believes in that sort of thing."

Michael looked down at me. "Can you sense anything?"

I shook my head and gestured to the rain that had begun to fall at a steadier pace. "I might have been able to scent the sulfur and wormwood if it wasn't raining."

"Sulfur and wormwood? I should be able to track that," Drummond said.

"Would you like some help?" Michael asked.

Drummond shook his head. "You won't be any good to me if you can't see him."

Michael nodded. "Regardless of what you find, come back to the house when you're finished. If you really are the only one her spell worked on, then it would be helpful to have you with us."

Drummond agreed and took off down Frederick Street. I certainly hoped his canine sense of smell would lead him to our ghost, but in this rain I had my doubts. As Justine walked ahead of us with Khalid, I realized for the first time that Bel hadn't followed us from the house.

"Do you believe him?" Michael whispered, nodding toward Khalid.

"I don't know," I sighed. "His reaction seemed genuine, but even if he was guilty I would expect nothing less."

"Yes, I see your point," Michael said.

"It was a good thought to invite Drummond to stay with us," I observed. "Though I was rather surprised you made the offer."

"Why?"

"Because, my jealous man," I said lightly, "that adds one more ruggedly handsome male to the household."

"There's a vast difference between Drummond Murray and Drake," Michael said.

"What sort of difference?" I asked.

"Drake looks at you as if he's cataloging all the things he'd like to do to you if he could get your clothes off."

"And Drummond?" I asked with genuine interest. Michael had my heart; I rarely noticed the way other men looked at me.

"He looks at you as if you were . . . kin."

At first I was surprised by his observation, until I'd had a moment to think about it. "I suppose that makes sense. He has been living at Glen Gregor with Aunt Maggie and the vast majority of my family on my mother's side."

"The poor man," Michael grumbled.

I shoved him. "Beast," I said.

He pulled me into his arms and kissed me roughly, making me melt against him.

"Why don't we go back to our room and I'll show you just how beastly I can be?" he whispered as he ran his tongue along the edge of my ear.

As we hurried into the king's residence, eager to get upstairs and out of our wet clothes, I noticed Bel and Drake standing just outside the library. Bel was regaling him with tales of the dresses and shoes we had found next door. Drake looked at me over the top of her head, and he certainly didn't appear to be undressing me with his eyes. It hadn't escaped my notice earlier tonight that his interest in me had cooled significantly. Briefly I wondered if that was due to my obvious reconciliation with Michael or the fact that I had smote upward of thirty vampires last night using black magic.

Michael and I had reached the third floor and I was happily considering which article of his clothing to remove first when our attention was drawn by raised voices coming from the king's bedchamber.

"That's Devlin's voice," Michael said.

We strode down the hall and threw open the double doors. My mouth dropped at what I saw. Quickly I pushed Michael into the room and closed and locked the doors behind us.

"Would someone care to tell me what's going on?" I asked.

Marrakesh was sitting on the edge of her bed in a diaphanous white nightgown and MacLeod was standing next to her, shirtless, looking ready to murder us all.

Devlin gestured toward them. "Justine and I were coming up to tell the king what we'd discovered when I heard a crash from the room. Thinking something was wrong, I entered without knocking."

I glanced at the silver tea service scattered across the floor amid MacLeod's discarded shirt and coat, along with the rumpled state of the bedsheets, and guessed what Devlin and Justine had interrupted.

"Marrakesh," I said. "It's good to see that you're awake and in such . . . good spirits."

MacLeod looked a little sheepish. "Aye, well, she's never been unconscious, not after the first few hours anyway. We decided it would be best if no one knew she'd woken. I was afraid you would want her to try to use her power again, and after what happened last time I absolutely forbid it. I will not put her in that position again. Of course, we didn't think it would take this long to figure out who was behind the attacks."

"So no one knows she's awake?" Michael asked. "Not Khalid, Hashim, not even Drake?"

MacLeod shook his head. "No one but she and I . . . and now the four of you."

"I think it's slightly absurd," the queen remarked, "but he insisted."

"Have you told him what happened out on the street tonight?" I asked Devlin.

He scowled. "We hadn't gotten that far yet. The

king was still berating me for entering his chamber unannounced."

I filled them in on Drummond's arrival and the incident with Khalid and what was quite possibly our ghost.

"Michael and Drummond and I will stay in the house next door during the daylight hours, but I honestly believe you need to take the queen out of here tomorrow night."

"I don't like abandoning my capital," Marrakesh protested.

"I'm sorry," I said. "I truly do think it's the best way to flush the villains out."

MacLeod nodded. "We'll go to Castle Darkness, but tomorrow night is too soon. There are arrangements that must be made before we can undertake such a long journey. It will have to be the following evening."

"Night after next, then," I agreed. "Michael and I will accompany you to see to your safety. I think it's best to keep the fact that Marrakesh is awake a secret while we're still in Edinburgh, though."

The king nodded. The queen did not look pleased.

"It will be all right, my dear," MacLeod said. "Aubert is an excellent Warden, and Khalid and Hashim will be here to see to anything that needs tending."

MacLeod looked at me, and we had a moment of perfect understanding. His dark eyes spoke volumes.

He was beginning to have doubts about his lieutenants. Marrakesh would never believe that the twins
would harm her, but it was MacLeod's duty, both as
her king and as her husband, to be suspicious.

# CHAPTER 36

Before dawn Michael and I moved some of our things to the townhouse next door. We were putting fresh sheets on the bed in the room where I had seen the ghost when Drummond rapped softly on the door. He looked tired, and he was soaked to the skin.

"I managed to follow his scent for several blocks before I lost it because of the damn rain," he said miserably.

"It's all right," I assured him. "Why don't you get some sleep? We'll be leaving for Castle Darkness north of Inverness tomorrow night."

He nodded. "I'll travel with you as far as Inverness, then I'll be heading back to Glen Gregor."

I handed him the bowl that contained the ash from the spell I'd cast. "Call us if you see anything."

He nodded and retreated to one of the other bedrooms.

\* \* \*

Several hours later I snuggled against Michael's chest, my hair still damp from the hot bath we'd shared, and sighed contentedly.

He kissed my forehead and said, "I like it much better when we come into a town and the Regent points out the bad vampires and we kill them."

I laughed. "Isn't that the truth. What are we missing here, Michael? I couldn't see the ghost but it certainly didn't appear that Khalid was talking to anyone. To me it looked like he was just walking quietly down the street. Everything seems to point directly to him and Hashim—Clarissa's death, what happened to the queen just before she touched Khalid, the ghost tonight. But we have no proof of their involvement in anything. To be quite honest with you, I've been so wrapped up in our troubles these past few weeks that I've paid little attention to either of them. Have you seen them do anything at all suspicious?"

"Not a thing," he said. "MacLeod has spent most of his time with Marrakesh. He rarely leaves their room. Khalid has been taking care of MacLeod's day-to-day business and Hashim just lurks about, watching us watch them. Nothing unusual has happened, but then again, did we honestly expect it to? There haven't been any more suspicious bodies showing up in Surgeon's Square, but that doesn't necessarily mean anything. If someone was trying to implicate the queen in these murders, it would defeat their purpose to have another human killed while she's comatose."

"Except for the fact that she's just as awake as you or I," I pointed out.

"Ah, but our villain doesn't know that."

"That's what I don't understand. If he's in league with our ghost, doesn't it seem that he *should* know it? You can't tell me that the ghost doesn't know she's awake."

"Aye but he's damned either way," Michael observed. "If he keeps up the murders and we never find out the queen is truly awake, then he's proven her innocence. If he stops the killings, then it points to her guilt—unless we find out that she hasn't been in a coma after all."

I was quiet for several moments. "What if we never figure this out?" I asked, miserably.

"Whoever is behind this will slip up sooner or later," Michael assured me. "If he thinks he's losing control of the situation by the king and queen leaving town, then perhaps we'll force him to make that mistake. And on the off chance that the queen is honestly stark raving mad and running about killing people, that will become readily apparent as well. It's a good plan, Cin." He chuckled. "But are you certain you didn't come up with it simply to get us out of town before your aunt Maggie arrives?"

I glanced up at him. "Would that be so bad?"

He blew out a breath. "Hell, no."

# CHAPTER 37

Michael and I spent such a glorious day making love and sleeping in each other's arms that I hated to leave the house at all. With no one else about, it was easy to imagine we were the only two people in the world—except for the werewolf prowling the halls. Drummond would sleep for an hour or so and then I'd hear him moving through the house, as if on patrol, before he retired to his room again.

Sunset came earlier than I would have liked. Michael dressed quickly and went to speak with Drummond. I looked in the mirror and admired my new gown. I'd picked this dress up in London on our way to Ravenworth and hadn't worn it yet. It was made of emerald-green velvet, tight through the waist and full in the skirt, with little cap sleeves. The bodice was cut low enough that my breasts swelled temptingly above it. I should have brought my breeches instead. I was hungry tonight and I needed to feed, but I was also vain enough to want Michael to see me in a new gown before we spent the next week or more cooped up in a carriage. I gathered up my throwing knives with their wrist sheaths, and the short sword in its spine sheath, unwilling to strap them on quite yet and ruin the elegance of my attire.

"That's new," Michael said.

I turned to see him lounging in the doorway with a hot, predatory look in his blue eyes. The candlelight cast dark shadows under his sharp cheekbones, and his beauty made my breath catch. I walked to him seductively, enjoying the way the velvet skirt swayed as I moved.

"Do you like it?" I asked.

He ran the backs of his fingers over the swell of my breasts. "I do," he replied huskily. "And I'll enjoy taking it off of you later, *mo ghraidh*."

I smiled. "I'll enjoy letting you but right now I'm hungry."

He offered me his arm. "Let me give Drummond the key to the house and we'll go out."

"Oh, damn," I exclaimed. "I forgot my cloak when we moved our things last night. You go see Drummond while I run next door and get it. I'll be right back."

As I opened the door to the king's residence, the sound of Justine's rich soprano voice filtered into the foyer from the hallway that led to the kitchen. I recognized the song from the role of Malwina in Marschner's *Der Vampyr,* which we had seen in Leipzig earlier in the year. I stood there a minute, listening with pleasure to the aria, then raced upstairs to retrieve my cloak.

Drake was waiting in the foyer when I returned. He smiled at me, and it was not a nice smile. "Miss Craven, might I have a word with you?"

I gritted my teeth in frustration. I didn't have the time or the inclination to enter into a conversation with him at this particular moment.

"What is it, Drake?" I asked, my voice sounding more impatient and waspish than I'd intended it to.

"Oh, my," he said in a cavalier tone that grated on my very last nerve. "Temper, temper. What are you going to do? Turn me to dust with your black magic?"

I narrowed my eyes, waiting to see where this topic would lead.

"There were rumors," he said, "that you'd killed a dozen humans in Venice by the use of dark magic. We were inclined to disbelieve these rumors because of your status with The Righteous. I wonder what the High King would say if I told him there is now undeniable proof?"

"No one has seen me kill a human."

He shrugged. "Maybe not, but it's certainly not a far stretch from what they say you did then to what the entire vampire population of Edinburgh saw you do to that group of rogues."

I glared at him but said nothing. What could I say? He was right.

"What? Not rushing to declare your innocence?"

"I certainly do not owe you an explanation and I have nothing to say on the matter, regardless."

He stalked toward me with a hungry, predatory grace. "I am the High King's representative and you will speak of it if I wish it."

I looked up into his face, only inches away from mine. "I answer to a higher power than you or the High King, Drake."

"There is no one greater among our kind than the High King and he heeds my counsel. You would do well to remember that, witch."

"Really? Because the goddess Morrigan herself acquitted me of any guilt concerning that incident and told me that if the High King took issue with it, he should speak to her." Drake snapped his head back in surprise.

I shook my head. "What did you think was going to happen here, Drake? That you would threaten to tell the High King what I did to that band of traitors and I would fall to my knees and offer you anything in return for your silence?" I laughed at him. "That's just . . . sad."

Sometimes I don't know how to quit while I'm ahead. Drake growled and his hand shot out, forcing me to stumble backward to avoid his grasp. Before I could even think of calling my magic another hand came from somewhere behind me, clamping down on Drake's wrist until I heard bones snap.

"I should have done this a long time ago," Michael said as he stepped in front of me and punched Drake squarely in the nose. "If you ever lay a hand on my woman again, Drake, I will kill you."

Drake lunged at him and the two of them grappled, knocking over the Chippendale table. A very expensive-looking vase shattered against the marble floor, and a heavy brass candlestick rolled across the foyer. I backed up, moving to stand against the wall next to the front door to give them room to maneuver. It was hard not to stop this, but it was a fight that had been years in the making and neither of them would thank me if I intervened. I winced as Drake landed a hard hit to Michael's ribs, but Michael came back with a solid punch to Drake's jaw that snapped the Sentinel's head back. While he was dazed, Michael swept his feet from under him and Drake landed on the floor with a violent curse, bleeding from his nose and a cut on his lip.

"Have you had enough yet?" Michael asked.

Battered as he was, Drake stood with one swift, graceful movement and the two of them squared off once again. I was so engrossed in the confrontation that I shrieked in surprise when the front door flew open and Devlin marched into the hall.

He took one look at the bloodied men in the foyer and yelled, "Stop it this instant, the both of you!"

Michael's head turned at Devlin's booming command and Drake used that moment of inattention to rush him. He threw himself at Michael and the momentum sent the two of them sailing past Devlin and me and down the front steps of the townhouse. I winced as I watched them tumble down the stone stairs. I was concentrating so much on Michael and the probable extent of his injuries that at first I didn't see the woman standing on the sidewalk in front of the house. Drake and Michael took swift notice of her, however, as she rapped them both sharply with the heavy silver ball that topped her walking stick.

"That's what I was coming to tell you," Devlin whispered in my ear.

Drake and Michael scrambled to their feet like two errant schoolboys. I looked down into the woman's eyes and inwardly sighed. This night was just going from bad to worse.

"If these two ruffians are quite finished," the woman said in an icy contralto I remembered so well, "perhaps you'd be good enough to invite me in out of the cold."

"Michael," I said wearily, "would you please escort Aunt Maggie inside?"

# CHAPTER 38

Mary Margaret Macgregor was barely five feet tall,
but every inch radiated her absolute belief in her own
power and authority. She carried herself like a queen
and in her world, at Glen Gregor, she was treated as
such. That had not changed. Indeed, time had changed
very little about my aunt. Her dress was black, high-
necked, and long-sleeved, as it always was. I hadn't
seen her in any other color since Uncle Richard had
died twenty years ago. The tall, silver-tipped cane
was new, though she wielded it more like a scepter
than a walking stick. Her hair, which had been a
lovely coppery red when I was young, was now solid
white and pulled back into a simple but stylish
chignon. Maggie's features were strong and square,
yet somehow managed to be delicate and feminine at
the same time, and her face was so finely lined that
she looked a good ten years younger than I knew she
was. I wondered briefly if this was what my mother
would have looked like now, if she'd lived.

Aunt Maggie's beautiful cornflower-blue eyes never missed anything, and tonight they quickly darted over the room full of vampires that had gathered during Michael and Drake's brawl. With the exception of Marrakesh and Drummond, everyone in the residence was milling about in the foyer.

"Where are your manners, child?" Aunt Maggie scolded. "I know that my sister raised you to be a better hostess than to neglect making introductions."

"Of course, Aunt Maggie," I said, rushing forward. To my astonishment, eight vampires, including the King of the Western Lands, lined up like subjects waiting to greet a monarch. I shook my head at the surreal tableau and took Aunt Maggie's arm, leading her first to MacLeod, as protocol dictated.

"May I introduce His Majesty, MacLeod, King of the Western Lands. Your Majesty, my aunt, Mary Margaret Macgregor."

MacLeod claimed her hand and bowed while my aunt bobbed a small curtsy. I wasn't sure if the shallow depth of the gesture was in deference to old bones or the fact that MacLeod was nothing more to her than another vampire. Whatever the case, he didn't seem to notice and was very gallant toward her.

"Mrs. Macgregor, welcome to my home. I trust your journey was uneventful?" he asked.

She sighed. "As uneventful as these things are at my age."

Reminded of why she was here in the first place,

I said a little sharply, "You made excellent time. We did not expect you for several more days."

Maggie cut her eyes at me and replied in a patronizing tone meant to put me in my place, "Really, dear, you shouldn't let being dead prevent you from keeping up with current events. There's a lovely new invention called a steamship that managed to get me here from London in two days."

I nodded, gritting my teeth at the way she reminded me that I was less than human and then made me feel stupid, all in two succinct sentences.

MacLeod stepped in. "It would be my pleasure to offer you the hospitality of my home while you're in Edinburgh, Mrs. Macgregor."

"You are too kind, Your Majesty, but I would not wish to intrude. I've taken a room at the Star Hotel on Princes Street."

I introduced Khalid, Hashim, and Bel next. Khalid and Hashim were gracious but aloof, regarding my aunt with quiet curiosity. To Bel she said, "You are truly a beauty, my dear. Surely this is a face that would launch a thousand ships." Bel blanched and took a step back, and I wondered what it was about Maggie's comment that had unnerved her. Apparently my aunt didn't notice Bel's odd behavior because she moved on to the next vampire without so much as a backward glance.

"Devlin, my boy," she said. "Must you always hover up there around the ceiling?"

Devlin leaned down from his great height and

gallantly kissed Maggie's hand. For some reason Devlin and Michael were the only ones who were exempt from her well-placed barbs.

*"Mademoiselle."* She addressed Justine. "You're looking lovely as ever. Such a pretty girl, it's no wonder you turned the heads of kings."

Justine pasted a smile on her face, trying her best to ignore the fact that my aunt had basically called her a whore. Justine was not ashamed of her past, but Maggie had a way of hitting you where you were the most vulnerable. She made a point of reminding you of your faults and shortcomings, but she did it all with pretty words and gracious compliments so that you couldn't truly take issue with anything she said.

Maggie walked to stand in front of Michael, tapping her silver-tipped walking stick sharply on the floor, narrowly missing the toe of his boot.

"Well, young man, I see you finally intend to do the right thing by my niece."

Michael smiled. "You noticed that, did you?"

Maggie glanced at my ring. "One cannot help it. It's such a gaudy thing."

"Ah, Aunt Maggie, nothing is too grand for your niece. I had to make sure I chose a gem worthy of the beauty of the Macgregor women, did I not?"

He took her hand and bowed, kissing her knuckles and bringing a smile to her face. "Silver-tongued devil. I don't know why she puts up with you."

"Of course you do," he said with a wink.

Maggie snorted and curled her fingers around his

wrist as he tried to withdraw his hand from hers. She looked at the broken skin on his knuckles and then glanced at Drake, catching him in the act of dabbing a bloodstained handkerchief to his nose.

"Fisticuffs in the house," she scolded. "In my day we defended a lady's honor with pistols at dawn."

Michael shrugged. "But this was so much more enjoyable than just shooting him."

Drake scowled at Michael, and Maggie chuckled. "You are a handsome rogue," she said to Drake "But you might as well give up the chase, dear boy. You'll never come between those two."

Drake stiffly inclined his head, and I think he was acutely grateful that Maggie's attention turned quickly from him to me.

"Aunt Maggie, would you care to accompany me to the drawing room?" I asked. "I'll have some tea brought in."

"That won't be necessary," Maggie said as she sailed past me like an ominous dark cloud.

Reluctantly, I followed.

"Well, niece, you don't seem surprised to see me," Maggie observed as she removed Justine's bag of yarn and knitting needles from one of MacLeod's velvet-upholstered chairs and sat down.

I cursed inwardly. Drummond would not thank me for her knowing that.

"Just as I thought," she remarked. "Wolves will be extinct in England once again when I get my hands on that boy."

"You know Drummond is a werewolf?" I asked incredulously.

"Of course I do. Neither my senses nor my eyesight have dulled with age. You, however," she said, looking pointedly at my hair, "seem to have forgotten the first spell you ever learned."

Self-consciously one hand reached up to touch my hair. Maggie watched me intently, as if she expected that I would use glamour to turn it from scarlet to copper just to appease her. I pulled my fingers from the curl I had been touching and crossed my arms over my chest, arching an eyebrow at her in defiance.

"Oh, I remember it perfectly well," I said.

Maggie glared at me, confident that her stern gaze could bend me to her will. When I was younger that cold look of disapproval had always worked, but I had faced far more frightening creatures than Maggie Macgregor since I'd become a vampire. At least that's what I told myself as I tried not to squirm under her penetrating gaze.

"I suppose Drummond's told you why I'm here," Maggie finally said.

I was somewhat surprised that she would broach the subject in such a straightforward manner. Then again Maggie never was one to beat around the bush. Like me, she was often outspoken and forthright to a fault.

I nodded. "He has."

"And?" she asked.

I'd had plenty of time to think about her impending visit and what I would do if I didn't manage to make it out of town before she got here. I squared my shoulders and said, "And, nothing. If knowing me all my life doesn't convince you that I'm not evil, Aunt Maggie, nothing I say now will do so."

"You are the walking dead, niece, and nothing about you or your magic is natural. You're going to destroy yourself one day, and take innocent people down with you. I cannot allow that, not if I can stop it."

"First, I am a vampire, not the walking dead. I've seen the walking dead and there is a vast difference, trust me. Second, who are you to say that my magic is not natural? It's as natural to me as yours is to you. Nothing about it is evil." *Well, except for the dark power inside me that can suck the life out of a human or a vampire,* I thought, but that was hardly helpful to the matter at hand.

"It's not that I think you're evil, necessarily, dear—"

"Yes, you do," I snapped, interrupting her. "You see only the vampire, you don't see that inside I'm the same girl I was before, the same girl who has loved you and worshipped you her whole life." I shook my head. "My mother, your sister, would be ashamed of you."

Maggie's face turned so red I thought her head might explode. "Your mother would be horrified at what you've become."

"You're wrong, Aunt Maggie. She would be glad that I used my power to protect the innocent and that I'm not dead and buried next to her. If you think any differently then you really didn't know her at all." I shook my head, saddened beyond words that we had come to this. A part of me had hoped that Drummond was wrong about Maggie's arrival and her intentions. I was disappointed and more than a little angry that she had come here for this purpose. "I'm tired of arguing about this. I know you, and I know that once you've made up your mind about something nothing will sway you from your course. Do what you feel you need to do, Maggie."

Her eyes narrowed as she regarded me. "Just like that?"

I nodded. "Just like that."

"Why?" she asked, her voice laced with suspicion.

"Because I don't think you can do it." It was probably not the smartest thing I'd ever said, but it was the truth.

Maggie leaned forward. "You doubt my power?" she asked, her voice low and angry.

"No," I replied. "I'm sure you're fully capable of working whatever bit of nastiness you please. I don't think you can do it because I don't think the goddess Morrigan will allow it."

She leaned back and laughed. "My dear, you think too highly of your worth in this world."

"And you have never thought highly enough of it,

but Morrigan does. I am her creation and I doubt she will allow you to take my power as easily as you imagine."

Maggie stopped laughing and looked at me. "What are you babbling about?"

"I'm telling you, Maggie, that I've seen her, talked to her. We walked up Hanover Street together the other night. She is the patron goddess of vampires. We are all hers and I, in particular, am her creation."

"You're deranged," Maggie whispered.

"Not at all. If you don't believe me, ask Michael or Devlin or Justine. I'm sure even Drake has seen her."

I reached for Justine's knitting bag and ignored the fact that my aunt recoiled in her chair, as if she was afraid I would attack her. I drew out a small pair of scissors from amid the balls of yarn and Justine's string of unfinished knitting. Pulling my hair up, I snipped off a long red lock from underneath where it wouldn't be noticeable. I'd read binding spells before. I knew that Aunt Maggie would need something of mine, preferably blood or a lock of hair, to work the spell. That was probably the only reason she'd shown up on my doorstep in the first place.

Dropping the hair in my aunt's lap, I said, "If your fear and resentment of me runs so deep that you'd stand against a goddess to bind my powers, then so be it."

I turned on my heel and stalked out the door.

Michael had been loitering in the foyer, and his

vampire hearing had picked up every word Maggie and I had said. "Do you think that was wise?" he asked.

"I don't know if it was wise or not," I replied, snatching my cloak and weapons up from where I'd dropped them earlier, "but I recently remarked to Devlin that I didn't think any witch was strong enough to bind my powers. I suppose now we'll see." I strapped on my blades and looked at Michael. "Would you make sure she gets to her hotel safely?"

He nodded. "Where are you going?"

"Out," I replied tersely, "before I forget that I'm not evil and eat her."

# CHAPTER 39

Michael had intended to hire a carriage to take us into the city, and I realized after I stormed out of the house that I didn't have any money with me. So I walked. At the moment I wished I could walk straight out of Edinburgh and Scotland altogether. I didn't bloody well care what happened with Marrakesh or Aunt Maggie anymore.

I stopped and took a deep breath. That wasn't the truth; I did care. There were times, like now, when what we, The Righteous, did overwhelmed me, and I desperately needed a holiday, but I truly did enjoy the life I'd made for myself. I made a difference in the world, and there was great satisfaction in that. I couldn't imagine living as many vampires did, with eternity spread out before me and no greater purpose to occupy my time than the pursuit of pleasure. What I did as a member of The Righteous was worthwhile. I served the greater good and I would have it no other way . . . but just now I wished the greater good would bugger off and give me some peace.

As usual, that wasn't likely.

I was passing by Greyfriars when I heard low voices coming from the other side of the cemetery wall. The western gate was just ahead and I stopped at it, peering through the long shadows cast by the gravestones, and into the darkness beyond. The Resurrectionists were at work tonight.

They were a brazen pair of bastards, I'd give them that; it was barely nine o'clock. They were too far into the cemetery for a human to see them from the gate, but the grave robbers couldn't hide from my heightened vampire senses. I could see them and hear them just fine. The trouble was, I couldn't touch them. Oh, certainly I wouldn't kill them, but even harming a human on consecrated ground was asking for more bad luck than I could afford just now. I would have to wait until they left the cemetery, but it would be worth it. If ever anyone deserved to be bitten, it was someone who would dig up a grave, rob the body, and then sell the corpse to someone like Dr. Knox. I paced at the gate, and it made my stomach turn to know that I could do nothing more than watch and wait while these blighters defiled a grave.

A movement in the shadows caught my attention, just to the left of where the grave robbers went about their gruesome work. I smiled when I realized what it was. I pushed the gate wide open and fell back among the shadows of the wall. A low growl hummed through the night, followed by the very satisfying sound of men shouting. The Resurrectionists literally fell over themselves trying to get out of the cemetery and away from the feral wolf that dogged their heels all the way to the western gate.

I let the first man run past me, but reached out and snatched the second man by his collar. His feet flew out from under him as I jerked him back and he fell to his knees in front of me, screaming like a school-girl. I reached around and turned his face to mine.

"Lady," he pleaded as he finally stopped scream-ing and caught his breath, "get out of here. There's a wolf back there!"

I smiled, feeling my canine teeth long and sharp in my mouth. "I know," I said. "Now look at me."

He looked up into my eyes, confused, and I knew the second I had bespelled him. I could feel it like a soft click in my head. He was mine now and I could do whatever I wished to him. I jerked him up to his feet and pulled his head back at an uncomfortable an-gle. Normally I was gentler than this, but the man had offended my sense of decency. I was a vampire and I respected the sanctity of holy ground. Was that too much to ask of humans as well?

I sank my teeth into the soft flesh of his neck and groaned in pleasure as his blood flowed warm and sweet into my mouth, fueling whatever magic made me a vampire. I drank him down, not realizing until that moment how hungry I had been. His blood filled me, calling softly to the darkness inside me. The dark magic liked blood, but I firmly pushed it down, as I always did when I fed.

The man's knees buckled under him and I pulled back from his neck, realizing that I had taken more than I should have. "Look at me," I said. His eyes turned to mine, dazed and unfocused like those of a drunk. "When you wake you'll go straight home. You won't remember anything after you passed through these gates." He nodded and I moved my face closer to his. "But know this, the next time you enter a churchyard they'd better be carrying you in feetfirst, or I'll be coming for you."

I closed my eyes and exhaled softly, breaking the vampire magic that had bespelled him. His eyes fluttered closed, and he sank into what appeared to be a drunken stupor against the cemetery wall. The wound in his neck would heal before he woke, and he would remember nothing except a wolf in a cemetery and a distinct aversion to continuing his career as a grave robber.

Something tugged at my skirt and I turned, seeing the large black-and-gray wolf pulling gently on my dress.

"Oh, for the love of Danu," I muttered, swatting at the wolf's nose. "Get your teeth out of my new dress, Drummond." The wolf took several steps back and sat, its tongue hanging out and what appeared to be a grin on its face. I sighed. "Drummond, as long as you're here I need to speak to you."

The wolf stood and its body seemed to shimmer, wavering until it was hard to discern what I was looking at. A moment later Drummond stood before me, naked as the day he was born. I snapped my eyes skyward.

"I hate it when you do that," I said.

"Would you rather talk to me with the fur coat on?"

"No," I said, taking off my cloak and waving it in his general direction. "What are you doing out here anyway?" I asked.

I heard the sliding of fabric over flesh, and when I turned back Drummond was decently covered. He looked ridiculous standing there huddled in my cloak with his bare feet and legs sticking out from beneath it, but it was a vast improvement on having to converse with him while trying to keep my gaze from wandering south.

"I might have a lead on who your murderers are," he said.

"Who? How did you—"

Drummond shook his head and interrupted me. "I don't want to get your hopes up. What I heard sounds rather far-fetched but I'll check it out and report back."

"I appreciate that," I said.

"What was it you wanted to speak to me about?" he asked.

"Aunt Maggie is in town," I replied grimly.

"Have you seen her?"

"I certainly have," I said. "And I owe you an apology. I'm afraid I'm not a very good actress. She realized quickly enough that I wasn't surprised at her arrival and she knew that you'd come here to warn me. If you're lucky you'll only end up with your head stuffed and mounted on her wall. I am so sorry, Drummond, especially after all you've done to help us."

"Ah, don't worry," he said. "I knew I'd never get away with it. Someone back at Glen Gregor would have let it slip that I'd disappeared right after she left. Even if you'd made good on your escape she would have figured it out. I was hoping we'd all be gone by the time she got here, though, and she'd have the whole trip home to cool her temper."

"One more day and we would have made it," I said. "I shouldn't be surprised. Nothing else has gone the way I wanted it to for weeks now, so why should that? Do you know what I need right now?"

"Vampires," Drummond replied.

"No, I've had it up to here with vampires. What I need is for Maggie to go home, for us to figure out who is tormenting the queen and see him punished, and for Michael and me to get married and have a nice, long honeymoon without any—"

"Vampires," he said again.

"Exactly!"

Drummond glanced over my shoulder and then looked back at me and rolled his eyes. "No, you nit, there are vampires behind you."

I whirled around, pulling the short sword from its sheath along my spine as I did so. When I realized that it was only Aubert and Warden Ross I exhaled in relief and resheathed the weapon. Turning back around, I found my cloak in a pile on the ground and Drummond gone. Where the devil was he off to now?

Exasperated, I snatched my cloak up, which now smelled faintly doggy, and turned back to greet Aubert and Ross.

"I saw the king just before dawn," Aubert said. "He mentioned that you wished to speak with me, but you and your consort had already retired for the day."

"Oh. Well, I did, but the matter resolved itself this evening." He looked at me questioningly. "My aunt was to arrive in Edinburgh within the week and I was hoping you could have someone keep an eye on the port for me. She was early, though, and arrived tonight."

Aubert shook his head. "The happenings in port seem of great interest to everyone these days."

I frowned. "What do you mean?"

"Bel has asked me to notify her whenever a Blood Cross ship came into port."

"Is she leaving town?" I asked. She had mentioned it, but I wasn't sure I wanted anyone in that house to leave until we'd fully resolved the situation there, even if it was only Bel.

"I don't think so," Aubert replied. "She asked this of me when she first arrived in town. Whenever a ship of the line comes in, I tell her."

"Why does she want to know?"

Aubert shrugged. "All she asks is the name of the

ship. I assume someone is probably looking for her
and she doesn't want to be found."

"That's just . . . odd."

"We all have our secrets, do we not?"

"I suppose so," I murmured, wondering if it had
something to do with her former lover.

"She was out when I called at the king's residence
just now. If you see her, would you tell her that the
*Falcon* made port in Leith this afternoon?"

I nodded. "I will."

"Are you having any luck catching your ghost?"
Warden Ross asked.

"Not much," I replied.

"Ah, well, you're not the only one with complaints," Ross said. "The whole town is rife with them
recently."

"Complaints or ghosts?" I asked flippantly.

"Both. It's an old city and we have places that are
known to be haunted, but the bloody ghosts seem to
be coming out of the woodwork recently."

A shiver ran down my spine as a nebulous
thought began to form in my head. "How recently?"
I asked slowly.

Ross and Aubert looked at me, confused by my
tone.

"I don't know," Aubert replied. "The past six
months or so."

*Oh, bugger.* "Since the queen came under suspicion for killing those people?"

He thought about it for a moment and I held my breath, silently praying that I was wrong. "Actually, yes," he said. "Perhaps a bit longer."

I exhaled and leaned back against the iron gate of the cemetery, stricken, my mind whirling. Bits and pieces of what had been happening since we arrived in Edinburgh flowed through my head. The way the house smelled of dark magic and an herb used to summon the dead. The way the queen had been taken onto the roof against her will. I was an idiot. I should have realized that no mere ghost could control a vampire of the queen's age and power. I clutched my head, thinking. The entity in the townhouse next door had felt both alive and dead to me, but it wasn't a ghost. It was something much more dangerous than that.

"Oh, bugger," I moaned.

Aubert reached for me. "Are you all right?"

I thought of the fact that Clarissa had seen the queen delivering a body to Surgeon's Square, even though MacLeod had sworn she was with him all night. It made me remember something Khalid had said after we found Clarissa's ashes. *If she tried to cover up what she believed to be the truth, then she feared the Red Witch of The Righteous would know her for a liar.* Not the truth, but *what she believed to be the truth.* I'd thought it was an odd turn of phrase at the time, but now it all fell into place. I finally knew how Khalid had orchestrated this whole thing.

It had taken Ross's casual mention of the rise in ghostly phenomenon to finally make me see what should have been obvious all along.

I grabbed Aubert by the lapels of his coat. "I know what's happening to Marrakesh. The werewolf who was here when you arrived, can the two of you find him for me?"

His eyes widened. "I—I think so."

"Track him down, Aubert, and tell him that I need him at the king's residence now. Tell him that it's a matter of life and death."

I started to leave, but Aubert grabbed my arm. "If there is trouble, we should be at our king's side."

"No!" I said forcefully, then took a deep breath and tried again in a more reasonable tone of voice. "You'll be a liability. The last thing I need is more vampires."

Ross shook his head. "Why?"

"Because," I said with fear in my voice, "he has a necromancer."

# CHAPTER 40

I slammed the front door as I rushed into the house. The sound of it reverberated through the marble foyer and made me stop and take a calming breath. I didn't want to alert Khalid or Hashim to the fact that I knew anything, at least not until Drummond got here.

Bel came floating down the stairs in a high-waisted lavender gown of a style popular around the turn of this century. It was a stunning dress. The little cap sleeves were off the shoulder and a fringe of stiff silver lace stood up from the edge of the sleeves, wrapping around the back of the bodice so that it looked as if she were framed in a ring of silver snowflakes. Her black hair was pulled up high on her head in artful curls and her lavender eyes regarded me with curiosity.

"Where is everyone?" I asked.

"They're busy and I'm lonely," she said with a pouty expression. "Your friends all went out and MacLeod is being tedious. He's locked himself in his room with the queen, though what possible fun that can be, I have no idea. Khalid and Hashim are up in the king's study and I have no idea where Drake's gotten off to."

I walked over and glanced into the two receiving rooms to the right of the staircase. They were both empty.

"Bel," I said, "you need to get out of the house tonight."

"Do you want to go to a ball?" she asked, hopefully.

"No, I need you to find someplace else to stay tonight. Go to a hotel."

She jerked her head back, offended. "I will not. I live here. You can't just order me out."

"Trust me," I said, crossing the foyer to check the library, noticing that someone had cleaned up the mess left behind from Michael and Drake's scuffle. "You don't want to be here tonight."

The library was empty as well.

"Where is Drake?" I asked. If Michael, Devlin, and Justine were out, then Drake, as much as I disliked the prospect, was the person I needed to speak to. He could deal with the king and queen. They were not going to be pleased that Khalid, and undoubtedly Hashim as well, had betrayed them, and the news would probably be better delivered by the High King's Sentinel than myself.

"I told you, I don't know where he is," Bel said, grabbing my arm. "What is going on?"

"Nothing you need to concern yourself with," I said, extracting myself from her grip. "Just take my advice and find someplace else to be tonight."

The last thing I needed was Bel getting in the way of what was going to happen here shortly.

"I'm not going anywhere until you tell me what's going on. No one ever tells me anything. Everyone thinks I'm obscene."

I frowned at her. "Everyone thinks you're what?"

She rolled her eyes. "You know . . . stupid."

"You mean, obtuse?"

She smiled. "Yes, that's it. I'm not, you know, and if you don't tell me what's going on then not only am I not leaving, I'll just follow you around all night until I figure it out for myself."

Which, knowing my luck, would be about halfway through the fight that I was certain was imminent. Against my better judgment I said, "I figured out exactly what's been going on here, how it's been accomplished, and who the ghost—who is not really a ghost—is. It ends tonight and you don't want to be here when that happens."

Her eyes widened and her face, for once, took on a serious and thoughtful expression.

I nodded. "Go to a hotel tonight, Bel," I said, and turned to go upstairs. Perhaps Drake was in his room.

"Well," she said flatly. "This truly is unfortunate."

I turned to ask what she meant by that. The last thing I saw was a heavy brass umbrella stand being swung at my head.

# CHAPTER 41

Michael's scent filled my nostrils. I groaned, turning my head so that my face pressed against the soft fabric of his shirt.

"She's awake," Justine whispered.

My head jerked up at the sound of her voice and I looked around, confused. I was in MacLeod's holding cell in the basement of the house along with Michael, Devlin, Justine, Drake, MacLeod, Khalid, and Hashim. They were gathered tightly around me, their faces a mixture of anger, fear, and frustration.

"How long have I been unconscious?" I asked.

"A couple of hours," Michael said.

"So long?" It took incredible strength to knock a vampire unconscious. I wouldn't have thought Bel had it in her. Apparently I'd misjudged her on many levels. We all had.

"You would have woken sooner, but we kept you sleeping," I heard Bel say.

Michael helped me to my feet, and I turned toward the sound of Bel's voice. Bel stood in the center of the room . . . and she had a long dagger with a wickedly curved blade pressed to my aunt's throat. I looked into Maggie's eyes. She didn't look frightened; she looked angry. A young man of perhaps eighteen or nineteen stood behind them.

"Bel, let Maggie go," I demanded.

"Oh, I think not," she replied. "I'm the one holding the knife and you're the one in the cage. I give the orders now. We're leaving Edinburgh on the morning tide, and if you try to follow us I'll kill the human." Her voice held a strong, commanding tone and her whole face had a new, cold look to it. Gone was the vacuous expression that she had wielded so well over the past months. Her eyes now glittered with calculating intelligence. She was an incredible actress, but I was a fool to have not seen through it. The helpless-female charade was one I had used many times to my advantage, though I was an amateur compared to her.

"Break the door down," I ordered.

Michael looked at me sheepishly. "We can't."

"Why not? I don't believe this cell is strong enough to hold eight vampires!"

"Because I ordered them not to attempt to escape," the boy said.

I turned my attention to him. "Necromancer," I spat.

He nodded. He was young, tall, and very thin, as if he was not accustomed to regular meals. His black hair was shaggy and tousled, falling into his bright blue eyes. His nose and lips were almost feminine looking, but his face was saved from being delicate by a square jaw and strong cheekbones. He was a pretty boy who would be a handsome man in another twenty years. He must have been the young man who Drummond had seen on the street, walking with Khalid. The fact that we vampires hadn't been able to see him had nothing to do with the intricacies of my spell. The boy had power over the dead and he hadn't wanted us to see him. He couldn't control what Drummond saw, though. I wondered briefly if the necromancer had known that Drummond was with us and had purposely allowed himself to be observed walking next to Khalid in order to throw suspicion toward the lieutenant. By the gods, the amount of power it took to accomplish everything he'd done was incredible, especially for one so young. But I had power of my own.

I called my magic, felt it rise inside me. The necromancer cocked his head to one side, as if he sensed it. My power welled up like a pot ready to boil over. I held my hand out toward the boy . . . and nothing happened.

The necromancer smiled. "I'm stronger than you are."

No, I thought, he wasn't. I'd worked magic in his company before. In the townhouse he'd been powerful enough to cloak his appearance, but I'd still been able to call my magic. Cold terror gripped me, and I turned to Maggie.

"What have you done?" I whispered.

She turned her blue eyes to me. I had never seen anything but confidence in those eyes, but now they held regret and, for the first time since I'd woken, fear. "I'm sorry," she said with a strangled whisper. "I worked the binding spell and now we're all going to die. I am so sorry."

I couldn't think about the implications of this right now. With my magic gone the only hope we had was to keep them here until Drummond arrived.

I turned my attention back to Bel. "If we do as you ask and allow you to leave the city, what becomes of my aunt?"

"I give you my word I'll set her off in London, unharmed," Bel replied.

There was movement on the steps that led to the cellar. Bel hadn't heard it because she wasn't expecting it, but I had.

"Why would you do this?" I asked her, trying to keep her attention on me. "What were you hoping to gain?"

"Yes, I look forward to hearing that as well," said a masculine voice from the doorway.

We all turned, but it was not Drum Murray who strolled into the room. It was Christian Sinclair, captain of the *Falcon* and, according to those who believed that The Templar was a myth and not a man, the owner of the whole Blood Cross fleet.

He wasn't tall, but there was a dangerous quality about him. Indeed, I'd heard tales of more than one unruly vampire whom he'd pitched over the side of his ship and left to the elements. The one time I'd met him he had been quite charming, but he was not a man I would wish to cross.

He was dressed as you would imagine a pirate to dress, in black breeches tucked into tall leather boots, a cream shirt, and a crimson frock coat with wide, turned-back cuffs and a multitude of gold braiding. There was a sword and at least one large knife strapped to his waist and he carried a black buccaneer's hat trimmed with a large crimson ostrich feather. His brown hair was shoulder length, thick and straight, and he wore gold hoop earrings in each ear. At the moment his warm brown eyes flashed with irritation.

His presence seemed a shock to Bel because she dropped the hand that held the knife as she silently watched him. Maggie took the opportunity to try to get away but Bel latched on to her arm, squeezing until my aunt stopped struggling. And all the while Bel never took her eyes off Sinclair. There was longing, disbelief, and fear on her face. I wondered now if all this could have been avoided if I'd remembered earlier to tell her that the *Falcon* was in port.

"Captain Sinclair, stop moving," the necromancer ordered.

Sinclair stopped abruptly, looking at first surprised and then mildly annoyed.

"Tristan Mahone," he said. "Your father is looking for you."

The boy's face paled at Sinclair's remark. It wasn't

hard to guess that Bel had probably offered Tristan a way out of a bad situation if he helped her.

MacLeod pushed forward, coming to stand beside me at the front of the cell. "Sinclair, what are you doing here?" he asked.

The captain's eyes locked on Bel's. "I've come for my wife," he said.

MacLeod looked from Sinclair to Bel. "Son of a bitch," he spat, leaning forward and resting his forehead wearily against the thick iron bars.

"What?" I asked.

The king took a deep breath and shook his head. "The fair Belinda, or Bel as she's been calling herself, is Sinclair's wife. Ladies and gentlemen, meet Belladonna, the Deadliest Flower of the Caribbean."

# CHAPTER 42

We all stared at her, having a hard time reconciling the woman we'd come to know with someone who deserved such an epithet.

"She nearly brought the Furies down on herself, back in the late 1600s," MacLeod said. "The High King ordered them to investigate allegations that she was luring men into brothels that she owned in Port Royal, Jamaica, and killing them."

"I don't suppose she was innocent?" I asked.

MacLeod laughed. "I doubt it. But there was an earthquake and two-thirds of Port Royal, along with any evidence against her, sank into the sea before the Furies ever left the Continent."

Bel smiled. "Yes, that was quite a stroke of luck," she said.

"Sinclair imprisoned her on his island after that, and the High King let the matter rest," MacLeod explained. "She was not supposed to leave there, Sinclair."

The captain smiled ruefully. "Yes, well, she had other ideas."

"Why come here?" I asked. "Why would you go to all this trouble to depose the queen?" Other than the need to stall her, I truly wondered at her motivation. Sinclair was a handsome man, and he clearly cared for her or he wouldn't have traveled all this way to find her.

Almost as if she could hear my thoughts, Bel growled in frustration and shoved Maggie toward Tristan. Maggie glanced at me, as if to ask whether she should fight him, but I shook my head and she stood still. With Bel still in possession of her blade and no help forthcoming from any of us, I didn't want Maggie to do anything to draw attention.

"You," she said as she stalked across the room, waving that wickedly sharp dagger in my direction. "How could you possibly understand why I had to do what I did? You're so young, so in love. Perhaps I should kill you now and save you the trouble."

Michael came to stand behind me, placing his hands on my shoulders.

Bel laughed, and it was not a pretty sound. "He'll break your heart, you know. He'll build you up and then piece by piece he'll tear you down."

"No," I whispered. "He won't."

She shook her head. "I see the way you look at him. I looked at Christian that way, too, when I was young and foolish. You're in love now, but it won't last. It never does. One day you'll notice that his eyes don't light up every time you walk into a room anymore. And then he'll stop telling you that you're beautiful. The times when he tells you he loves you will come fewer and farther between, until he never says it at all anymore." She glanced back at Sinclair, but he simply stood there, making no effort to appease her. Smiling bitterly, Bel turned her attention back to us. "You'll miss the nights when you used to lie together and talk about the future, or about nothing at all. You'll feel him slipping away from you like water between your fingers and there will be nothing, *nothing,* you can do to stop it. Before you know it, sex is all that's left between you and even that will leave you cold in the afterglow, wondering if you were just a little bit better, would he love you again? You'll spend days, years, trying to figure out how and where you lost his love, and wishing with every fiber of your being that you could get it back. It'll tear a woman apart, wondering what she did wrong."

Finally Sinclair spoke, and his voice was hard and angry. "If our lovemaking leaves you so cold, Bel, why is it that you spend all your time trying to get me into bed?"

She turned to him and said in a flat, emotionless voice, "Because the only time that I feel you care for me is when I'm naked."

Sinclair glanced away, and I wondered how much of what she was saying was the truth. I looked into her eyes, saw the pain there, and I genuinely felt sorry for her. She was the embodiment of everything I had feared about the future. Was this how I would end up as well, if I ever lost Michael's love? As though he felt the effect Bel's words had on me, Michael took my hand and his fingers toyed with my ruby engagement ring, the small gesture reminding me of his love. No, I thought, he and I would never walk this path. We would not allow this to happen to us.

"So what was your purpose in coming here, Bel? To have the queen set aside so that you could take her place?" I asked.

"Why not?" she replied, indignantly.

"For God's sake, woman," Sinclair spat. "He's been in love with Marrakesh for over six hundred years. Did you think that he'd just forget about her and fall in love with you?"

"He's a man," she said frankly. "Given enough time he'd feel the need for a woman again—and I can be very persuasive. As for his love . . ." She paused and looked back over her shoulder at him. The edges of her lips quivered as she said, "I will always love you and only you, Christian. I didn't need MacLeod to love me. I just needed a place in the world."

"Your place is with me," Sinclair snapped.

She whirled on him, suddenly angry. "Where? Locked away on Rose Island while you sail off for months at a time, leaving me alone while your blood whore shares your cabin?"

*Blood whore* was a derogatory term for a human, male or female, who regularly fed the same vampire.

I couldn't imagine Bel's vanity allowing Sinclair to keep one.

"Well, I have to eat, don't I?" he shouted.

I glanced around and all the men in the room, including Tristan, were looking at Sinclair as if he were the greatest fool alive. Bel shrieked and flew at him, burying the knife in his chest. He looked down in shock and she stepped back, her hand flying to her mouth as if she couldn't believe what she'd just done.

"You stabbed me, you bloodthirsty shrew!" he yelled.

Her eyes narrowed and she reached out and jerked the curved blade from his chest, twisting it just a bit as she did so. "If I had a stake, I'd drive it through your black heart, you pompous ass," Bel shot back.

While the two of them argued I tried once more to call my magic. I even reached down into the darkness and attempted to draw on the black magic's power, but still nothing happened when I tried to free it. I grunted in frustration and pain as the magic fought to push its way through my skin and failed. I turned to Maggie.

"If the binding spell had worked, would I still be able to feel my magic?" I called out to her.

She dragged her gaze from the warring vampires and focused on me. "I—I don't know," she replied.

I glanced at Tristan, who was also absorbed in Bel's quarrel. I'd been certain that Maggie's spell was responsible but, truthfully, this felt less like a binding and more like something interfering with my power. I wondered if he'd learned how to obstruct my magic since the last time we'd crossed paths. Was he truly that powerful?

"I broke vows I made to God for you!" Sinclair was shouting.

"And you've resented me for it ever since," Bel wailed. "Let me remind you that I never asked you to break them. I didn't turn you without your consent. You came to me of your own free will!"

Bel stomped across the room and grabbed Maggie's wrist, jerking her forward. "We're leaving," she said, waving the bloody knife in my aunt's direction. "And if you try to follow us, I'll kill her."

A low, inhuman growl filled the room and I nearly shouted for joy as Drummond stormed down the stairs. His eyes were locked on Bel, and I wouldn't have wanted to be in her place for anything in the world. When I'd first seen Drummond in that warehouse in London, I hadn't known what he was. Looking at him now, I didn't know how I'd missed it. Even in human form he looked every inch the wolf protecting his pack.

"Tristan, stop him," Bel commanded.

Tristan shouted for Drummond to halt, but the werewolf kept coming. Drummond smiled a feral smile, and his teeth looked whiter and sharper than a human's should.

"I'm not a vampire, boy," he snarled. "You have no power over me."

Bel let go of Maggie's wrist and stepped back,

raising the knife in a defensive position. Perhaps she thought that if she released Maggie, he would back down. It was a grave mistake. Maggie ran toward me and Drummond rushed forward, his body shifting as he ran until the man was gone and the wolf moved in for the kill.

# CHAPTER 43

All hell broke loose as Drummond pounced on Bel and the two of them went flying in a shrieking, growling blur of fur and lavender silk. Sinclair was screaming for his wife, and all the vampires in the cell were jostling for a better position to watch the brawl. Tristan had fallen back to one side, clearly wanting to help his benefactor but unsure of what to do. My magic rushed up again, as if it was eager to get out and join in the fray. I let out a grunt of pain and turned to Maggie.

"Take my hand," I called to her. "I don't think it's your spell, I think it's his necromancy that won't let my magic work through a dead body."

I threw back my head as the magic pushed to get free and a strangled laugh escaped my throat. Even to me it sounded frightening, laced with pain and frustration. Maggie stared at my outstretched hand and shook her head.

"Bel!" Tristan cried and then turned to Sinclair. "Captain, kill that wolf!"

My gaze swung to Sinclair as he pulled his sword. Maggie's eyes grew wide and, unable to do anything else to save Drummond's life, she thrust her hand through the bars and clasped mine. The moment she touched me my power rushed outward, through her.

Her eyes widened and she stood transfixed as the magic that had been building for so long inside me finally burst free. A rush of power surged through the basement like a thundering explosion. The door of the cell was blown completely off its hinges and everyone on the other side, except Maggie, was caught up in its wake. Bel and Drummond were thrown into the far wall, the impact dazing them both enough to halt the fight. Tristan's head made a sickening *thud* as it collided with the stone wall. He lay there, unconscious but alive, as I stepped through the gaping hole that had once been the cell door.

Bel struggled to sit up but the wolf had recovered first, its bloody muzzle hovering mere inches above her throat.

"Drummond," I said softly. "That's enough. She's lost."

The wolf looked at me, then turned back to Bel, snapping its jaws in her face, then falling back to sit and watch. Somewhere to my right Captain Sinclair was picking himself up off the floor. As soon as he gained his feet he rushed forward to tend to Bel, but I ignored them both. Instead I crossed the room to stand over Tristan's body. I didn't need to check for a pulse. I could hear his heartbeat from where I stood. Staring down at the boy, I wondered what we were going to do with him. Hashim stepped forward, pulling the scimitar from its scabbard.

"What are you doing?" Maggie demanded.

He looked down at Tristan and then back to me, as if I would take his side in this matter simply because I was a vampire.

"He cannot be allowed to live," Hashim said. "He is a danger to us all."

Maggie turned to me. "Do something!" she exclaimed.

I didn't know what to say. Certainly I wouldn't allow Hashim to kill the boy, but he did have a point.

Whatever solution I might have come up with was forestalled as the sound of wood scraping against stone drew our attention. One of the wine shelves swung outward, and we were all surprised (some of us more than others) when the queen emerged from a passageway behind it. MacLeod smiled and went to her.

"My love," he said, kissing her cheek. "How long have you been there?"

She smiled up at him. "Since they abducted you from our room. I was waiting for an opportunity to help, but you all handled everything nicely. Hashim, put the sword away. We won't be killing some poor human boy just because he was foolish enough to fall in with Belladonna's mad scheme."

Tristan groaned from his prone position on the floor. "Kill me," he croaked. "Would rather die than go back there."

Sinclair came forward with his arm around Bel. She was bloody and her lovely dress and flawless skin were torn, but she would live. Drummond, still in wolf form, trotted along at her heels, waiting for her to give him a reason to sink those sharp teeth into her flesh again.

"His father," Sinclair volunteered, "is the Reverend Mahone of the isle of Jamaica. Naturally, he thinks his youngest child is an instrument of Satan. He's kept him locked away his entire life. I'm not excusing what the boy's done here, but if you'd lived the life he has, you'd have taken whatever means of escape was offered to you."

"Be that as it may, Sinclair," MacLeod said, "I cannot allow him to stay on my lands, especially after I've seen firsthand the damage he can cause if he wishes."

"What if he wasn't on *your* lands?" Aunt Maggie asked. "What if he was on mine?"

MacLeod looked at her and cocked his head to one side. "I'm listening."

"What if I take him back to Glen Gregor with me and promise you he'll not set foot off my land again?"

MacLeod regarded her for a moment, then addressed the boy. "What say you to that, lad?"

Tristan looked up at Aunt Maggie as if she were his savior. "Yes," he whispered.

"Fine," Hashim growled, "but I do get to kill her?"

He turned to Bel, and Sinclair stepped in front of her, drawing his own sword.

"Over my dead body," the captain threatened.

"That can be arranged, too," Hashim assured him.

Khalid moved to stand with his brother. "Not only has she committed treason against our queen," he said, "she's killed over a dozen humans and the vampire Clarissa in the process."

"I didn't kill anyone," Bel protested.

Drake intervened. "Someone killed all those people and made it appear to us as though the queen had done it. If it wasn't the boy, then it had to be you."

"It wasn't us, it was the humans," Bel said. "None of you knew it, but Tristan and I were in town well before I presented myself on the king's doorstep. We were staying at the White Hart Inn when I allowed a man to lure me back to his lodgings. I thought I would have a quick taste of his blood and be off, but the bastard tried to kill me! That didn't work, of course, but when I realized the scheme he and his friends had in place I thought I could use it to my advantage."

"Do you honestly expect us to believe such tripe?" Devlin sneered.

Beside me Drummond whined and, as I turned to look down at him, his wolf's body shifted. In the blink of an eye he was human again. Maggie and I were the only ones who averted our eyes and blushed at his nakedness.

"As much as I hate to admit it," Drummond added,

"she's telling the truth. The culprits' names are William Burke and William Hare, and I have their address written on a scrap of paper in my coat pocket," he said, motioning to the pile of clothes that had seemed to melt off of him earlier when he'd changed forms.

"How did you come by such information?" I asked incredulously.

"As you once said, I can go places you cannot. I've also never made a vow to protect humans," he replied with a wolfish grin.

I decided that perhaps I didn't want to know the particulars.

"She still killed Clarissa," Khalid argued.

"I did not. He did," Bel said, pointing to Tristan.

We all looked down at the boy.

"Actually, I didn't," he replied with a sheepish glance in her direction. "She's locked up in the basement next door."

Bel narrowed her eyes, clearly irritated that he'd gone against her orders, but she wisely kept her mouth shut.

"I searched the ground floor of that house myself," Devlin said with certainty. "I saw no basement door."

"I didn't want you to see it," Tristan said. "It's where I hid whenever you came into the house."

MacLeod nodded. "There is a basement. The layout of the other two houses is exactly the same as this one."

"There's still the matter of treason," Hashim reminded us.

"Let her go," Marrakesh said softly.

"My queen, you cannot mean that," Hashim said, aghast.

"Why would you show her mercy, after all she's done?" Khalid demanded.

Arguments broke out all around. MacLeod, I noticed, was silent on the matter. Perhaps he knew his wife better than her lieutenants did. The bickering continued for several minutes before Marrakesh herself put an end to the matter.

"Her crimes were against me, and it is I who will decide her punishment," she stated. "I show her mercy because she is what we females fear becoming." She turned and glanced sadly over her shoulder at Bel. "A woman who loves a man who is no longer in love with her. Take her back to Rose Island, Sinclair, and keep her there this time," Marrakesh said harshly. "Mark me well, Belladonna, if you ever set foot on my lands again, I will kill you myself."

"Agreed," Sinclair said readily. "And you have both of our sincere apologies for the trouble she has caused, don't they, dear?"

He squeezed her arm until Bel murmured an apology. Sinclair must have decided that this was the best result he could hope for because he started toward the door, pulling Bel along with him. She stopped in front of me, and he paused and turned back.

She smiled sadly. "Despite everything, I rather like

you, Cin. You remind me a bit of myself when I was young and the world was fresh and full of promise. Enjoy it while it lasts because one day you'll look back on these years and know that you'd do anything to have them back. They'll be the memories that keep you warm at night when he's grown cold. Don't be afraid of anything . . . there will be plenty of time for fear later."

Sinclair tugged on her arm and she followed him, a look of quiet desperation on her face. I reached out and took Michael's hand, silently praying that I would never have cause to think back on this day and feel the sting of truth in her words.

# CHAPTER 44

Michael and I were married the following night in the Presence Chamber of the King of the Western Lands. Justine and Devlin stood up with us as we pledged our love and trust to each other for eternity. It was not the church wedding I'd thought I would have when I was human, but the bonding ceremony was more beautiful than anything I had ever dreamed up in a schoolgirl's fantasies.

Justine had gifted me with a stunning gown for the occasion, a copy of the late Princess Charlotte's wedding dress. For years she'd had it tucked away in the bottom of one of her many trunks, waiting for this moment. It was fashioned of gold netting and Brussels lace over a cream tissue slip and had a longer train than any woman could reasonably manage. It was perfect.

Aunt Maggie attended the ceremony, though Drummond remained behind at her hotel, to keep an eye on Tristan. Maggie had not apologized for attempting to bind my powers, and I'd not asked her to.

We seemed to have come to an unspoken truce, she and I, and I was content with that.

At the reception I sipped champagne and watched Maggie speaking with Marrakesh. When the queen took Maggie's hand and patted it I noticed that Marrakesh was not wearing her gloves. She looked over Maggie's head and her eyes found mine. Perhaps she would tell me later what she'd seen in my aunt's heart, perhaps she wouldn't. I was pretty certain that I already knew.

The whole of Edinburgh was abuzz with talk of the arrests of Burke and Hare. After Bel and Sinclair had departed the previous night, MacLeod and Marrakesh had taken a trip into the city, traveling in an open carriage so that Edinburgh's vampires could see their queen and know that she was once again a force to be reckoned with. Marrakesh had swept into Hare's lodging house and had impressed upon him and his wife the fact that if the humans didn't get them, she would if their names were ever breathed on the night air in her lands again. She then told what she knew of the crimes to a constable who was involved with one of her court ladies. Both men and their wives were arrested, and Jacques Aubert informed the queen that a final victim's body had been discovered in Dr. Knox's classroom. The good doctor would be lucky if the mob didn't lynch him along with the men.

*Speaking of lynching,* I thought as Drake made his way across the room to me.

"I believe I owe you an apology," he said, somewhat uncomfortably.

"You think?"

He shifted his weight and swirled the champagne around in his glass. It had to be hard for a former king to apologize to one of us lowly peons, but I certainly wasn't going to make it easier for him.

"Bel made me realize something last night," he said finally.

"And what was that?" I asked.

"That I was chasing after you because I was envious of what you and Michael have. Elspeth and I . . . we were in love like that. I will never forgive myself for her death, and it galled me to see you and Michael with the happiness that I'd once had, and lost."

"So you thought you'd seduce me and take that happiness from us?"

Drake grimaced. "It wasn't a conscious thought—I'm not that big a bastard—but yes, on some level perhaps that's true. At any rate, I'm sorry."

"Apology accepted," I said, feeling that I could afford to be magnanimous at my own wedding. "I think that perhaps living in such close proximity to a powerful necromancer made us all a little crazy."

"I hope there's truth in that," Drake said, rubbing the bridge of his nose. "I would apologize to Michael, too, but I believe it'll be a while before I put myself within striking distance of his right hook again."

I laughed. "I'll convey your sentiments," I assured him.

"Ah, I do believe our fair queen is hailing you," Drake said.

I nodded to Marrakesh and then turned solemnly back to Drake. "What do you intend to tell the High King about me?" I asked.

"That you are a very dangerous woman," he said honestly. "And that we are lucky you're on our side."

"I will happily come to Castle Tara to make my obeisance and sign my name in the Book of Souls," I assured him.

Drake regarded me silently for a moment, as if unsure of how to delicately phrase his reply. It was quite obvious from the look on his face that he was thinking of what I'd done in that alley. Perhaps he was even wondering if I could make a successful bid for the High King's throne, should I choose to do so.

Finally, he said, "I believe it is best to keep you at a safe distance, Cin. At least for now."

I nodded, extremely uncomfortable with the fact that the High King might believe I was a danger to him. There was little I could do to remedy the situation, however, so I excused myself and made my way to Marrakesh's side.

"So?" I asked, nodding across the room to where my elderly aunt was flirting shamelessly with Jacques Aubert and my new husband.

"I was hoping to thank you for all your help by being able to mend things between you and your aunt," Marrakesh said.

"That bad?"

The queen shrugged. "She is afraid of your power, but I think you already knew that."

I nodded.

"She's a complex woman, your aunt. She harbors a great deal of jealousy."

I frowned. "About what?"

"The fact that your mother, as the eldest, was supposed to be the Macgregor Witch, but instead she married your father and moved to England."

"But Aunt Maggie loves being the Macgregor Witch," I argued.

"That is true also. I think you of all people, though, know what it's like to wonder what your life would have been like if things had turned out as they should have, instead of as they did."

"I do. I wouldn't change anything, but the thought does creep up from time to time."

"Your aunt feels much the same way. She's also jealous of you, of your magic, even though it frightens her. She wonders what it would be like to wield such power, and there is a part of her that resents the fact that you were chosen to bear it."

"Because I'm a vampire," I stated.

"Because you were so young when it was given to you, and she doesn't think you had to sacrifice anything for such an enormous gift."

"I gave up my life," I protested. "I sacrificed everything I knew to save those I loved."

"She sees only that you are young and beautiful and powerful, and you will still be that way when she is long in her grave."

"How do I make her understand?" I asked.

"You don't," the queen said. "Cin, for all I've just told you, your aunt loves you. One thing you'll learn when you live as long as we do is that people rarely change. If you're going to have someone in your life, for however long you have them, you can only love them for who they are. Take the good with the bad and love them for all of it. If you expect people to be who you want them to be, and not who they truly are, then you're going to be disappointed time and again. Maggie is your aunt and her problems are hers. They were not caused by you, and they are not yours to fix. Enjoy the time that you have together and don't worry about the things you cannot change."

For several moments I stared across the room at my aunt, thinking about what Marrakesh had said. It was not the answer I had hoped for, but we had all come through this ordeal unscathed—even Clarissa, who had survived the past few weeks on butchers' blood, would soon regain her health—and I wouldn't mar the joy of this night by wishing for things that would never be.

I looked back at the queen. "I'm glad I met you," I told her.

She smiled. "I'm glad I met you, too. I want to thank you for believing in my innocence. If it hadn't been for you, I'd probably be locked up in Castle

Tara and Bel would be well on her way to sitting on my throne."

I shuddered at the thought, very glad that the *Falcon* had left port on the morning tide. I didn't envy Christian Sinclair his trip home.

"If you'll excuse me," I said, "I think I need to go speak with my aunt."

I'd almost made it across the room to Maggie when I was intercepted by Khalid and Hashim. I smiled at them uncomfortably, feeling rather guilty that I'd been so sure that Khalid was responsible for the attacks on the queen.

"We wanted to thank you for everything you've done for our queen," Khalid said.

"There's no need," I replied. "I believe I owe you an apology for suspecting you of treason."

Khalid shook his head. "You were only protecting Marrakesh, and we respect that. I would have faulted you if you hadn't suspected us."

As soon as was polite I excused myself from the twins and made my way to Maggie's side.

"I'm glad you came, Aunt Maggie," I said.

"Would I miss my niece's wedding?" she asked, the champagne having put quite a glow in her cheeks. "A bit odd, if you ask me, but if that's the way you people do things . . . I'm just happy to see you settled."

My life was the farthest thing from "settled," but I thanked her anyway.

Maggie put her hand on mine. "I want you to

know that I won't be making any more attempts to bind your powers."

I cocked my head to one side. "Why the sudden change of heart?" I asked.

"I've had no change of heart," she said, leveling that iron gaze on me. "There's darkness in your magic, niece, don't think I didn't feel that last night. I still say your power isn't natural, but then, the things you fight against aren't natural, either. I think you need your magic just as it is in order to do the things that you do."

That, I knew, was the best I would get from her. I hugged her and she stiffened in my arms for a moment before relaxing and patting me on the back.

"Thank you, Aunt Maggie," I said.

Someone had moved a piano into the Presence Chamber, and Aubert was finally coerced into playing for us. Justine was drawn to the instrument like a moth to the flame and before long her voice rang out in accompaniment to Aubert's music.

Michael came up behind me and kissed the back of my neck.

"Oh, I almost forgot," Maggie said as she opened her reticule. "Drummond asked me to give this to you. He said you'd know what it meant."

Michael looked on as I unfolded the piece of paper. There were two phrases written on it:

*Macmillan Parties, Privateer*
*Saint Claire, templar vampire*

"Oh, my God," Michael whispered.

"What does it mean?" I asked. Macmillan Parties, Privateer, was the official name of the Blood Cross line, but I didn't understand what it had to do with the second phrase.

"It's an anagram," Michael said. "You know that *Sinclair* is a bastardization of the original French *Saint Claire,* right? Well, if you rearrange all the letters in *Macmillan Parties, Privateer*, what you end up with is *Saint Claire, templar vampire.*"

I choked on my champagne. "Are you telling me that Christian Sinclair is actually The Templar himself?"

Michael grinned. "That's what I'm telling you."

I shook my head, remembering how much I'd pitied Bel when I had thought that she'd been taken in by some rogue pretending to be The Templar. All this time she'd been married to him! Come to think of it, that the man was a former monk certainly explained a lot. Still, you'd think even a monk would learn a thing or two about women in five hundred years, now, wouldn't you?

Aubert struck up a waltz and Michael grinned down at me. Even now, more than ten years after its debut in London, the waltz was still considered vulgar by many people.

"My beautiful wife, may I have this dance?"

"Why, certainly, husband," I replied and looped the train of my gown over my arm before he swept me into the waltz. "Do you think we'll scandalize my aunt and all the older vampires with such dancing?"

"Oh, I do hope so," Michael murmured, pulling me closer. "Where do you want to go for your wedding trip, *mo ghraidh*?"

"Will you take me home to Ravenworth?" I asked. "I want to sleep with you in my own bed."

"Ah, one of my favorite places in the world—the bed where we made love for the first time," he said, smiling down at me with a rakish grin. "How could I refuse such a request?"

"I promise it'll be much better than the first time," I said. "You won't have to kill me afterward."

Michael's face grew serious and he whispered in my ear as he spun me around the room. "You know, I may be nothing more than a crusty old vampire, but I hear tell of a strange new invention called a steamship that can get us all the way to London in only two days!"

I laughed and laid my head on his shoulder. "That sounds lovely," I sighed.

Read on for an excerpt
from Jenna Maclaine's next book

# MORTAL SINS

Coming soon from St. Martin's Paperbacks

Le Havre, France, 1864

The House of the Crescent Moon was a brothel where the blood whores plied their trade. For a few coins a vampire could get a quick meal. For a few more, you could buy an evening's entertainment. I had no need for the latter, but it was nice, on occasion, to drink from a willing donor—someone who wasn't a rapist, cutthroat, or thief who had the misfortune to accost the wrong woman, namely me, in a dark alley. Buying blood certainly didn't carry with it the same thrill as hunting in the aforementioned dark alleys, but the drinking was undeniably more pleasant. Instead of a rank, filthy alley, tonight I was reclining on a chaise longue in a private parlor that was sumptuously decorated in silks and satins of varying shades of blue. The young man whose blood I had purchased was no ruffian smelling of sweat and gin. He was beautiful, blond, and shirtless—and perfectly willing to let me sink my teeth into any vein of my choosing. Yes, quite a departure from my usual fare.

I looked at the young man again as he silently ran his fingers through my long, curling, blood-red hair. He was undeniably lovely, but I knew that I could never grow accustomed to drinking from a blood whore on a regular basis. Many vampires do, but, to me, it was rather like feeding a tiger in a cage. The tiger would live, it might even thrive, but it would always miss the hunt. Sometimes, however, a change of pace was nice, and the vampire brothels were convenient.

The blood whores actually commanded quite a lucrative trade. Even in the smallest cities, vampire brothels were on a par with the most exclusive houses of prostitution in Paris or London. Vampires, as a rule, had expensive tastes and were willing to pay for the luxuries these houses provided. The men and women who served in such places were the most beautiful creatures that money could buy. And why wouldn't they be? If selling your body was your chosen profession, you couldn't find a better place to do it. The houses were magnificently well-appointed, the money they made was ten times better than what they could have earned in even the best human brothels, and the clientele was . . . well, suffice it to say that there were humans who would pay a high price for the pleasures to be found in a vampire's bed.

Thoughts of such passions made me turn my attention from the human to the vampire lounging on a sofa across the parlor. I watched as his sensual lips moved against the lovely, pale throat of a buxom brunette, searching for the perfect spot to strike. She clung to him, her head thrown back, and when his teeth slid into her flesh, she clutched his dark blond hair and let out a moan of pleasure. I felt a twinge of jealousy at the sight. He was my husband, after all.

*Let her enjoy it while she can*, I thought.

As if he sensed my gaze on him, Michael looked up at me. His need for blood almost quenched, there was now lust in his eyes. And it was directed at me. He pulled back from the brunette's neck and a trail of crimson blood flowed down her white skin. Never taking his gaze from me, Michael caught the trickle of blood on his tongue and licked his way up the side of her throat in one long stroke. A shudder ran through me as I imagined taking him back to the hotel and letting him fulfill the promise that was evident in that one smoldering look.

"Come to me," I said to the human.

The young man sat up, and I rolled onto my back, stretching out across the velvet-upholstered chaise. He leaned over me, and I admired the way the muscles in his arms and shoulders tightened as he moved closer, exposing his neck. I stared into his chocolate-brown eyes until I felt the familiar click in my head that meant he was now under my control. You could certainly drink without bespelling a human, but I didn't want him to feel the pain of my bite, only the pleasure. When you took someone's blood, you made a mental connection with them, sharing their thoughts and feelings. It could be horrifying, pleasant, or downright erotic, depending on who you were drinking from and to what degree you allowed that connection. I thought of it as a door inside my head and I controlled how far I opened it. Considering the caliber of men whose blood I generally took, I usually kept that door firmly closed. When I was a young vampire, I'd learned very quickly that I didn't want to know what went on inside their minds. Tonight, though, was different, and I thought it only polite to allow this human to experience some measure of the satisfaction I felt in taking his blood. I opened the door in my head, wanting him to feel what I felt as his hot blood poured down my throat and filled me with life. I was not prepared for the reciprocating feelings and images I received from him.

Hot pleasure rolled over me in waves, and I was aware of him moving between my legs, pushing against me. As I drank from him, I closed my eyes and was overwhelmed with flashes of what he was thinking. He was imagining me on top of him, moving down his naked body with the cat-like grace of a vampire, parting his legs and sinking my teeth into his femoral artery. I quickly severed the connection, pulling away from him as he threw back his head and shuddered in rapture against me. I let out a shaky breath as he looked down at me with glazed eyes.

"Buy me for the night," he pleaded. "Let me make love to you."

Suddenly his weight was pulled from me, and

Michael was standing between us. His blue eyes glittered and his sharp cheekbones seemed even more pronounced when he clenched his jaw that way. I smiled up at him, my body humming with excitement at the predatory look on his face.

"Sorry, boy," my husband said sharply as he held his hand out to me. "The lass has other plans tonight."

I placed my hand in his and let him pull me up from the chaise. When I'd gained my feet, he snaked one strong arm around my waist and pulled me against his body.

"Tonight and every other night," I promised.

He kissed me swiftly. "For eternity, *mo ghraidh*," he whispered against my lips.

As we left the house, I turned my face into the cool breeze, which carried with it the salty scent of the ocean. It was a clear, crisp night, and the Hotel Frascati was a few blocks away. It seemed longer, though, with Michael whispering naughty things in my ear every few minutes. I was strolling along, happily contemplating the rest of my evening, when my vision began to blur and a sharp buzzing sound took up residence in my head.

"Dear Goddess," I mumbled, stopping short and pressing the heels of my hands to my eyes.

"Darling, what's wrong?" Michael asked.

"I don't know," I replied. "It feels like there's a nest of bees in my head."

I stumbled backward, as if I could somehow get away from the sound.

Michael grasped my upper arms to steady me. "Is it the blood?" he asked worriedly. "Was he tainted?"

"I don't think so," I replied, shaking my head as I tried to clear the buzzing sound from it. I'd often fed from drunks and several varieties of drug addicts. The aftereffects of taking in tainted blood varied, but you could always tell if a human was . . . polluted in any way . . . the minute their blood hit your tongue.

I pulled away from Michael and staggered off the sidewalk. I had the feeling that if I could keep moving, I could somehow dislodge that horrible sound. Michael plunged into the street after me, catching my arm and pulling me back just before I walked in front of an oncoming carriage. I hadn't even heard the rumble of the wheels on the cobblestones over the racket that was in my head. As I stood in his arms, facing the opposite side of the street, the sound lessened.

"I'll hail a carriage and we'll drive back to the hotel," Michael said.

He put his arm around my shoulders and began to steer me back onto the sidewalk in the direction we'd been headed. The buzzing sound returned, violently. I stopped again and glanced across the street. I grabbed Michael's hand, looked both ways, and marched across the street.

*Better*, I thought. *This is better.*

"Michael, what lies in that direction?" I asked, pointing to the darkened row of shops lining the street in front of me.

"The harbor is in that direction," he replied. "Why?"

I pinched the bridge of my nose between my fingers. "When I performed the summoning spell that brought you to me when we first met . . . what did it feel like?"

Michael frowned and then the tension eased from his body as he realized what was happening. "It felt exactly like a nest of bees in my head, and it only stopped when I went in the direction that would take me to you."

"I didn't know what it would feel like," I said. "I'm so sorry to have put you through this."

Michael cupped my face with his hands. "Don't ever apologize for that. It brought me to you, did it not?"

I smiled up at him, able to think more clearly now that I knew I wasn't losing my mind. "I suppose we must go to the harbor," I said.

Michael shook his head. "I am not running after some witch powerful enough to do this to you without first knowing where we're going and why."

He was right about that. At this point I'd have run headlong into no telling what sort of danger, just to get this infernal buzzing to stop.

"Let's just go have a look," I suggested. "First we'll see where the magic wants me to go."

A muscled ticced in his jaw, but he finally relented and hailed a carriage to take us to the docks. The harbor was filled with all manner of vessels, from small fishing boats to larger steamships. I appreciated the convenience of the new steamships but, in my opinion, nothing could match the grace and beauty of a sailing vessel. I laid my head on Michael's shoulder and closed my eyes as I nestled against his chest. He put his arms around me, and we sat in silence as the carriage lumbered along. The buzzing, which had diminished from a dull roar to a soft hum the closer we'd gotten to the harbor, suddenly softened until I could barely hear it at all.

"Here," I said, and Michael rapped on the roof of the carriage. The driver brought the conveyance to an abrupt halt, and I peered out the window, taking in the sleek lines and tall masts of the ship that someone's magic wanted me to board.

A sailor passed by the carriage, an Englishman by the sound of his voice as he softly sang a rather vulgar ditty.

"Pardon me," I called out to him. "Do you know this ship?"

"Aye, miss," he replied, smiling at the sound of my English accent. "That's the *Charlotte Ann*."

"Where is she bound?" I asked.

"London on the next tide, miss," he answered.

I thanked him and sat back with a sigh. "Well, that's a relief," I said. "We should return to the Frascati and find Devlin and Justine."

Michael frowned. "Cin, just because that ship is headed for London doesn't necessarily mean whoever is summoning you is a friend."

"You're right, of course. But how many witches do you think there are in Britain who would not only work a spell to summon me specifically but are also powerful enough to do it?" I gazed out at the silent harbor, the water silver in the moonlight, and keenly felt the pull of the spell. "Someone is calling me home."